WIESBADEN, GERMANY, U.S.A.

The Second Life of Brencie Jessup

A Novel

REBECCA LONG HAYDEN

outskirts
press

This is for Brian, who did everything he could to make this book possible.

Acknowledgements

I'm privileged to name those individuals who made significant and direct contributions to *The Second Life of Brencie Jessup*.

Brian Hayden supported me every day for a year, freeing me from many other tasks, and with unflagging good humor.

Thanks to Sue Allen, author of *Water Beyond the Bridge*, a fine work of fiction, and *Lilacs, A Fortnight of Fragrance on Mackinac Island* (with Jeff Young). Sue took time away from her own work to offer the kind of critique only a seasoned writer could give.

Dorothy Howe Brooks, an amazing poet, gave me a single suggestion without which this book might not have been written. Dorothy's most recent poems have been collected and published in *A Fine Dusting of Brightness* and *Subsoil Plowing*.

Shannon Hayden read the *Brencie* manuscript many times. Her keen eye for detail (including mistakes) and her insightful suggestions were invaluable.

Sam Hayden read the book and gave me a male point of view. Perhaps most important of all, he encouraged me to keep going when I thought I might not.

Amy Morrison Hayden produced the author's picture on the back cover. Amy took hours away from her schedule as a professional photographer to take hundreds of pictures, just to be sure I had plenty to choose from.

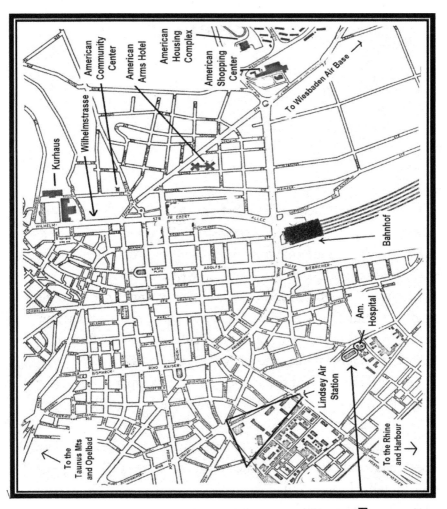

Wiesbaden 1968

Kurhaus

Wilhelmstrasse

American Community Center

American Arms Hotel

American Housing Complex

American Shopping Center

To Wiesbaden Air Base

Bahnhof

Am. Hospital

Lindsey Air Station

To the Taunus Mts and Opelbad

To the Rhine and Harbour

Amelia Earhart Hotel

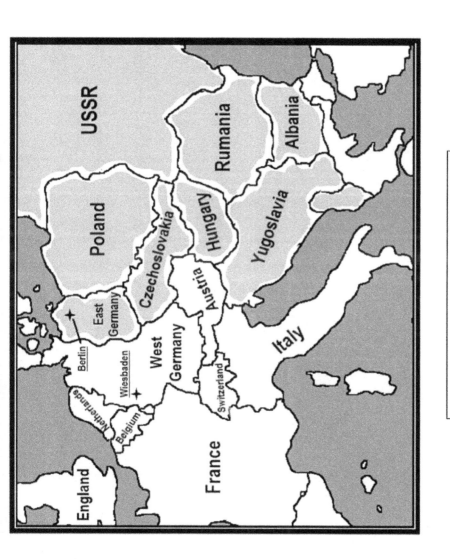

Iron Curtain Countries in Gray

Chapter 1

Brencie Jessup swayed on the tightrope of panic. Dizzy and conspicuous in the crowded terminal, the last words of her personnel contact at Ellington Field looped in her head: *Someone will meet you in Frankfurt. Someone will meet you in Frankfurt.*

Staying on her feet increased her visibility, so if *someone* showed up they might see her, somehow know her, *meet her* for hell's sake. Fatigue from the transatlantic flight made her woozy, and the acrid smell of vending-machine coffee cranked up a tilt-a-whirl in her stomach. She sat down and rested her head on her knees until the nausea passed.

Three days ago, she became an employee of the U.S. Air Force in Wiesbaden, Germany. She possessed a passport, her first, olive green, gold seal, issue date October 9, 1967, signed by Secretary of State Dean Rusk. She had expected the flight to be glamorous. It wasn't. It was nine hours on a government-leased DC-8 full of children, military wives, and a few civilian employees like herself. Glamorous? More like a Saturday matinee at the Showboat theater in her home town of Friendswood, Texas—crowded, disorganized, noisy, kids in the aisles, sticky stuff on the seats.

On the flight, six-year-old Rusty sat between his mother and Brencie, and when he finished his meal, he emptied his chocolate ice cream onto Brencie's light-blue dress. The more his apologetic mother rubbed the spot with a napkin, the more the napkin disintegrated. Now the saucer-sized stain looked like dried blood sprinkled with coconut.

Becoming more anxious as *someone* still didn't appear, Brencie fished in her tote bag, drew out a blue folder, and reread all sixteen numbered paragraphs of Special Travel Order A-1688 issued to Brenda Cecelia Jessup. Surely she could find something helpful, a clue, a hint, a wink. Although it wasn't useful, paragraph nine remained her favorite.

9. In the event of limited war, Traveler will contact the military base that arranged transportation. In the event of general war or if the continental U.S. is attacked by a foreign force, Traveler will report to the nearest active military installation.

She dusted off a tidbit from her well-stocked mental warehouse: *Traveler* was the name of General Robert E. Lee's horse. Years of voracious reading provided her with amusing information and a good vocabulary, but that wasn't helpful now. As for *limited* war, her transportation had been arranged at Ellington field near Houston, so contact would be impossible. If it came to *general* war, she was covered. The nearest military installation was right where she sat, *Rhein-Main* Air Force Base, Frankfurt, an American facility attached to the commercial airport. It was supposed to be Germany, but the signs were in English. She heard nothing but English spoken and had no sense of being outside the United States. Had she taken a wrong turn and ended up in Amarillo?

General war called forth images of mushroom clouds, kids diving under schoolroom desks, and the belief that nuclear annihilation was a certainty. Only *when* was unknown. As Brencie left Houston the plane had banked away from the Gordian knot of freeways, and a slogan scrawled on an overpass caught her eye: Peace in Vietnam. Not a general war or any kind of war. The people in Washington insisted Vietnam was a police action.

Travel Order A-1688 ended with a distribution list, and the last entry tickled Brencie. "Copy to the Pentagon," as if the Pentagon gave a hoot what happened to Brencie Jessup. She laughed a few decibels too loud, beginning with an intake of breath, something like a sob, that caused strangers to think she was going to cry. In this case the laugh gave a man seated nearby an excuse to speak to her. "Did you say something?" He smiled.

"Should I call the Pentagon?" she replied. "They might know where my reception committee is."

The man had been glancing at her from behind his newspaper. At twenty-one years old, Brencie knew men looked at her, but she didn't know if they stared at her in particular or if it was a male version of window shopping, trolling for a short skirt or a bit of cleavage.

Either way the attention made her uncomfortable. In eighth grade her waist-length pony tail was the target of too much male interest. They touched it, tugged it, lifted it up and said, "What's under the pony's tail?" Fed up, one day after gym class she had taken a scissors to her pony tail, right up to the skull. A classmate looked at the heavy pile of dark hair filling the sink, then said, "Nice going. Now you look like a boy."

When she got home, Brencie's stepmother, Agnes-Rose Jessup, didn't change expression. She tilted her head and said, "Well. Who knew your hair was curly when it's short."

Agnes-Rose sat Brencie in front of a mirror. "Not for nothing do I own a beauty shop. I can fix it." She snipped away, and when she was finished, she said, "Look, honey. What do you see?"

Brencie stared. A late-bloomer, the previous year she hadn't needed a bra. This year she did, finally, but with or without breasts, she did not look like a boy. And she liked the short haircut. "I look like me, with short hair."

"There. Listen to the voice in the mirror. It will tell you the truth," Agnes-Rose said. "It's more important to fit in your own skin than to fit in."

As for the man sitting across from Brencie in an airport, years away from that eighth-grade epiphany, his suit, briefcase, even his socks were so ordinary she wasn't surprised when the Pentagon remark caused him to lose the smile and duck back behind his *Wall Street Journal*. Her wit often fell flat when practiced on strangers, yet she liked to see if she could predict the response. The man's retreat was what she expected down to the snap of his newspaper as he disappeared from view.

Remembering the "fit in your own skin" remark made Brencie think of her stepmother without bitterness for the first time in five months. Five months ago Agnes-Rose's despicable behavior blasted Brencie out of her own orbit, and if this overseas fiasco ended in catastrophe, Brencie would blame rhinestone-booted, scarlet-haired Agnes-Rose. It was all her fault.

There was an imaginary volume in Brencie's head called *The Book of Agnes-Rose*. The book was full of her stepmother's advice, which from time to time seemed inexplicably brilliant. If she were here, she might say "Relax and take advantage of the consequences." The consequences of this adventure looked bleak so far.

Oh, give me strength, Brencie thought.

A man in fatigues entered the waiting area holding a hand-lettered sign. The last name scribbled on the cardboard was Jester. *Jester?* Or *Jessup?* Brencie got up so quickly her belongings fell to the floor. She gathered them up and scrambled to join a cluster forming around the sign.

The man in olive drab carried a bullhorn, but he didn't use it. The voice of command rose from his thin body. "I'm Sergeant Tinker, your detail leader. Please answer when I call your name." He flipped the sign into a waste receptacle and unfolded a piece of paper. Brencie held her breath until he read the final name, the only girl on the list. "Miss Brenda Cecelia Jessup."

"Yes! Here!" Heads swiveled in her direction.

"Right," the sergeant said. "That's everyone. Five to Wiesbaden Air Base, one to the American Arms, one to the Amelia Earhart, and three to Lindsey Air Station. Questions? No? Good." He led them outside to a dark blue bus. "*Autobahn*, here we come. The Air Force gave me a speed limit, but for everyone else, it's a full-on grand prix. Gird your loins, people."

Brencie wasn't sure where a loin was, or how to gird it, and when they were underway, the *Autobahn* didn't seem different from any Texas freeway, except for the signs. *Ausfahrt. Eingang. Flughafen. Biebrich.* She didn't know a word; she didn't even know the time of day, and there was no sun to offer a hint. The sky was overcast and spitting rain. The flight had arrived in the morning, but the time dribbled away in disembarking, luggage scrambling, and waiting. She tapped the shoulder of the man seated in front of her. "Can you tell me the time, please?"

"Sure. It's fifteen thirty. We should be at the base by sixteen hundred."

She thanked him and did the math: Fifteen thirty, as he pronounced it, minus twelve hundred, or 3:30 p.m. It cheered her up, to sort out military time. She leaned her forehead against the window. Elfin villages in soft gray, tan, and taupe rose and fell with the rolling terrain. Germany, after all?

They left the Autobahn and drove past a guard station onto Wiesbaden Air Base, which looked similar to Ellington Field. America redux. The first passengers disembarked and then the bus left the base and lumbered down a highway to exit into a kind of park, or an outdoor gallery. The bus window framed an exhibit: A patch of grass bordered by white mums. An antique gaslight next to a wrought iron bench. A hanging basket dripping pink petals on a gravel walk. It wasn't the United States. It wasn't a park or a gallery. It was the town. It was Wiesbaden.

The bus lurched to a stop in the driveway of a gray stucco building adorned only with a marquis: American Arms Hotel. The first paragraph of Brencie's travel order said she would be "billeted" at the Amelia Earhart Hotel, and this was not it. She was glad. The sorry-looking heap should be known as The Dismal Arms. One passenger left the bus, and the sergeant turned off the engine and followed. As soon as the passenger's suitcase was retrieved from the hold, the sergeant climbed back into the driver's seat, and they were underway again.

Fifteen minutes later they pulled into a circular drive and stopped in front of a building some forty yards from the street. The simple blue letters over the entrance said Amelia Earhart Hotel and seemed too modest for a structure half the length of a football field. Its nine stories towered over its suburban neighbors and six mature trees dotted the lawn. Brencie wasn't sure what she expected, and it didn't matter. Nothing was happening as she expected.

The Amelia seemed newer than the American Arms, and although Brencie was beginning to believe she was in Germany, the place screamed U.S.A. as loudly as a drill sergeant.

The floor-to-ceiling windows on the ground floor, punctuated by brick-red columns, revealed a restaurant to the left of the entrance. To the right was an open arcade of shops, a beauty salon, a delicatessen, a dry cleaner. Above the ground floor the segmented façade looked like a honeycomb painted the colors of the flag, white stucco walls, red balcony screens, and blue railings. Flower boxes added color to random balconies, softening the geometry.

Sergeant Tinker retrieved her suitcase from the hold, put it down, and got back on the bus without a word. She blinked back tears in the fading light, as the only person she knew by name on this terra firma drove away. Another bus pulled into the circle and disgorged a dust devil of girls. Coming home from work?

Brencie went to work for NASA right after high school graduation, and she was proud of looking like a "NASA girl," backside girdled to midthigh in sheaths or shirtwaists, skirts and blouses or the occasional suit. Compared to the coordinated casualness of these girls, in her gingham dress Brencie felt like Minnie Mouse in a tablecloth.

For lack of any other plan, she followed the ungirdled butts of this new species into the hotel, where expectations collided with reality again. Not a cuckoo clock in sight. The lobby suggested a medium-priced hotel in the Midwest circa 1955. Leatherette furniture, light-colored wood veneer tables, and parchment shades on chrome lamps. There were two elevators on the back wall, and a gaggle waited to ascend. Behind a polished reception desk three clerks in blue blazers retrieved mail and handed out keys. A limp version of "Good Vibrations" played in the background, and Brencie laughed out loud. Right. "Good vibrations." She loved the place.

Thankfully no one noticed the laugh, and Brencie spotted a sign by an office door. Christine Holloway, Manager. The office wall was glass, and an older woman, forty-ish, was on the telephone. "Bozena, I need it today not next week," she said. When she hung up the phone Brencie knocked on the door frame and introduced herself. The woman stood up and offered her hand. "Welcome! I'm Christine Holloway. We've been expecting you."

Brencie almost fainted with joy. *We've been expecting you.* She was no longer a phantom on the sidewalk in a chocolate-stained dress. She was Brencie Jessup, who was expected.

"Your sponsor's Lulu Greenholt." Christine Holloway checked her watch. "She should be here. Well. She'll turn up. I'm sorry to say a FRELOC group came in unexpectedly, so I had to give your apartment to them. I won't have another available for two weeks. I called the American Arms and arranged a temporary billet. You might even decide to stay there permanently."

Brencie had been unimpressed by the Arms, and she had no idea what FRELOC was, but she got the point. The Amelia Earhart was full. The sound of breaking glass drew her attention to the lobby, but Christine didn't look up. "Lulu, no doubt," she muttered.

A girl about Brencie's age clutched a bouquet and stared at a broken bottle of red wine at her feet. When a maid brought a mop, bucket, and rags, Lulu-no-doubt stepped out of her shoes, took a rag, and swabbed her ankles. Then she picked up her shoes, sidestepped the glass, and made her way to the office. Even in stockinged feet, she looked elegant in a black silk blouse, tweed miniskirt, and a gold chain belt on her narrow hips.

Brencie shifted her handbag to hide the chocolate stain.

The girl greeted Christine and turned to Brencie. "Are you Brenda Cecelia Jessup? I'm Lucille Marie Greenholt, your sponsor. Call me Lulu. Sorry I'm late. Here's a copy of *Stars and Stripes*. Everybody reads it. Progress in Vietnam. Postage Stamps Go Up. I dropped the wine meant for you, but the tulips survived. They grow after they're cut. My favorite for a new arrival." She handed the bouquet to Brencie and put on her shoes.

"Thank you. Umm. Call me Brencie."

"I'll help you get settled," Lulu said. "You'll have a million questions. Is your apartment ready?" Christine Holloway explained the situation. "Hmmm. Not good," said Lulu. "I'll show her my apartment, then we'll get a taxi to the Arms. Can she leave her suitcase here for a few minutes?" When they were out of earshot, Lulu said, "Chris hates me, and we don't call her She-Who-Must-be-Obeyed for nothing. Well, I wouldn't want to manage a hotel full of hormones."

"Why does she hate you?" They were in the elevator, and the top half, above a railing, was mirrored. Brencie saw herself in unflattering contrast to Lulu's perfect makeup, slim figure, and light-brown shoulder-length hair so shiny Brencie wanted to stroke it.

Lulu shrugged. "Long story. Short version? I painted my foyer black. Residents are allowed to paint if you get the color approved. I didn't. Black's *verboten*. She made me re-paint it. It took five stinkin' coats." A walk down the sixth-floor hall, and Lulu opened her door. "All the apartments are the same except for the view. The view from the apartments on the back isn't that good, although you can see the Rhine in the distance."

Brencie followed Lulu into the once-black now-yellow foyer. A half-open door on the right revealed a white-tiled bathroom, and at the end of the foyer was a mini kitchen with two burners, a tiny refrigerator, and overhead cabinets. Although it was a studio, the apartment was well-designed, spacious, and twice as big as the studio Brencie had rented in Friendswood. The room accommodated an apple-green sofa, coffee table, two armchairs, a chest of drawers, and a desk. A small TV sat on a metal stand in a corner. "You won't have a TV or a stereo unless you buy them yourself," said Lulu. "At least the best BX in Europe is right here in Wiesbaden."

A window above a low radiator ran the length of the exterior wall, and a French door in the left corner led to the balcony. Flower boxes hung from the blue railing, where yellow, purple, and pink petunias competed for brilliance. Transfixed, Brencie stepped outside as the sun broke through, casting a post-rain light that seemed to come from within everything it touched.

Lulu followed and stood by Brencie's side. "The view's something, isn't it? Up in the hills, that's a Russian Orthodox church, St. Elizabeth's. Built by a German duke for his dead bride. Our own tiny Taj Mahal."

The front lawn sloped to the street, and the town sat in the valley beyond, punctuating the horizon with church spires and low buildings, mauve, blue, and gray. The sun went back behind the clouds and street lights chased the dusk. On the other side of the valley, the Taunus mountains created a flawless backdrop, and the onion dome of St. Elizabeth's nestled in the foliage like a golden teardrop.

There was little traffic, and a solitary runner passed by on the street below. "I don't recognize him," Lulu said, "but he's an American. Only Americans run when no one's chasing them. Come inside. It's getting cold and I'm late."

As an exercise in seeing things more clearly, Brencie liked to sketch, and she made up her mind to sketch this view as soon as she could. "It's so peaceful," she said.

Lulu shrugged. "Hard to believe we're in the heart of Naziland." They went inside, and Lulu closed the drapes. "Last year the MPs raided the trees out front and dragged down a dozen guys with binoculars. She-Who-Must-Be-Obeyed issued a memo to all residents, *suggesting* we close up at night. Jules—that's my boyfriend—said for that much trouble the Peeping Toms deserved a little bedtime skin show."

Brencie realized what was missing. "Where's the bed?"

"The sofa *is* the bed. You'll have to make it up every night, but the maids put it away every day. You can request a double bed, but then the apartment looks like a bordello with a waiting area." Lulu checked her watch. "I'll get you to the Arms, but I have a voice lesson later. Do you sing?"

"A little. I was in the high school choir and a couple of musicals." *Naziland? Peeping Toms? Maids?* Before Brencie could ask about anything, Lulu donned a red leather bomber jacket and picked up her purse.

"Angelika can always use another pupil, and there's a theater group too. We do two dramas and one musical every year." She glanced at Brencie, now without the cover of her tote bag. "Oh, my God. What happened to your dress? Is that blood?"

"I was gored by a unicorn in the airport ladies' room."

Lulu raised one sculpted eyebrow. "And I thought unicorns were extinct."

They laughed, and Brencie explained. Rusty-the-kid. Chocolate ice cream.

"You'll have to throw the dress away. No loss," said Lulu. "Oops. Sorry. No offense."

"None taken." They left the apartment and passed several girls in the hall. "Who lives here? Mostly Americans?" Brencie asked.

"Only Americans." Lulu looked at her watch and pushed the elevator button four times. "The Amelia's owned and operated by the military for single females. Secretaries like us. A good many teachers and some nurses. The U.S. regional hospital is right next door. There's about thirty-five thousand Americans in the area, if you include the whole Rhine valley."

"Thirty-five thousand?" said Brencie. "That's way more than my hometown. Where do they all live?"

"Single men live in the barracks or the BOQ. Families live at Hainerberg, the American compound. Higher ranking officers sometimes live in town or up in the Taunus Mountains."

Downstairs, they retrieved Brencie's suitcase and got into a taxi waiting in the drive. "So you don't own a car?" Brencie asked.

Lulu shrugged. "Some girls do, but you can go almost anywhere in town for about a dollar. A car's too much bother and expense for me."

They left the driveway, and they were back in Germany. "This is the Wilhelmstrasse. Expensive but fun," said Lulu. She nodded toward a well-lit restaurant. "That's the Park Café. Very chic." Waiters could be seen slithering among the tables like eels, black trays balanced overhead.

When the taxi stopped at the American Arms, it looked shabbier than ever. "Here we are. AKA the Open Arms." Lulu paid the driver. "It's the BOQ."

AKA; Also Known As. BOQ was a new one for Brencie and the second time Lulu had used the term. "Lulu, let me pay. Oh. I don't have any German money."

"Dollars are accepted everywhere," Lulu replied. "Four Deutsch Marks to the dollar, but I'm an official volunteer sponsor, so don't worry. I'll be reimbursed."

They entered the lobby through a revolving door. Relentlessly beige, the lobby was half the size of the lobby at the Amelia, but

with a similar arrangement, restaurant and bar to the left, reception
to the right. A sign said Call to Arms Lounge, listing Happy Hour
and the dinner special in the *Oak Leaf Restaurant*. Meatloaf and
mashed potatoes. And American apple pie.

"Twenty-five cents for a cocktail?" Brencie remarked.

"It's a wonder we aren't all alcoholics," Lulu said as they waited at
the desk. "The food isn't great, but you'll only be here a week or two,
unless you decide to stay."

"That's what Christine Holloway said. Are the apartments nice?"
Brencie gave the clerk her name and a copy of her travel orders. He
rummaged under the desk and handed her a key.

Lulu looked puzzled. "Ah. You never worked for the military.
BOQ stands for bachelor officers' quarters. Chock full of single men.
Some girls like it here."

"I'm not looking for a man," Brencie snapped. "Never again!"

"Never again?" said Lulu, as they got on the elevator. "Bet there's
more to that story than . . ."

The best-looking man in the world stepped into the small space,
and he didn't turn around to face the front. "Hello, Lulu. You look
like you stepped off a Paris runway as usual."

"And Air Force blue is your color, Captain Charming," Lulu replied. "Haven't seen you lately. Been deployed?"

"Roger that. Leaving again next week. After Christmas I should
stay put for a while."

"Chase, this is Brencie Jessup," Lulu said. "Just arrived from
Friendswood, Texas. Brencie, Chase Dellasera."

He took Brencie's hand. "Welcome. I hope you'll like it here."
His olive skin made his eyes beyond blue, and his uniform fit his tall,
trim body as if it were custom made.

Brencie mumbled something; she wasn't sure what. Probably the
dullest remark ever made by anyone.

"Nice to meet you, Brencie. When I see you again you can tell me your decision." When the elevator doors opened, he released her hand, took a step back, and then he executed a right-face in the hallway. He walked away, leaving them to stare at his straight back and square shoulders.

"Do they all walk like that?" Brencie had no idea what decision he had referred to in his parting remark.

"Standard military bearing," said Lulu. "Attractive as hell, and he's got that fighter pilot cockiness."

"And gilt hair," Brencie said.

"Premature gray in the blond. Odd effect. Handsome, smart. Southern Ivy League. Heartthrob of the *Rheingau*. When I first met him, I teased him about defending democracy, and he quoted Winston Churchill. 'I'm not a lion but my job description requires me to roar like one.' Something like that."

Although it sounded like a practiced remark, maybe there was more to Captain Dellasera than godlike self-confidence. "You know him well?" Brencie asked.

"We had a couple of dates," Lulu said. "His unit moves from base to base, so he's gone a lot, then he got deployed during the Six Day War . . ."

"I thought that was in Israel."

". . . it was, but it's the usual Cold War crap. If the commies had decided to help the Arabs, then we help the Jews and all hell breaks loose. It's escalation time and the fighter squads in Europe get the job. So red alert. Anyway, while Chase was gone, I met Jules."

"Did Chase call when he got back?"

Lulu laughed. "You had to ask. Actually, he didn't. And before you ask, we didn't sleep together, either." Lulu shot Brencie an impish grin. "Ah-ha. I've shocked you, haven't I. Thought I might. It *is* 1967 you know."

"Not where I come from."

"What is it where you come from?"

"I don't know, 1957?"

"Fabulous. You're about to step into another decade, and single men outnumber single women by three to one. Disheveled as you are right now, you're attractive. You'll probably have a date by the weekend. Even ugly girls find some version of love." As they left the elevator Lulu said, "Tell me how you ended up here. Short version."

"At NASA they circulate overseas job announcements. I applied, interviewed, and got the job." Brencie didn't mention the calamity of her broken engagement. Time for secrets when she knew Lulu better.

As they made their way down the hall they passed another man. "Come to the Open Arms, Lulu, and bring your cute friend," he said. "The scotch and water's fine."

"Some other time, Ray." When he was gone Lulu rolled her eyes. "See what I mean? New girls are like blood in the water. Avoid him. He brought the clap back from Vietnam and shared it with a few unlucky ladies."

Brencie took a breath and laughed.

"I like your laugh," said Lulu.

"My laugh? It's embarrassing. I tried to change it but Agnes-Rose said I shouldn't."

"And Agnes-Rose would be ...?"

"My stepmother."

"She's right. You're too symmetrical. Keep the kooky laugh. Here we are," Lulu said. "Number four one seven. Don't expect too much." She switched on the dim overhead light to reveal muddy green walls, a dingy brown couch, and a bed with a faded chenille spread. The bathroom appeared to be clean, but nothing more.

"Officers get a suite, living room, bedroom, and bath," Lulu explained. "You don't have rank so you get a lousy room." She picked up a clock. "I'm setting the alarm for oh eight hundred. I'll meet you in the lobby at oh nine fifteen and take you to the air base for in-processing. When I lived here the bus came every half hour. I doubt it's changed but we can take a taxi if we must."

"You lived here?"

"Another long story. Short version? It got to be over the top. Too much booze, too many *Guten* Howdy *Wieder* Bye-Bye parties, hello and goodbye, which is life around here. Then at a rooftop party an officer literally went over the top. I'd had enough. I moved to the Amelia."

"You don't mean he fell off the roof! It's what? At least four stories."

"Five, and he didn't die. He fell onto soggy turf. Broke a lot of bones but if he had landed on the driveway, I can't imagine he would have survived. It was a costume party and the padding helped. He was dressed as Humpty Dumpty."

"Humpty Dumpty?" Brencie studied Lulu's face, looking for the impish expression.

She shrugged. "Oh, all right. He wasn't dressed as Humpty Dumpty, but it was a costume party, and the rest of it's true."

"What was he dressed as?"

"Peter Pan."

Brencie abandoned her expectations about this place, a combination of now and then, fairy tales and foreboding. "First star to the right and straight on till morning." In this place someone could fly from a five-story building and survive. She laughed out loud.

"I know," said Lulu. "Welcome to Disneyland on the Rhine."

Chapter 2

B rencie collapsed into the dingy armchair. Despite Lulu's warm welcome, Brencie was glad to be alone, beyond the demands of polite conversation and a long day.

She picked up a postcard from a stack on a side table. The card featured a drawing of the American Arms, elongated and elegant, technicolor sunshine on an Oz green lawn. The description sounded like the place Brencie had expected to be.

> *The American Arms in Wiesbaden, gateway to the Rheingau* (Rhine Valley). *Rheingau wine has written the history of this sundrenched land, rich in monasteries, castles, and country inns. From spring until autumn there is happy turmoil along the Rhine.*

She had promised to let Agnes-Rose know of her safe arrival, so she addressed the card and scribbled three words on the back. *Arrived safely. Brencie.* Agnes-Rose wasn't forgiven, and she would know it.

Brencie closed her eyes, just for a moment, and woke with a start at 2:00 a.m., stiff from sleeping in the chair. By the time she rummaged in her suitcase for pajamas, brushed her teeth, and crawled into bed, she was hyper alert. At 5:00 a.m. she decided she might as well get up, but she put her head down and fell back into a deep sleep. A pounding on the door forced her to her senses. Lulu was there, shined up and tucked into a light gray dress with a red print scarf.

Staring at Brencie's Betty Boop pajamas, Lulu said, "It's oh nine thirty. Half past nine. Oh, don't look so stricken. It's perfectly normal. Jetlag *über alles*. I see you knocked the alarm clock to the floor, and you didn't hear the phone, either. Get dressed. I'll wait."

Brencie hurried to the bathroom and glanced at her matted hair. Deader than roadkill. No time to wash it, but the shower spray would perk up her curls. After minutes in a dark stall that smelled like mold, she wrapped herself in a towel and applied a touch of makeup before returning to the bedroom. Lulu puffed on a cigarette. "First one today. I'm trying to quit."

Brencie took her first-day outfit from her suitcase and laid it on the bed, smoothing the skirt with her hands, but Lulu shook her head. "Too wrinkled." Wrinkles weren't the issue. When Brencie had selected the outfit, she thought it was the best thing in the world. Today, in its pepto-pinkness, it looked like the worst thing in the world.

Lulu crushed her cigarette in a cracked ashtray and started tossing items from the suitcase. She settled on a caramel-colored blazer, black skirt, and sleeveless cream-colored knit top. "There, but not the pearl earrings. Too dressy. The gold ones, and you'll save some earlobe agony if you get your ears pierced."

Brencie went to the bathroom to finish dressing, and when she came back, she looked in the mirror. "Listen to the voice in the mirror." Queen of the mixed metaphor, Agnes-Rose meant something more complicated than clothes. Brencie smiled at her own reflection and nodded to Lulu. "Nice. Thanks. This outfit says *Brencie*, but better."

"Exactly. Now lose the headband and let's go."

Brencie obliged, then picked up the postcard she had written last night. "Can I get a German stamp at the desk?"

"Your mail goes through APO with U.S. postage. Let me see

that. Thought so. These are prepaid. Wow. The Open Arms never looked this good. We'll drop it in the mail slot."

They reached the lobby as the bus arrived outside, and in twenty minutes they were on the air base a few miles out of town. Lulu walked Brencie to the personnel building. "It will take some time," she said. "I'll come back at thirteen hundred. That's 1:00 p.m."

———— ((●)) ————

Lulu was back five minutes after Brencie finished the paper-work. "I've been assigned to Materiel, on Lindsey Air Station."

"That's lucky," said Lulu. "Only blocks from the Amelia. I'm with OSI, Office of Special Investigations, so I have to trek out here every day, and I can't talk about the work. I even answer the phone incognito: 'Five five four six two, Miss Greenholt.' I'd rather be at Lindsey, but I like my job. Let's go to the officers' club for lunch. You'll get over jetlag quicker if you eat at regular times."

Brencie wasn't prepared for the jolt that smacked her between the eyes as they walked into the club. Advancing through the smell of french fries and the clatter of metal trays was Rick Smith, her ex-fiancé.

In a millisecond she realized it was a doppelganger, an ordinary guy who resembled her ex. The stupefying thing was, the doppel-ganger looked like Rick plus twenty-five years of hard living, and the added years made Rick look like Anson Jessup, her own father. How had she not seen that her ex-fiancé looked like her ex-father? Brencie was frozen in disbelief.

"What's the matter?" asked Lulu.

"Nothing. I thought I saw someone I knew." As they found a table, Brencie heard her stepmother's voice clearly, as if she were standing right there. "Look at Rick more closely." Agnes-Rose had

— 18 —

said it three times, on different occasions, but Brencie thought she was meant to examine his character, not his countenance.

After lunch Lulu showed Brencie the library and the gym, and then they got on the bus. Brencie got off at the American Arms, and Lulu continued to the Amelia. It was after 1600 hours when Brencie walked into the lobby.

Chase Dellasera, still in uniform, stood up from a wingback chair. "Hello, Miss Friendswood. Can I buy you a drink?"

Brencie was seldom tongue-tied, but she couldn't summon the wit she was known for.

"I know you can speak," he said. "Maybe you don't remember. I met you in the elevator, with Lulu Greenholt. I'm Chase Dellasera."

"Of course I remember. I'm tired and jetlagged." She was accustomed to an ordinary amount of male attention, but he was extraordinary. "Do you remember my name?" she said. "It isn't Miss Friendswood." It sounded snarky.

He laughed. "It's Brencie, and I was hoping to run into you."

"Really? I doubt it." First snarky and then hostile. *Say something enchanting*, she told herself, running her fingers through her curls.

Before she could sensibly decline his offer of a drink or gracefully accept, he took her arm and guided her to a table in the bar, removing a copy of *Stars and Stripes* from the chair. He glanced at it. "Same version of 'Progress in Vietnam' every day. Good progress. More progress. One time it dared say 'Progress Temporarily Stalled.'"

"At least it's on the other side of the globe," she said.

"Geographically, but it's starting to get all over everything. What will you have?" he asked.

"Scotch and water." She had never tasted scotch, but it was the first thing that came into her head.

He ordered scotch for both of them. "Have you decided? About being happy here? When we met, you said you would be happy if you decide to be happy. Quoting someone called Agnes-Rose."

Relief mixed with irritation. She hadn't said anything stupid, but not clever, either. "I've been here forty-eight hours. I'll need a few more minutes to decide for sure." To her surprise, four drinks arrived. Happy hour. She took a sip and willed herself not to make a face. It tasted like cold, liquid spinach.

"So where were you before you landed here?" he asked.

"I worked at the Manned Spacecraft in Clearlake. A few miles from Houston."

"NASA? Really? An astronaut? Or just a secretary?" He smiled.

"I was selected to be in the next round of astronaut-scientists, but I decided to come here and be *just* a secretary instead." *Just-a-secretary* was like *damn-Yankees*, and it made her cross every time she heard it.

"Sorry. It was only a question. Do you not like pilots? Or is it captains? Everyone hates captains."

"I met a fighter pilot at a NASA party. He flew missions over Cuba during the missile crisis, and he was disappointed he didn't get to drop his bombs. I didn't believe him."

"When you're locked and loaded, you want to do what you're trained to do," he said.

Small talk was getting easier with each sip of her drink, and it was tasting better. She noticed a discreet V attached to one of the ribbons on his uniform. The ribbons stood for medals; she knew that much. "What's the V stand for? Vietnam?"

"I earned it in Vietnam, yes."

"And all the others? Very colorful. I'm impressed." *Like every girl you meet*, she thought.

"Don't be. Most of them are just for showing up."

Perhaps he realized he was too smooth, too good-looking. As for his confidence, that seemed to be of the inborn variety. "Why do people hate captains?" she asked.

"Captains are like squirrels chasing their tails, trying to leap up to major. I don't like captains myself, and I am one."

"Perhaps I can learn to hate captains too," she said.

He threw his head back and laughed. "You don't talk much, but when you say something, so far, at least, it's never what I expect." He leaned closer and put his hand on hers. "If you plan to hate captains, I'll have to make major as soon as possible."

He was flirting, but she wasn't ready for a new man, especially an irresistible one. She withdrew her hand and collected her things. "Thanks for the drink. Drinks." She had finished both.

He motioned for the check. "I'll take you upstairs." His tone said something seductive, smooth and down south. Not I'll *walk* you upstairs. I'll *take* you upstairs. Did it mean *my place or yours?*

"No." She should have said *No, thank you.*

"OK, then." He stood up, but he made no move to walk her out. She left the bar confused, a little tipsy, wondering if Captain Dellasera preferred girls he could *take* upstairs.

—«(•)»—

On Monday morning Brencie caught the bus from the American Arms to Lindsey Air Station with confidence. She consulted *The Book of Agnes-Rose,* the one she carried in her head. *Everything's easy once you know how.*

Although Wiesbaden Air Base looked like other American bases, Lindsey did not. The white stucco buildings seemed organic, as if they had grown there for decades. While the squareness of curbs and sidewalks, parade grounds, flags, and signs screamed "military," the crenulated rooflines were more whimsy than warfare. She found the right building, pushed open the heavy double doors, and reported to the administration section on the ground floor. A secretary led her to an office off the reception area. "Wait here, please. Sergeant Hanik will be right back. He'll handle your paperwork and take you to meet your new boss." She smiled. "Welcome to Materiel."

Brencie remained standing and examined a map of Europe on the wall. The legend indicated NATO territory in blue, Soviet bloc in red. The aggressive swath of scarlet included the USSR. West Germany looked like an S-shaped afterthought, separating France and the rest of the continent from East Germany and Czechoslovakia.

A compact young man came in and filled the room with his presence. In a fluid motion he put down his coffee, placed a clipboard on a hook, and extended his hand. It wasn't possible, but she had the feeling she had seen him before. "I'm Nolan Hanik." His smile happened quickly, no twinkle of eye nor tilt of mouth, just an instant conversion of his serious face. His hand was dry and callused, and his grip stopped short of being too tight. "If you're Brenda Cecelia Jessup, I have your file."

He had her file. Christine Holloway had been expecting her, and there was the miracle of meeting Lulu. Days ago she felt alone and abandoned. Now she was expected. She had a file. She felt ecstatic. "I go by Brencie." She glanced back at the map "All that red looks threatening. How fast does a tank move?"

He looked at her with interest. "Good question, and it's not just threatening. It's *the* threat. It's four hundred kilometers to the East German border, roughly two hundred fifty miles. A little more to the Czech border. Russian tanks could be rolling down the Wilhelmstrasse in six or seven hours. U.S. military might is here to see that doesn't happen." He opened a folder. "I have everything except confirmation of your NASA security clearance. In the meantime, I'll administer the oath."

"I took it twice already, on my first government job and again when I accepted an overseas assignment."

"I know. It's General Novak's idea. He's the Deputy Chief of

Staff for Materiel, and he likes to remind civilians of their commitment. So repeat after me. . ."

She raised her right hand and recited the oath from memory.

"I, Brenda Cecelia Jessup, do solemnly swear that I will support and defend the Constitution of the United States against all enemies, foreign and domestic; that I will bear true faith and allegiance to the same; that I take this obligation freely, without mental reservation or purpose of evasion; and that I will well and faithfully discharge the duties of the office on which I am about to enter. So help me God."

"Impressive," he said.

"I wrote it," she deadpanned.

"You wrote it." He fought to keep away the quick smile. "Good job. Especially that 'true faith and allegiance' part."

He smiled.

She smiled back. "I had an English teacher who made us memorize a lot of poetry, said it was good for the brain. I like the oath, so I memorized it."

"Your teacher was right." He held her gaze, started to say something, and then looked down at his desk. "Have a seat. Seems like NASA would be an exciting place to work. Will they put a man on the moon by 1970?"

"Yes."

He looked skeptical. "You sound sure."

"I am."

He outlined a few administrative details, and in ten minutes, he said, "OK, sign here, and that's it until we get that clearance."

She signed, returned the papers, and looked at his name tag. "Thank you, Mr. Hanik."

"It's Sergeant Hanik, but call me Nolan." He pointed to the sleeve of his uniform. "Four stripes. Staff sergeant. I'll introduce you to the general and take you to meet your new boss." He escorted her to a corner office full of flags, plaques, and photographs of important-looking people. She met General Novak and was quickly escorted out.

"There's the ladies' room," Nolan said. "One on every floor, and there are vending machines on every other floor, candy and pop, watery hot chocolate, and awful coffee." When they encountered three people in the hall, he made introductions. "This is Audrina Remlinger from procurement. Wolfgang Ritter from the motor pool. And Captain Leah Crum, our chief administrative officer."

"*Willkommen*, Brencie," said Wolfgang. Trim and precise, his posture conveyed a military impression, though he was not in uniform. Audrina told Brencie where to requisition office supplies, and Captain Crum encouraged Brencie to come see her if she had any questions.

They left the group. "That's the first female officer I've ever met," Brencie observed, "plus I've been in Germany three days, and those are the first Germans I've met. Except for taxi drivers. The desk clerks are from Turkey. The waiters are from Italy. The maids are from Poland."

"*Gastarbeiters*. Guest workers from all over. German economy's booming. Wolfgang's quite a guy. We go for beers sometimes. Your office is on the fifth floor. No elevator. The first military buildings were built in eighteen sixty-eight. We took it over after the war. You'll like your new boss. He's from Texas too."

Although the marble steps were reinforced with metal strips, a hundred years of boots had carved depressions in the middle. When they hit the fifth floor, Nolan showed no sign of exertion. "Well done. Five flights, and you aren't breathing hard."

"I play . . ." she gasped. "tennis. But . . . you can see, I'm . . . hiding it."

"Thought so." He grinned and took her to meet Lieutenant Colonel Grover Foss, a tall man with a familiar twang. They would be sharing an office, her desk positioned by the door, his at the back of the narrow room by a high window. Nolan left, and Brencie and Colonel Foss congratulated each other for being born in Texas. "Are you over jetlag?" he inquired. "It takes time. I understand the Amelia had your apartment ready."

"I'm temporarily at the American Arms. An emergency made them give my apartment to someone else. Something that sounded a little like Prufrock?"

He laughed, not unkindly. "FRELOC. Fast Relocation from France. Must be the close-out group. All American forces were supposed to be out by now." He shook his head. "In August of 1944 I helped liberate Paris. I was twenty years old. That beak-nosed Charles de Gaulle has a short memory." He went to his desk, and Brencie took out her list of questions, starting with how to answer the phone. "Weapons Systems Support Division," he said. "We keep the weapons working, meaning airplanes."

He showed her a chart with the names of airplanes down one side and a weekly grid across the top. "NORS. Not Operationally Ready, Supply. If a plane can't fly because of a part, we get busy. Each sergeant in the division is responsible for one or more bases in Europe, and he cannibalizes the part from another plane, orders it from the States, or acquires it locally."

The newness must have registered on her face. "You'll understand operations over the next few weeks," he said. "Your biggest responsibility will be managing the classified documents. We don't handle anything higher than Secret, except for the morning readout, which is Top Secret. Only division chiefs see that. If we come under attack, all classified documents have to be shredded. Each safe has a team of two people, with a backup in case the primary team's disabled. You'll be on a backup team."

Brencie almost laughed, but the look on Colonel Foss's face indicated it wasn't a joke.

Nolan Hanik entered again, this time with a red folder. "Come in, Sergeant," said the colonel. "How's the world according to the Air Force?"

"Still code green, sir. An interesting TWX from Army HQ, though."

Brencie went to her desk considering words like "tanks on the Wilhelmstrasse, threat of attack, and primary team disabled." She didn't recall words like that in the job description they gave her at base personnel, though there was the bit about *limited* and *general* war in her travel orders. Maybe that wasn't a joke either. Five minutes later, Colonel Foss initialed a routing slip and handed the folder back to Nolan, who smiled at Brencie as he left. Colonel Foss explained that a TWX was a military telegram, gave her an organization chart and some reading material, and went to a meeting. When the phone rang, Brencie fumbled her answer and was relieved the call was for her.

"This is Chris Holloway, at the Amelia. An apartment's come available a week from Wednesday. It's a good one, fourth floor front with city views. That's the fifth floor, Stateside. I'm required to show it to you, and then have you fill out the paperwork if you want it."

"If I want it?"

"Once you're installed at the Arms, you have the option of staying there, or you could wait for an apartment on the ninth floor. Some girls want that."

"I won't be staying at the Arms," Brencie said. "Fourth floor front sounds great."

"Smart girl. I'll see you next week." As soon as the call ended, the phone rang again.

"Yeah, hi. It's Nolan. Sergeant Hanik? We got a TWX confirming your clearance. Stop by my office, today if possible, and I'll give you a startup briefing."

After a decent tuna salad sandwich and a cup of coffee at a crowded canteen, she reported to Nolan's office.

"Have a seat," he said. "How's it going with Foss the boss?"

"I wondered if they call him that. It's going good. He's nice."

"He is. OK, you're scheduled for in-depth security training next month, but I'll give you the general practice within Materiel." In a few minutes he said that was it. He got up and went to the map. "See this? Schierstein harbor, about five miles away."

He looked so serious. She wondered if the harbor was a primary nuclear target. It had been that kind of day.

Then he smiled. "There's a beer festival at Schierstein on Sunday. Would you like to go?"

It took her by surprise. "You mean with you?"

"No, with General Novak. He asked me to be his go-between. Like what's-his-name."

"Cyrano?"

"Right. Cyrano de Bergerac." He cleared his face of the grin, but she was pretty sure his tongue was still in his cheek. He sensed her hesitation. "If you're worried about working together, we don't. I'm manning this desk temporarily. My permanent assignment is with the judge advocate general, in the HQ building."

He was efficient and intuitive, qualities that didn't always go together, and he had a sense of humor. His dark brown hair, close-cropped military style, was so thick it looked like a cap; more-so because he had a slight widow's peak. There was something honest in his deep-set brown eyes, and at about five feet ten inches tall, Nolan Hanik looked solid, muscular, like his uniform strained the seams across his chest.

"I'm sorry. I've only been in town for a few days. I didn't expect anyone to ask me for a date." It wasn't quite true. She had thought Chase Dellasera might.

"I'm surprised I'm the first, considering the odds. If I don't ask quick, you'll be dated up through Christmas. The festivals are fun, and Schierstein's beautiful."

"I hear there's 'happy turmoil along the Rhein.' Can you guarantee happy turmoil?"

He understood she was teasing. The sudden smile. "Blood oath. I'll pick you up at fourteen hundred hours."

She went back to her office. Lulu was right. It would be hard to avoid romance. She liked men, and they liked her, but she could and would avoid any but casual relationships, no matter if he had the charisma of Chase Dellasera or the easy charm of Nolan Hanik.

Brencie wondered how she would describe her first day at work to Agnes-Rose. Or her first day in town. Or even her first new friend, Lulu. A new life? The beginning of her second life? Her first life ended in the bathroom of the house in Friendswood, leaving her fractured and miserable. But by the nature of her present assignment, this life would be temporary. She would one day go home, and that would be a new life, too. Cats got nine lives. How many did girls get?

In the late afternoon, march music drifted into the office, and Colonel Foss opened the window. "There's a tattoo, a kind of parade, for a retiree on the CINC's staff," he said. "That's the commander in chief. We can watch from here."

Brencie stood shoulder to shoulder with Colonel Foss as a marching band approached from the south end of the parade ground and halted below the flag. They struck up the "Stars and Stripes Forever," and it was irresistible. Brencie sang the silly lyrics. "Be kind to your fine feathered friends . . ."

To her delight, Colonel Foss joined in. "For a duck may be somebody's mother."

They looked at each other and laughed. When the parade was over, he told her about his wife, Flo, and daughter, Karen, who were with him on this assignment, and about his son back home at Sam Houston State College. Brencie liked her new boss, a good omen.

He checked his watch. "You might as well go, so you don't miss the bus to the Arms. In case you don't have your bearings, the Amelia's a few blocks from the front gate. Once you're living there, you can walk home if you like."

As she left the building, the melancholy sound of "Retreat" echoed from speakers on the parade ground. The bugle call signaled the day's end, a gentle transition from working mode to whatever the evening might bring. Men in uniform saluted and stood at attention, and civilians placed their hands on their hearts. Brencie did the same. It was dusk so far north, but a spotlight illuminated the flag as a detail of airmen lowered Old Glory and folded it away.

Chapter 3

After a promising first week on her new job, Brencie rode across town to the Amelia on Saturday morning. She hadn't taken a taxi alone before, even back home, and when she paid the driver and tipped appropriately, her confidence soared.

When she arrived, one of the desk clerks beckoned to her. "Here is a letter waiting." He handed her an envelope.

"*Danke schön.*" She read his name tag. "Herr Uzan? Did I say it right?"

"*Bitte schön.* Yes, I'm from Turkey. You're from Texas, and you'll be moving here on Wednesday. *Ausgezeichnet.* Excellent."

Ausgezeichnet. She repeated the word in her head. Aus-ge-sigh-snit. It sounded like *outta sight*, hippy slang, and it seemed to mean the same thing. Once on Lulu's floor, she could almost see the mouthwatering aroma of butter and cinnamon that oozed into the hall. The door was open, and Lulu flipped a slice of batter-dipped bread in an electric skillet. "Hi! What's new?" she said.

"I got a letter from my stepmother. She must have mailed it the day I left. The Amelia's the only address she has, and the clerk knew everything about me. He was so serious. I blew him a kiss, and he looked shocked."

"Oh, my God! You flirt! Herr Uzan, right? Now he's yours forever. The clerks know everything about everyone, including which GIs are living in." Lulu popped the cork on a bottle of champagne.

"Champagne for breakfast? That first time you and I rode up in the elevator, I looked for signs saying no men above the ground floor."

"I'm serving it in orange juice glasses. Big juice glasses." Lulu poured the wine and handed a glass to Brencie. "No men above the ground floor? Even Christine Holloway would play hell enforcing that. Tell me about your stepmother."

"That's like asking about water. Or air. Everything Agnes-Rose wears has a Texas logo." Brencie thought about it. "There's no defining her. When she married my father, I was six and furious about it. I hated her, except for her makeup table. I liked that. I never saw so many tubes and jars. I helped myself and dared her to do anything about it."

"Did she catch you?"

"Red-handed. She showed me how to use an eyelash curler and suggested a different shade of lipstick. My dad came in and had a fit. She said, 'Anson. Mind over matter. If I don't *mind*, it doesn't *matter*.' That's Agnes-Rose."

"She's a free spirit. What about your real mother?"

The thought came unbidden. *Agnes-Rose is my real mother in every way that matters.* Brencie took a swig and decided champagne in the morning was a good idea. "My biological mother died in a car crash. I was a baby. I don't remember her."

Lulu gave Brence a long look. "You don't remember her? That's the saddest part."

The look lasted so long Lulu forgot the french toast. "Shit. It's burnt. Well, call it a prototype." She removed the burned bread and turned off the skillet. "Let's enjoy the champagne, and then I'll start over." She brought the bottle to the coffee table and sat beside Brencie on the sofa. "Go ahead. Read your letter."

Brencie drained her glass and opened the letter as Lulu peered over her shoulder. "Not much of a speller," Lulu said. "Read it to me."

"She thinks every important word deserves a double letter. '*Dear Brencie, I was glad to hear you arrived safe.*'" Brencie looked up. "She got my postcard. How's that possible?"

"APO," said Lulu. "Read on."

Last week it was 85 degrees. Freakky in November if it wasn't Texas.

Mrs. Cobe dyed her hair sluddge green, but I fixed it. Didn't help, with her face.

The house is paid off as of the last installmant, but it's in Anson's name. Should I try again to locate him? I check with the police now and then, but except for a fling with an uneducated pig of a dispatchor, nothing. Rick wants your address.

Love your Bee Bee

Love your Bee Bee. Without the comma, Brencie understood it was a plea for forgiveness.

"Anson's your dad. Who's Rick and Bee Bee?" Lulu asked.

"Agnes-Rose is much younger than my dad. He called her Baby Bride, shortened to Bee Bee."

"Ah. Here's to Bee Bee." They clinked and drained their glasses for the third time. "And Rick? If he's a cheating boyfriend, I've heard it a million times"

"OK, short version, as you like to say. Not boyfriend. Fiancé. I caught him with someone else."

"And poof! You're on another continent." Lulu refilled the glasses. "To the Amelia Earhart Hotel, refuge of broken hearts. I read a book called *Whatever Happened to Amelia Earhart*. She disappeared over the Pacific before the war, and no one knows what happened to her."

"*Auf Wiedersehen*, Amelia," Brencie said.

"Elaine from Tulsa who lived down the hall got pregnant," said Lulu, "and it was *Auf Wiedersehen Elaine.* Gone. Left everything. Her stuff will be stored in the sub-basement for a year. *Refuse* of broken hearts." Lulu topped off their drinks and the bottle was empty. "Here's to Elaine, wherever she is."

"And to Amelia Earhart, a woman ahead of her time," said Brencie. "You speak German. How long have you been here?"

"Careful with that question," Lulu suggested. "In a military environment it means 'when are you leaving? Should I bother getting to know you?'"

"I didn't mean that." To hide her pique, Brencie went to the window. "It's starting to rain, but it doesn't stop that runner. There he goes."

"I know you didn't mean that, but you're new in town. I just thought you ought to know. My dad's in the military. I graduated from high school in Munich. When my family left, I came here and got a job. Six years ago." Lulu fetched another bottle. "What about yours?" She opened the bottle, filled their glasses, and went back to her cooking.

"My dad? He went on a business trip when I was ten and didn't come back."

"What? Your mom died and your dad left? Well. that's . . ."

Brencie interrupted. She hadn't meant to talk about her family. "Probably did me a favor. He drank. And speaking of drinking, I've had more to drink in a week than I had in a year back home. I had a drink with Chase Dellasera. Two of 'em."

"Really? Your clothes fell off when he took your hand in the elevator. Did you sleep with him?" Lulu was dipping bread in batter, and she stopped mid-dip. "You're blushing. You did!"

"I certainly did not."

"Why are you getting so agitated? Oh my god! You're not a virgin."

"Not exactly."

"Is that like a *little bit* pregnant?"

"I can't even believe we're having this conversation. If you must know, I slept with my ex after we got engaged. I was all of twenty years old. One thing I took away from *Sex and the Single Girl*. Don't marry anyone you haven't slept with. That seemed logical."

"And you're all about logic." Lulu dropped the bread into the skillet, and it sizzled. "And high moral standards."

"Maybe. Probably more about terror of pregnancy."

"So you aren't on the pill?"

"The pill? Single girls can't get the pill, and I'm not sure about the married ones. Not in Friendswood."

"And Friendswood sounds so friendly. At the American hospital they fill gumball machines with them, every day."

"That sounds too friendly." Brencie giggled. "Did you make that up?"

"No gumball machines, but if you want the pill, all you have to do is ask." Lulu refilled their glasses, then took two cobalt blue plates from a shelf.

"I broke up with Rick months ago, and I don't miss him. Or sex." Brencie squinted her eyes and stared at Lulu. "I can hear you thinking. Snap, crackle, pop."

Lulu laughed. "I'm thinking, you don't miss *sex*? Or you don't miss sex with your *ex*? Maybe he didn't get it right. Mediocre sex is more trouble than it's worth, though I doubt there's a man alive who would say that."

Brencie hiccoughed and then giggled, gaining speed, laughing harder. "I can't believe I'm actually enjoying this conversation. Are you trying to get me drunk? If so, it's happening."

"Sure. Why not. *In vino veritas*. That's what my boyfriend says. Tell me more about your ex," Lulu said. "Handsome? Rich?"

"Good-looking, yes. He looks a lot like my father. Agnes-Rose tried to point that out, but I only saw it recently. I don't know why it took me so long."

Lulu shrugged. "Not unusual for a girl to be attracted to someone who reminds them of their dad, and not to see it at first. Know what *auf wiedersehen* means, literally? *Wieder* means again. *Sehen* is to see, to look or watch. *Auf* is kinda squishy, but it means *on* in this case. So on seeing, or looking again. You'll see a lot of things differently when you've been here a while."

"Well, when I realized the resemblance I was stupefied. And horrified." Brencie started to laugh, and it was contagious.

Lulu laughed, too. "Are you going to tell me what we're laughing about? Dad? Sex? You have to tell me, or I'll die of curiosity."

"No, not Dad. About Rick. No reason not to tell you. In *vino veritas*. I'll never see him again, and you'll never meet him." Brencie punctuated her words with laughter. "Get a . . . load of . . . this. He . . ."

"He what? Stop laughing and tell me." Lulu was laughing harder too.

"He sometimes … passed wind when he, you know . . ."

It took Lulu three seconds. "Oh, no! You don't mean he farted when he *came*?" Lulu had to put down her glass, she was laughing so hard. "Are you kidding?"

"I said *sometimes*. Just a little toot-toot, not loud, and not every time."

"I don't see how you kept from falling out of bed in stiches. I had a boyfriend who sometimes sneezed. Gave me a little last-minute kick, as long as he remembered to turn his head." Brencie laughed even harder as Lulu managed to complete the task at hand. She turned the toast one last time, sprinkled it with powdered sugar, and put a plump, red strawberry on each plate.

"Thanks for the most fun conversation ever," Brencie said. "I haven't laughed so hard since a rude teenager swore at Agnes-Rose in the grocery store, and she hit him in the back of the head with an over-ripe tomato."

"Wow. I'm getting a pretty good picture of your stepmom. I love her."

"Everyone does. As for the pill, I don't need it this very afternoon, but I do have a date tomorrow." She took a bite of the toast. "Oh, my god. This is the best thing in the world."

"A date with Chase?" Lulu licked her fingers. "Umm. Sticky."

"A guy from work. Nolan Hanik. We're going to a beer festival."

"You have a date with Nolan Hanik? Everyone knows Nolan. He's on the base football team. He plays when the other guys have the ball."

"Defense." Brencie took another bite. "Wow. This is the best french toast I ever had."

"Nutmeg in the batter. Do you like to cook?"

"I don't cook," said Brencie.

"What?" Lulu flashed the impish expression. "If you are female, *Achtung*! You *vill* cook. '*Kinder, Küche, und Kirche.*' Old Nazi expression about a woman's place. 'Children, kitchen, and church.' Not far off all over the world. As for Nolan, he's as un-gay as it gets, but he doesn't date. Or didn't. Can Jules and I come? He's going to find you interesting. He finds everyone interesting. He gets out of jail today."

"He's in the pokey?" Brencie hiccoughed and laughed at the same time. "Excuse me."

"Pokey? Right. MPs raided the Café Ekstase downtown. It's off limits to GIs. Jules got caught."

"How did you meet Jules-the-Jailbird?"

"His last name's Pasternak, like the guy who wrote *Dr. Zhivago*. It means *parsnip*. We take lessons from the same voice teacher, and I arrived early. He was singing "La Donna è Mobile." "Women are fickle." I hate that song, and he insisted women *are* fickle, so I called him a big tenor *Scheisskopf*, which means . . ."

"I know what *that* means. You called him a dirty name, and he asked you for a date? Men are knuckleheads." Brencie got to her feet. "Whoa. I'll have to learn to pace myself. As it is, I've gotta get back to the Arms and take a nap. Glad I'm not driving."

Lulu walked her to the door. "Nolan has a car, right? What time will you pick us up?"

———— ((●)) ————

Brencie waited in the lobby at the Arms. When Nolan arrived wearing a jaunty flapjack hat and a dark blue jacket, he seemed ill at ease, but he brightened when he saw her. They were almost to the exit when Chase Dellasera came out of the restaurant in civilian clothes. "Good morning, *Fräulein* Jessup," he said.

Brencie nodded but kept moving until she and Nolan were out front.

"Who was that?" he asked.

"Chase Something. Lulu introduced us on the base." *Chase Dellasera*, she thought, absurdly pleased a man she hardly knew had remembered her name.

"An officer." A dark green Volkswagen Beetle waited at the curb. It wasn't new, but it was spotless. "Meet Grendel's Mother. Grendel was my badass football nickname in high school." He offered her the quick smile as he opened the car door.

"Lulu told me you play on some football team. I hope you don't mind about Lulu and Jules? It would have been awkward to say no."

When he got in the driver's seat, he said, "It's fine. I've met Lulu, and anyway, she won me over by volunteering to bring the food. I know Jules too. He's a medical corpsman. They call him The Genius. Straight A's through two years of college. Psychology major. And

— 37 —

it isn't *some* football team. It's the Wiesbaden Warriors, competing with American bases all over Europe."

"Sorry. I haven't been here long, remember. Why did he leave school?"

"Got burned out. I left school for the same reason." The sun appeared as they passed the Kronprinzen Park, and a breeze sent fallen leaves aloft like confetti. They passed an imposing brown brick building, complete with arches, high windows, a colonnade, and a clock tower. "That's the *Bahnhof.* Train station," said Nolan. "See the empty slabs over the arches? There used to be swastikas there."

"Why haven't they put something in the spaces?" she asked. "The war was a long time ago."

"Twenty years is nothing, for some things. Vietnam was my last assignment. Sometimes I wake up thinking I'm still there." When they stopped at a red light, he nodded toward the crosswalk. "That man? Fortyish? A former Nazi, probably, or Hitler Youth. Remember Wolfgang Ritter? You met him on your first day. He was fourteen when he went into the *Wehrmacht*, which means war machine. Besides being General Novak's favorite driver, he learned to be a mechanic. Jeep. Tank. Golf cart. Doesn't matter. He can fix it."

At the Amelia, Lulu was out front standing beside an oversized young man with black hair pushing military standards. He greeted Nolan, then surprised Brencie with a bear hug. Lulu and her bulging tote bag got into the back seat, leaving just enough room for Jules to squeeze in. When they got to Schierstein, they left their things in the car to explore the festival, and Jules immediately consumed a bratwurst and a hard roll.

Lulu pouted. "You won't want my beautiful sandwiches now."

"I'm a trained fighting man," said Jules. "Can't get enough sandwiches or sex."

The lemon-colored sunlight cast a spell on the day. The brats smelled spicier, the click of shoes on the dance platform resonated, and the band was an orchestra playing a polka. Nolan put his hands on Brencie's waist and spun her around the floor. Lulu and Jules followed, and when the number ended, everyone but Nolan was breathless. "You're a good dancer," Brencie said. "Let's go again. What is that?"

"A *Schottisch*," said Lulu. "German folk dance."

"Oh, we did that in gym class in high school. One-two-three skip. One-two-three turn. Let's try," said Brencie.

"One-two-three skip? Uh. No," Nolan said. "But I can waltz. Maybe they'll play one later. I like to waltz, but don't tell anyone. We trained fighting men don't waltz."

The guys went to the car for their things, and Lulu and Brencie found a grassy area above the river. The cooling air of the afternoon said winter was coming, and Brencie sighed. Lulu sensed her shift in mood. "Are you homesick?" she asked.

"That's not it, exactly. It's painful like that, but it's something else."

"*Sehnsucht*," Lulu said. "*Deutsche* word. It means missing someone you never met, or longing for something you never had. Even understanding something you'll never understand."

Nolan and Jules arrived carrying the picnic trappings. Lulu spread a blanket, opened a bottle of wine, and passed around Gouda and ham on flaky croissants. After they ate, Jules stretched out and surveyed the surroundings. "This country was rubble twenty years ago. Before you know it, Vietnam will be just another tourist attraction."

"Colonel Foss served in Vietnam," Brencie said, declining a second glass of wine. "Also in World War II and Korea. He's my boss."

"My old man had flat feet," said Jules. "Kept him home. I knew this master sergeant in 'Nam. When I got orders to Wiesbaden, he said, 'From hell to Wiesbaden, where WW Two's a memory and the Cold War's a party.'"

Nolan ripped up a handful of grass and tossed it into the air. The breeze scattered it. "My father served in the Pacific, but he won't talk about it. War's a waste. A GI jumped from that bridge a week ago. I saw the report. They dragged the harbor but didn't find him. He was fresh from 'Nam."

"From a clusterfuck war to the Cold War." Jules looked at the sun going down and the shining silver river. "When the Cold War ends, if we don't destroy the planet first, this little American raj will disappear. Of course, if we destroy the planet, everything disappears."

"So enjoy everything while it lasts," offered Lulu.

"Right. Sure," Jules said. "Adjust or jump off a bridge. I read a sci-fi novel about a planet where the ground was like a wet sponge or a cloud. Strangers had to find a different way of walking or sink and disappear."

"Change their way of walking," said Brencie. "But not themselves?"

Jules thought about it. "Well, they didn't grow an extra leg, so yeah. Their way of walking, but adapting is key." He lit a cigarette and flicked ashes on the blanket.

Lulu rolled her eyes. "The blanket isn't an ashtray."

"The world's an ashtray." Jules offered the pack to Lulu, then said, "Brencie doesn't smoke, I'm sure, and Nolan's in training. He jogs."

"I don't jog," Nolan said. "I run."

"That's it!" said Brencie. "I thought I'd seen you before. You go by the Amelia. I saw you the day I arrived, and yesterday too."

"Small world," Lulu said as she opened a tin of shortbread. "You know, Jules, it wouldn't kill you to get a little exercise."

"It might. Why risk it?" said Jules. "I gave up exercise after basic training. I sweated so much in 'Nam I didn't need to move at all."

"I was stationed near Da Nang," said Nolan. "The barracks stank like dirty socks and rancid rice, and the flight line got shelled. I thought they might lob a mortar on my cot with me in it."

Jules took a drag and blew an elegant smoke ring. "I was at Tan

Son Nhut. An Army kid from Daytona shot some gooks, right on the base. Two laundry girls and a mess hall cook. It was hushed up. Crazy, but army guys saw some shit." Nolan and Jules gazed at the horizon with the vacant look of blind men.

"Here we are," said Brencie. "Lulu and me, standing outside the treehouse. No Girls Allowed."

"Who wants to be allowed?" Lulu replied. "Men like to bash each other in the name of a cause, but really, they just like to bash each other."

"Know a lot about war, do you?" said Jules.

"I know a lot about men. They like to fight, so we have contact sports and wars. Ask Nolan."

Nolan smiled. "All football players aren't brutes."

Lulu shrugged. "Can we talk about something fun now? Like wine? Love? Music?"

"Ah, that distracting little shrug," Jules said. "They compare love and war all the time, so it's the same subject. Come sit by me, and we'll sort it out."

When Lulu moved close to Jules, Nolan helped Brencie to her feet. "Let's walk." It was peaceful along the river, and he asked about NASA, the astronauts, the space flights. "How did you get that job?"

"I fell into it. My stepmother owns a beauty shop called The Swank, where death-by-lacquer is the main hazard. I remember the exact day. She was hair-spraying her troubles away, and I was worried about graduation."

"And you didn't want to marry the lovesick beau, or you didn't love him?" They found a bench near the water and sat down.

"I loved him, but we were years too young. After the last customer left, my stepmother handed me an envelope full of cash, every tip she got for years, enough for business school. In the meantime, NASA came to Clearlake, and there was a hiring frenzy, rocket scientists, aerospace engineers. Lots of secretaries, clerks, cafeteria cooks. A lady came to my high school and tested the girls in typing and shorthand. I filled out a few thousand forms and got called for an interview."

A soccer ball rolled in front of them. In a smooth motion, Nolan stood up, tossed the ball in the air, and side-kicked it back to a small boy a few yards away. He smiled. "Did they put you to work as a cook?"

"Oh, sure. I hate to cook, though Lulu says it's mandatory for women. NASA offered me a job as a stenographer, and I took it. The business school money went for work clothes and a used car. You ask almost as many questions as Lulu. Tell me something about you."

"My middle name's Anthony. I like The Rolling Stones. I was pre-law at the University of Illinois, but like Jules, I got burned out."

There was something he wasn't saying, but Brencie let it go. She had her own secrets, and according to *The Book of Agnes-Rose*: "The way to keep a secret is simple. Don't tell anyone."

"I'll go back when I get out of the service. I like the law. Lawyers have status and make good money. What brought you here? You're younger than most of the ladies at the Amelia. They call it Menopause Manor. Did you know that?"

"That's mean," but she couldn't suppress a laugh. "I wanted to travel, and this is how I can afford it. Lulu says you don't date, but here we are."

"Lulu likes to talk. I asked you out because you recited the oath from memory and you aren't totally unattractive. I'm having trouble getting you to talk about yourself. Still waters run deep?"

"Look! The fireworks are starting. Come on football player. Race you back!"

She was halfway up the hill before Nolan caught up, and then they settled on the blanket with Lulu and Jules. The fireworks signaled the end of the fest, and when the last incendiary star fell apart and dribbled away, the crowd was silent, unwilling to break the spell. Softly, so only her friends might hear, Lulu sang.

Yes, we'll gather at the river,
The beautiful, beautiful river,

With one arm around Jules, Lulu put her other arm around Brencie who picked up the song. Jules added his polished tenor, and Brencie put her arm around Nolan. She nudged him, and he sang, keeping his voice low.

Gather with the saints at the river
That flows by the throne of God.
Shall we gather . . .
Shall we gather . . .
Shall we gather . . .

When the song was over, they packed their things and left, dropping Jules and Lulu at the Amelia. At the Arms, Nolan declined the invitation to have a drink in the bar. "Thanks, but it's an officers' facility. I'm not encouraged to hang out here. You'll be at the Amelia soon." He came around and opened the car door. "Do you expect me to ask you out again?"

"I thought you might. Do you expect me to say yes?"

"I thought you might. How's this? Five years from now we'll be married. I'll be finishing law school, and you can help me decide which of many job offers to accept."

It was ridiculous, and they both laughed, but she wanted to make one thing clear. "You're cute as they come, Nolan, but I'm not looking for anything long term."

"No one ever is." He brushed her lips with his. "I'll do that properly soon, but not today."

The following week Christine Holloway showed Brencie apartment four oh eight. The view was the same as from Lulu's apartment, as were the furnishings, except Brencie had a wine-red sleeper sofa instead of a green one. She was eager to sign the paperwork, so in Christine's office, Brencie read through the forms. "My obligation will be eleven dollars a month?"

"For the daily maid service and the phone," Christine said. "The maid is optional. I'm sorry. Sometimes the personnel people back home give the impression everything's free on an overseas placement."

"They said my expenses would be nominal, but eleven dollars? That's way less than I expected. And I want the maid."

Christine smiled. "Nearly everyone does. Here's the welcome packet and your key. Any more questions?"

"I'll need to do laundry soon . . ."

"Information's in the packet. There's a laundry room on the basement level. You can use the machines for free, or for a quarter a load, the laundry girls will take care of it and deliver it to your room, usually the same day. If there's nothing else, you'll be billed for what's left of October, and more good news. Your household shipment came. It's in the sub-basement. Who knows? Maybe they can find it again, and I'll have it sent up to your apartment ASAP."

Brencie taxied to the American Arms, packed her things, and settled her bill for less than twenty dollars. In an hour she was back at the Amelia, so she stopped by the deli on the arcade for a split of champagne. A s soon as she got to her new apartment, she called Lulu.

"Five five four six two. Miss Greenholt."

"Lulu-no-doubt. It's Brencie. I'm home. Apartment four oh eight. Stop by after work?"

"Fabulous! I'm leaving this minute."

Brencie hung up and went out onto the balcony. She looked down to see a flock of sparrows darting from branch to branch. The treetops were level with the bottom railing, giving her a new point of view.

Chapter 4

On the Friday before Christmas an early dismissal was in place, and Brencie did a walk-through in her division. All classified materials were stored according to regulations, so at thirteen hundred hours, she locked the safes, initialed the forms, and wished Colonel Foss *Frohe Weihnachten*. Merry Christmas. She ran into Wolfgang Ritter, the general's driver, as she left the building.

"*Guten Abend*, Brencie. I'm done for the day, but I can run you to the Amelia before I go back to the motor pool. It's still snowing a little."

She thanked him, but declined the offer. She couldn't wait to walk home in the fresh snow that had fallen all afternoon.

She swept snow from low walls along her route and shook it from fir trees. It was true what they said. Everyone's a kid again when the first snow falls. *Why not?* she thought. She lay down on an incline, flapped her arms, and then got up to survey her first snow angel. She was damp and shivering by the time she entered the Amelia.

In the lobby a fifteen-foot Christmas tree rose in a twinkle of white lights and silver ornaments. The scent of evergreen filled the air, and poinsettias in silver urns stood on either end of the reception desk. A quick trip upstairs to change clothes, and when she came down again, Lulu still hadn't appeared, though they had agreed to meet at fourteen hundred. Brencie collected her mail, including a card from Mary Ann, her best friend from Friendswood High.

Dear Brencie,

Sorry I haven't answered your letter, but my wedding's days away, so I've been busy! Can you believe it? I'll be a Mrs! Wish you were here to be a bridesmaid. The dresses are a fabulous shade of purple!

I hope you have a great Christmas! I still remember the green eggnog Agnes-Rose used to make. She loved Christmas! She put rum in it (we weren't supposed to tell anyone).

Love ya!
Mary Ann (Johnson soon-to-be-Glick)

Brencie had almost been a Christmas bride. She sighed. Letters from her friends ran together now. Someone got married, someone moved away. Birth announcements would be next, but Mary Ann was right; Agnes-Rose loved the holidays. The first Christmas after Anson left, she came home from The Swank to find Brencie in tears. "I know, honey. You miss him." She sat down and patted Brencie's knee.

Brencie took her stepmother's chapped hand. "Oh, Bee Bee. You said you would hire someone to help with the chemicals."

"Next year, if things keep going good." After Anson left, they got by, but with few extras. Agnes-Rose went to her bedroom and came back with a heavy box wrapped in Santa Claus paper. "Now seems like a good time for your gift," she said. "You know, I can deal with Anson's skedaddle, and for me there's a silver lining." She waited until Brencie looked at her. "Honey, you're the silver lining. It was a big hurt for you, but the best thing Anson ever did for me was not take you with him when he left. Maybe I'll find another man, but there's no one as special as you."

Brencie opened the gift and exploded with pleasure. Skates, white boots with wheels, the kind the kids wore at the roller rink. Renting skates marked you as a have-not, and the first time she wore her own, she sailed around the wooden oval like a queen.

A WASKI group entered the Amelia lobby chanting "One-two-three-ski." Members of the Wiesbaden American Ski Club would soon head to Austria, Switzerland, or Bavaria, and skis were stacked like teepees around the room. Along the back wall brass trays and candlesticks gleamed on two long tables. Local merchants were allowed to set up shop for two days at a time, and even though everyone joked about the bizarre bazaars, they bought wood carvings, camel-saddle foot stools, and pink alabaster grapes.

Brencie drew her small sketch pad out of her bag, hoping to capture the excitement in the lobby, but she was interrupted when Leah Crum walked by with an armful of packages. She wore a short, plaid kilt and a beige fisherman's sweater. It was the first time Brencie had seen her in civilian clothes, and although she looked good in uniform, trim and businesslike, today her ash blond hair was loose. She looked pretty and young.

Brencie put her pad away. "Hi, Captain Crum," she said. "Are you visiting someone?"

"Please, call me Leah. I moved out of the Open Arms. If I set foot in the bar there, I'm 'looking to get picked up,' and God forbid I leave with anyone. Here, I can have a drink in the bar of my habitat and I'm just having a drink. Are you working next week? Let's have a long lunch."

As Leah moved on, Lulu came in the front door clad in red jacket, red pants, and a red beret with a green rhinestone reindeer pinned to one side. She carried two huge bags of groceries, which she thrust into Brencie's arms.

"Oh my god! The crowds in the commissary. I'll be right back. Two more bags in the taxi."

Lulu had hosted Thanksgiving and was eager to have Christmas dinner too. Holiday dinners were served in all American installations, but Lulu nixed the idea. "Two years ago everyone who ate in Café Amelia, including me, got sick," she said. "Long story. Short version? We did the Turkey Trot for days."

"Joy to the World" played on the radio at the reception desk, mingling with "Green Grass of Home" from the bar. Lulu rolled her eyes. "Shit. Is that the only song on the juke box?" She swam through the crowd to retrieve the rest of her groceries, and then she and Brencie squeezed into the packed elevator. One last passenger elbowed in, jostling Lulu and launching an orange from the top of her brown paper bag. The orange escaped into the lobby as the doors closed.

"Never mind," said Lulu. "It will be juice before I can get to it." She turned to Brencie. "Come help me put the groceries away. I have two hours before play practice, all the way across town at the Community Center. You should come. It's nice. A mansion we took over after the war."

"Thanks, but Nolan's coming over. I thought you only had a walk-on part."

"A *tiny* walk-on. Servant Girl Number Two, yet I have to be there every night, like I had the damn lead. Well. It *is* an Arthur Miller play."

"We read *The Crucible* in advanced English," Brencie said. "But I *am* an experienced thespian. In high school I was Cowboy Number Three in *Annie Get Your Gun*."

"*Cowboy* Number Three? You should join the American Players. You need some hobbies."

"Living *is* my hobby. At least that's what Agnes-Rose says. Besides, I read. I knit. Well, I hated knitting. I sketch now, instead. I play tennis. Do you play?"

"Of course not. I ski a bit because it's glamorous, but otherwise, I'm an indoor girl. You saw the courts behind the hotel? Too cold now, but I think there's a tennis club."

In Lulu's apartment they put the perishables to one side. Her tiny refrigerator was full of beer and wine, but there were two huge community kitchens on each floor, with six full-sized American refrigerators in each. Lulu had reserved a kitchen for use on Christmas day, and the perishables would be stored there. She pulled a long chain out of a cabinet, and they transported everything down the hall. Once the food was in the fridge, Lulu wound the chain around the back and through the front handle, securing it with a padlock. "It's a hotel full of hungry women. In more ways than one." They returned to the apartment. "Speaking of hungry, if I don't have a cigarette, I'm eating a bag of chips." She lit up. "Angelika wants me to quit. It affects my voice, but it's a struggle."

"My stepmother says food is to women as sex is to men."

"Jules says *mother* is a powerful thing, step or otherwise. He says I don't like myself because my mother doesn't like me. He says Agnes-Rose is probably a big flirt."

"He says a lot. What does that even mean? He doesn't know her. Or me."

"No, but he watches you dangle your gentleman linebacker. Are you sleeping with him?"

"You and Jules gossip and like old ladies."

"Well, I don't get it," Lulu said. "You like him, and he's crazy about you. He's got that bad boy kind of attraction without being a bad boy, and you've been seeing him for weeks. What does Agnes-Rose say?"

"About what? About sex? She probably started having sex when she was fourteen, so cautioning me about it would have been tough. If there's anything she isn't, it's a hypocrite."

"I like her more all the time. She must have said something."

"Her advice. Let's see. 'Don't do anything you don't want to do. You never have to apologize or explain your choices to any man.' That's all I remember on short notice. Oh. She cautioned me that a normal young woman has needs. 'Be on the lookout for that,' she said."

Lulu was laughing. "You seem like a normal young woman to me."

"God, Lulu. I get more normal every time I'm with Nolan. I just want to go slow. Now that he's captain of the Warriors, he's gone a lot," said Brencie. "That takes the pressure off. He's leaving tonight and won't be back until Christmas day."

Lulu shrugged. "I'll bet Nolan Hanik could do a better job than your famous farting fiancé."

"I shouldn't have told you about that. In my world there are good and bad girls. The rules are changing, but sex is more than something to do."

"Oh, don't take it all so seriously," said Lulu, "which you do sometimes. Oh, crap. I forgot the stinkin' sorbet. It's dripping. I'll be right back." She left her cigarette in the ashtray and hurried down the hall with the sorbet.

Brencie went out on the balcony to survey the snow-covered valley. She gathered some flakes from the railing, but it was too powdery to make a snowball. The particles floated away like fairy dust. Out on the street Nolan ran by, his feet leaving depressions in the snow like a dotted line tracing his route.

Lulu joined Brencie. "I caught my neighbor trying to jimmy the lock on the fridge." She saw Nolan as he turned the corner and disappeared. "He's a machine. Brrr. Let's go inside."

Lulu arranged cheese and crackers on a red plate, and placed several leaf-shaped green gumdrops on the side. "Jules is stopping by. He settles down better in the presence of food." Lulu looked at her watch. "Still an hour till play rehearsal. Guess what. I ran into Chase

Dellasera at the base. He's been deployed and was heading to the States for the holidays. He asked about you. I told him you were living here, which he knew. He said he called you twice, but you didn't answer. He had lots of leave saved up after Vietnam, so now he won't be back until February."

So he had called. No one had ever had such an enduring effect on Brencie. She couldn't stop thinking about him, even now. "I thought I might see him here in the bar some time."

"What? Here? At the Amelia? Officers don't come to the Amelia. The ladies go to the Arms."

"We're supposed to go to them?" Brencie said. "There's something shabby about that."

"Shabby. Just the right word. Well, if you ever get over your broken engagement, Nolan is standing by."

"You know what, Lulu? There's something I haven't told you about that . . ."

There was one solid bang on the door, and Jules came in wearing medical corps whites and smelling like disinfectant and snow. He swept Lulu into his arms. "God, Lucille. If you get any more beautiful, the world can't stand it. I'll have to kill you."

Lulu laughed. "If you get any more full of shit, the world will run short of toilet paper."

"OK, you two," said Brencie. "I'm outta here."

⟫•⟪

On Christmas morning, Brencie answered the door in her nightgown.

"Oh, red silk." Nolan kissed her, a long kiss, and she felt his erection against her hip. "How's it possible to miss what I haven't had?" he mumbled into her neck.

"*Sehnsucht?*"

"Great word." He kissed her again, and she felt the thin fabric of her nightgown riding up her thighs, desire rising with it.

"Nolan, don't. Not yet."

"Do you have any idea the effect you have on me? You do, don't you. You answered the door in your nightgown. This is foreplay." He didn't release her.

"You're an hour early. If you had been on time, I would have been dressed. I'd call it flirting, not foreplay." She laughed, and he let her go.

"There's something about your laugh," he said. "It's sad and happy at the same time."

"That's what Agnes-Rose says." Brencie got her clothes and went to the bathroom, leaving the door ajar, aware it was provocative. Soon it would be a new year. Maybe New Year's Eve would be the night. "What time is it?" she called. "Are we late yet?"

"Why don't you wear a watch?"

"I used to. It stopped working and I decided I didn't need it. There's clocks everywhere."

"Except in the bathroom," he answered.

When she was dressed, she poured him a cup of coffee and noticed a flat package on the table.

"Oh, gifts now? Looks like a book. We've given each other the same thing." She went to her tinsel tree and handed Nolan a foil-wrapped present. "You go first."

He opened the package and found a history of football in two volumes. He grinned. "You're doing your damnedest to avoid romance."

"I warned you about that, and anyway, you've given me a book too." She tore the wrapping off and found a leather-bound five-year diary, with a lock and a gnat-sized key. "This is more romantic than a history of football. I love it."

"You love a lot of things, Brencie. Reading. Food. Dancing. Lulu. Snow. Foss the Boss. Robins. Even Wolfgang Ritter, the general's driver, for hell's sake. What about me?"

"You love things too. Beer. Football. Also dancing."

He didn't smile. "That's not what I meant."

"On our first date I told you I wasn't looking for that kind of trouble. Did the Warriors win?"

"We did, so we're in the playoffs. I'll be gone more if we keep winning. When we play in Mainz, you can all come. It's just across the river. You can drive Grendel's Mother, if you can drive a stick shift."

"I learned to drive on a 1948 Studebaker pick-up truck. I can drive anything." Brencie stood before the hall mirror applying lipstick, the last touch before they went up to Lulu's. "I'll get an international license. I want one, just so I can write to my friends about it."

They were upstairs in time to help set up the buffet. Jules and Nolan took Lulu's Christmas tree onto the balcony, trailing pine needles, and when they moved the couch, Jules clutched his chest. "Dr. Bernard can do me a heart transplant, so I might survive. If you make me a sandwich."

"You're heartless to begin with," Lulu said. "No sandwich. Besides, the guy who got the heart transplant died. But it's amazing all the same."

The guests were assembled by noon, including two colored GIs from Jules's unit. Brencie had been surprised to see them at Lulu's Thanksgiving dinner. She wasn't even sure *colored* was the right word. At NASA if a luncheon group was inclusive, someone called the restaurant to ask if bringing *Negroes* would be a problem.

The Christmas group also included two girls Brencie hadn't met, petite Dierdre Goode with a red pony tail, and skinny Margo Caufield, blond hair to the middle of her back. Brencie barely said hello before the two girls began batting the conversation back and forth.

"Margo and I are from St. Louis. We went through nursing school together and went to work in the same hospital. Then we applied for jobs here. We came before the start of our contracts, so we could check things out," said Dierdre, "and at the airport we met some back-packers . . ."

"Who persuaded us to hitchhike to Spain," Margo said, "and when our money and time ran out, we hitchhiked back to Wiesbaden . . ."

"Where our jobs were waiting, but boy . . ."

"Was Spain fun. We ate paella and drank sangria.

"We got drunk and fat . . ."

"And here we are," Margo finished. "Dierdre's running the whole nursing staff and pissing off the doctors because she knows more than they do. We've been here two years."

"A year to go," said Dierdre.

Lulu clapped her hands three times. "Buffet's open! Come and get it!"

By 1900 hours all the guests were some combination of tipsy, stuffed, or sleepy, and it took Nolan and Jules both to clear everyone out. Lulu wanted Jules and Nolan gone too, which they were as soon as she mentioned the kitchen down the hall stacked high with greasy pots and pans.

Lulu and Jules left for Paris the day after Christmas. Brencie's favorite sergeant at work rotated back to the States before the holidays, and another one would leave soon. Nolan was in town this week, but who knew where the infamous Chase Dellasera was? He was still on her mind, though, and occasionally in her dreams.

During the Christmas-to-New-Year's slowdown, Brencie had Tuesday lunch with Leah Crum, and mid-week Nolan suggested they grab a bite at a popular *Gasthaus* a few yards from the back gate of Lindsey. The sun was shining for the first time in weeks, so the sidewalks were crowded and slushy. The saluting ritual slowed the foot traffic more than usual, and Nolan didn't see a passing officer. He failed to salute.

"Sergeant!" barked the pasty-faced second lieutenant. "You salute your superiors. Stand at attention!" They were in the middle of the sidewalk, forcing people to walk around them.

"Sorry, sir. I didn't see a *superior* officer."

"Excuse me?" The lieutenant peered at Nolan's name tag. "Sergeant Hanik."

"I said, I didn't see a *superior* officer." He leaned forward to read the lieutenant's name. "Lieutenant McBride."

McBride shot Nolan a withering look, but Nolan didn't wither. His body seemed to expand, and the skin above his collar turned deep red. Brencie held her breath.

"I'll take that salute now." McBride's tone changed. He must have realized he had stumbled onto dangerous turf. This could go wrong, and it would be as bad for him as for Nolan. Nolan saluted in slow motion, and the lieutenant walked away.

Nolan set a clip toward the Gasthaus, and conversation was impossible. They were seated and their drinks were served before he spoke. "Self-righteous bastards because they have rank on their shoulders. Especially shitty little shavetails no older than me. You wouldn't believe the crap they pulled in 'Nam. I should have flattened him." He took a swig of his beer. He didn't usually drink in the middle of the day.

"You were surly. If you did any more, there would have been consequences," she said.

"I came close to not giving a damn. He humiliated me."

"Holding your temper kept you from spending New Year's in the brig, and without Jules for company. He's been good lately. Lieutenant Knucklehead was no match for you physically." It was true, and it would soothe his ego.

"Good point." His smile seemed genuine. "If I hadn't left university before graduating, I'd be an officer. Then I could bully the lower ranks. Maybe that's what gets under my skin."

"You've never told me the real reason you left school."

He paused, like he wasn't sure he wanted to tell her. "Something happened. Remember at Schierstein, when Lulu said guys bash each other for fun? When I was fourteen I was skinny, and I got picked on. I worked out with weights, so I could pick back. I liked knowing I was strong. I still do."

He took a deep breath. "I was at a big Rotary Club barbecue. My dad was on the board at the time. I was scuffling with my brother. There's something in me. Anger's hot. This other thing. It's cold. Relentless. We fell across a picnic table and rolled off, taking a lot of food with us. My brother tried to stop, but I wouldn't, until I knocked him backwards into a folding chair. When he went down, I felt powerful. Proud."

"Obnoxious, maybe, but not the end of the world."

"I'm not done. A little girl named Debbie was all tangled in the chair. She was eating a piece of pie when the chair collapsed. When she got up there was a plastic fork buried in her eye. Her mother screamed, and her dad took her to the emergency room. He would have killed me if he could, and I deserved it. An inch deeper and the fork would have penetrated her brain. I was twenty. I knew actions have consequences, but I thought they could be predicted. They can't. I caused a child to lose an eye. I embarrassed my family. I left school."

"It was an accident. You never meant it to happen."

"Doesn't change it, and I learned to channel that cold thing. It's what turns me into a wall on the football field. No one's getting by me. It will help me get through law school. I joined the Air Force for room and board and a salary, so I could pay Debbie's medical bills, which I paid off four months ago." He flashed the smile. "And now I can afford to date."

He had revealed himself in a way that didn't necessarily show him in a good light. It was brave, and it made Brencie want to confide in him, tell him about her falling out with Agnes-Rose, tell him about her broken engagement. She reached out to touch him, to open that confessional, but the food arrived with a shuffle and clatter, and the moment passed.

Happy New Year 1968! The optimism of a new year expressed itself in an enormous banner over the bandstand.

The long folding wall dividing the Amelia restaurant from the bar area was opened up to create a ballroom. Silver streamers dropped from the ceiling, and bits of confetti and glitter adorned the tables. Jules caused a glitter explosion just by sitting down. "Christ! There's glitter in my eye," he said. "Ouch. Ouch. It hurts. Lulu, help me!"

Lulu tilted his head back. "Look up." She dabbed at his lower eyelid.

He blinked. "It's gone. How did you do that?"

"One of my many talents. Now stop thrashing around and be happy. It's a new year." The band, hired from England, launched into "Satisfaction."

"All right," said Nolan. "My favorite song from my favorite band." The tables emptied and the dance floor filled. By the time the medley ended with "Let's Spend the Night Together," Brencie was ready to remove her high heels. "Hmmm. 'Let's Spend the Night

Together.' It might be my new favorite," Nolan said. "They can't even use those lyrics in the States. So I'm told."

The band slowed it down with "Nights in White Satin," and Brencie liked the way his hips moved to the melody, sexy, immediate. The lyrics ended with "I love you," and he held her so tight she could hardly breath. She felt a surge of something she couldn't run from, and why should she?

The band took a break, and Nolan led her back to the table. "Great party," Brencie said as they sat down.

"It is." Jules nodded. "But wait till Fasching. That cranks up in February."

"What's Fasching?" Brencie asked.

"Carnival. Better than Mardi Gras. A frenzy of self-indulgence and then damn. The self-denial of lent. You know the Krauts and their rules. You aren't allowed into any of the big parties around town unless you're in costume. Forces everyone to wear fancy dress and lose their inhibitions."

Dierdre and Margo arrived wearing identical light-blue dresses with horizontal ruffles circling the dress from shoulder to hem. Jules and Nolan got two more chairs.

"Where did you get those dresses?" Lulu kept her tone neutral.

"Sears catalogue, page fifty-two," said Dierdre.

When it was time for the global *wieder* bye-bye 1967, *guten* howdy 1968, the countdown began. Five, four, three, two, one, Happy New Year! To the bittersweet melody of "Auld Lang Syne," Nolan whispered in Brencie's ear, "Don't send me back to the barracks tonight."

Midnight kisses were bestowed on strangers and lovers, and the party was over.

Nolan exuded expectation as they walked the long hallway to Brencie's apartment, and when they stepped inside, he slipped his arms around her. She wanted to melt into him, let it happen, but she wavered. She was afraid. *No. Not afraid*, she thought. *Unsure.*

He sensed her hesitation. "Brencie, is it about your ex-fiancé? I'm pretty sure I don't remind you of your dad."

She pulled back. "What? How did you . . . oh. Lulu-no-doubt."

"She told Jules. Jules told me. It's not a big deal."

"I'll want a word with her." Thank God she hadn't told Lulu everything. *To keep a secret, don't tell anyone.* Nolan's use of what he wasn't supposed to know felt like manipulation. The sexual tension turned into anger. "It's a big deal to me."

"I'm sorry. It was the wrong time to bring it up," he said. "But you could have told me. Your dad and your fiancé resembled each other. Why's that a big deal? You learned why I left school because I told you. I haven't told anyone else."

"Maybe this has nothing to do with anything except I don't want to go to bed with you."

"Your body temperature goes up every time I touch you."

"In your imagination. The male ego's a wonderful thing."

"This isn't about ego," he said. "Stop judging all men by one man. It's childish."

"Childish?" She broke away. "Don't you dare try to bully me into bed."

"Childish was a bad word choice, but do you think for one minute I'd *bully* you? About anything? I've never made an aggressive move on you, even when you invited me to."

"What? I said 'hello' and you thought 'She wants me'?"

"That's bullshit. Don't pretend you didn't know how parading around in a thin nightgown would affect me. You enjoyed it. I think you're afraid to get laid, so you're getting mad instead."

"And I think you're just another vulgar GI. Go ahead, accuse me of being a tease. Then you can leave, and I don't have to give you a reason."

"And I don't need one."

He stormed down the hall, and he didn't wait for the elevator. He ducked into the stairwell and disappeared.

Chapter 5

Fasching settled on the Rheingau like a long-running prank. Weekend parades and masked balls ramped up to a frenzy the closer it got to *Fastnacht*, the Tuesday before Ash Wednesday and cold-hearted Lent. Decorations, more gaudy than those favored for Christmas, lined shop windows all over Wiesbaden. Even the street cleaners wore harlequin vests, and the *Polizei* made their rounds with jaunty feathers in their hats.

According to Lulu, the Fasching ball at the *Kurhaus* was the highlight of the season, so she had hauled Brencie to a costume rental shop, and now Brencie sat on the sofa in Lulu's apartment wearing an outfit that looked like Pocahontas as imagined by the Brothers Grimm. The black leather miniskirt had four inches of fringe around the hem and the bottom of the matching vest. Every time Brencie moved, the fringe revealed more leg and midriff. Under the vest she wore a black bikini top, even though Lulu suggested the vest should be worn with nothing under it. An unwieldy war bonnet and a red plastic spear completed the ridiculousness. "I'm showing more skin than a stripper already," Brencie said. "I'm not showing my bazooms."

"Bazooms?" Lulu put a plate of cucumber sandwiches and a half dozen shortbread cookies on the coffee table and then tugged a long yellow dress over her red bra and panties. She placed a circlet of daisies on her head. "I wore this dress to a wedding last year." She rummaged in a jewelry box. "Where's that pin? Oh. Here." She hiked the long skirt up on one side and pinned it at the waist with a rhinestone brooch. Her shapely leg peeked from the opening. "I'm spring. The sexy season." She surveyed herself in the hall mirror. "I look amazing. What do you think?"

"You have the best legs in the world, and you do look amazing," Brencie agreed.

Lulu adjusted the showy brooch. "My mother gave me this. I got a long letter today, all about her. What's new with Agnes-Rose? Her letters are frequent but short. Eat something. It's going to be a wild night."

Brencie took a cookie and then fished in her purse. "She sent a picture. Here." It was a photo of Agnes-Rose, hip cocked, arms akimbo, wearing one of her custom-made aprons from The Swank with a big pocket shaped like Texas.

"This is your stepmother? I was expecting an old lady with a bun and wire-rimmed glasses."

"I told you. She's thirty-six, but if she were ninety-six, she wouldn't wear a bun."

"Rochelle's almost fifty and wearing a flip like Marlo Thomas."

"You call her Rochelle?"

"She doesn't like 'mother.' Being called one, or being one. She says we're lucky because of the pill. She tried to have no kids, and took what she got. I told you I have three brothers."

"I remember. It must have made you special, to be the only girl."

"Not really. My mother saw me as the competition. Read me your letter."

"OK. She says, 'I ate lunch at the cafeteria at Gulfgate. It was crap, but I did find a cute sundress. Two of my regulars died last week. Not from anything I did to their hair, ha ha. Fasching sounds like fun. Should I send your Raisin Maid outfit from tenth grade?'"

"Raisin Maid? You do look like the Raisin Maid, with short hair." She inspected Brencie's outfit. "Would you like to know what Jules says about you?"

Brencie thought about it. "No."

"He says you're loaded with sex appeal. And you don't see yourself as others see you."

"Is that important?"

"Isn't it?" said Lulu. "Maybe you're yourself, but aren't you also how others see you?"

Brencie bit into a sandwich. "Mmm. That's really good. I've never had a cucumber sandwich. Agnes-Rose is a philosopher, like Jules, and she was big on being yourself. She said if you pay too much attention to how others see you, you start to shape yourself to meet their expectations." She finished the sandwich and considered herself in the mirror. "I don't look like Brencie."

"That's the point of a costume," Lulu said.

"I look like a floozy. Too bad I don't have my Cowboy Number Three outfit, you know, from *Annie Get Your Gun*. Handlebar mustache and cow-print chaps. Even a rifle. It makes more sense than this stupid spear." She took another sandwich.

"What the hell are cow-print chaps?" Lulu asked.

"Chaps go over your jeans, to . . . never mind. It's western wear. And I'm not taking the spear." The war bonnet slipped down over her eyes. "Shit."

Lulu grinned. "Why, Brencie. You know you *never* swear."

Lulu helped adjust the war bonnet, and the cigarette between her fingers caught one of the feathers on fire. She swatted the tiny flame, but before it was out, there was nothing left of the singed feather except the shaft. "Crap. I'll have to fix the stinkin' thing somehow. The *Deutschers* are particular about property damage."

"You could have set *me* on fire," Brencie said. "Do you still have Servant Girl Number Two from *Crucible*? You could have worn that." The play had been excellent, quite professional, and Lulu had nailed her part, tiny two-liner that it was.

"The costume manager came after it like it was sable instead of sackcloth. No sex appeal, either."

"Well, you make a great spring, and your self-confidence is better than sex appeal."

Lulu shrugged. "I know what I have. Amazing eyes and great legs. I have a receding chin, though, and the rest of me is medium. Not bad. Not great. No sense getting into flaws of character." She held a gold-sequined mask to her face and then leaned toward the mirror and flicked a stray sequin off her nose. "You already know I talk too much. And I may have done that again."

"Oh, Lulu. What now?"

Brencie and Lulu had had a dust-up on New Year's Day, after the rift with Nolan on New Year's Eve. "I'm sorry, Brencie," Lulu had insisted. "I didn't mean to spill the beans about Rick-the-fiancé-father. I honestly didn't know it was a secret. I promise, if you tell me not to tell something, I won't." Lulu had been contrite, and the breech was forgiven. Not for the first time, Brencie was glad Lulu couldn't tell the revolting story of her broken engagement, because she didn't know it.

Lulu hiked the yellow dress a little higher. "Don't get mad," she cautioned, "but I had lunch last week at the O Club, and there was Chase Dellasera. He asked about you. Again. He smiled down at me with those dimples, and I mentioned we would be at the Kurhaus tonight. Is that awful?"

"Ready, *fire*, aim. That's you." Brencie tried to raise a flicker of anger at her friend, but it didn't come. The truth was, she wanted to see Chase again, and though the argument with Nolan had been smoothed over, they were in a holding pattern. Brencie finished the last cookie. "I thought you were rooting for Nolan."

"I am, but Chase? Well, when I haven't seen him for a while,

I'm still impressed." There was a knock on the door. "Dierdre and Margo," said Lulu. "I can't wait to see their costumes."

Arms around each other, Dierdre and Margo stood hip to hip and shoulder to shoulder, or as close to it as they could, given the difference in their statures. They seemed to be wearing matching purple-sequined dresses, until they stepped apart to reveal one single big, weird, stretchy dress.

"Oh my god!" said Lulu. "*Ausgezeichnet!* If I don't stop laughing, I'll ruin my eye makeup. You look like one girl with two heads. Isn't it crowded in there?" She opened her purse, took out her Instamatic, and snapped a few pictures.

They stood farther apart, and the dress pulled open as though it were made of fish net. The loose weave revealed glimpses of what was underneath: matching hot pink bikinis. "If we get uncomfortable, the dress can go," said Dierdre.

"Brencie ate all the cookies, and most of the sandwiches," said Lulu. "Only two left. Grab them, and let's go. It may be hard to get a taxi." When they got downstairs the lineup of taxis was longer than usual, anticipating steady fares all evening. The driver spoke, and Lulu translated. "He said we're the prettiest yet."

"Kurhaus? *Rhein Main Hallen*? Scotch Club?" the cabbie asked. He knew where the parties were.

"Kurhaus, *bitte*." Lulu turned to her friends. "I was at a party at the Arms last year. You should have seen my harem girl outfit. Whew. What a night! Long story, and there's no short version."

Partygoers lined the sidewalks. It was cold, so oversized clown shoes flopped along the pavement beneath long coats, and Frankenstein masks popped up above Burberry capes. It was a spectacular show, and almost too soon, they reached their destination.

The Kurhaus sat back from the Wilhelmstrasse at the end of a rectangular park, which featured two fountains, tiered like wedding cakes, water cascading from each level. Tonight the building was a palace dressed up for a ball. Six thick pillars ran along the front, each wrapped top to bottom with ribbons and flowers. Every inch of the structure glowed from lighted windows, ground lights, and spotlights high on corners and in niches.

"Oh, my gosh," said Brencie. "Why didn't the Americans take this over?"

"As a matter of fact, they did, right after the war, but do you believe it? They gave it back in nineteen fifty something. There was an American Eagle Club where Bob Hope and Frank Sinatra played. Man. Those were the days.

"Seems to me these are pretty good days," said Brencie.

Taxis waited one behind the other, inching forward to discharge their passengers under the portico, but Brencie couldn't wait. She paid the driver and got out of the car, followed by her friends. They walked the last few yards to the grand front doors, handed over their discounted tickets from Armed Forces Services, and stepped into the rotunda.

A silver-gilt maypole rose from the black-and-white marble floor to the center of the cupola. Ribbons of every color floated from the top of the pole, and dancers weaved in and out, clockwise and counterclockwise, wrapping the ribbons tight along the pole. A "horse" with Apocalypse written on its chest fought with "Poseidon" over an unclaimed red ribbon. Mahatma Gandhi in a loincloth ogled Eve wearing a flesh-colored bikini and a floor-length blond wig. There was a giraffe and a kangaroo and animals of every ilk.

"Brencie," said Lulu. "Your mouth is hanging open. And you're burping cucumbers."

"I'm flabbergasted. I never saw anything like this, even in the movies. Look! An armadillo!"

"It's a rat. You can take the girl out of Texas . . ." Lulu observed. "There's another Indian maiden costume like yours. Nothing under the vest. You look better, anyway."

Although no one was admitted unless they wore fancy dress, traditional German attire was accepted. There were a few men in lederhosen and many women in dirndls. A grinning Pagliacci, painted tear glued to his cheek, blue rubber nose, walked directly to Lulu.

"My favorite tenor. Hi, Jules," she said. "I thought you weren't coming."

"Heaps of shit. How did you know it was me?"

"I'd know you with your face removed. Isn't the nose supposed to be red?"

"I got to pick the color. I chose blue so I wouldn't look like all the other clowns. There's one here with a yellow-green nose. Looks like a wad of snot."

"I'm glad you picked blue. And glad you came."

"Awww. Lucille. I'm surprised you admit it. Hi, Brencie. And Dierdre. Margo. What the hell are you wearing?"

They stepped apart to reveal the dress for two, and Jules hooted. "Holy shit! Best sight gag ever." He turned to Brencie. "I called Nolan's office. They said he almost made it back, after all, but there was a football controversy, whatever the hell that means, so he had to stay in Bitburg. Let's go. My buddy's holding a table on the mezzanine."

Jules led them to an immense ballroom in the heart of the building. They took the stairs to the open mezzanine, which had a view of the brightly lit ballroom below. A ten-piece brass band, heads bobbing and elbows bouncing, made music from a platform in the middle of the room, and fantastic figures whirled around the platform like a *Glockenspiel* come to life. Jules took them to a long table, where a hobo in a homemade costume presided over four pitchers of beer. Lulu snagged a waiter and ordered champagne. When the band launched into an even friskier tune, the floor emptied, and a spotlight fell on a couple in traditional German costumes.

"Ah. A floorshow," said Lulu.

The music slowed and the couple moved in a stately manner until another man cut in. As the tempo increased, the rejected partner swatted at the interloper, who turned and kicked his tormentor in the seat of the pants. Both men began pounding their own thighs, kicking each other, slapping their heels, until a third man stepped in and claimed the girl.

"They're just getting started," Lulu whispered. "It's called *Schuhplattler*. Shoe-slap dancing."

The girl faded into the shadows, and six suiters bashed each other faster and faster, until it seemed impossible to avoid injuries. When the mock brawl ended, the audience was on its feet cheering.

"Damn!" said Jules. "Music as an excuse to slap people around. I *love* Fasching. I hear you can't get a divorce because your spouse fell off the fidelity wagon during Fasching."

"Often repeated," said Lulu, "but not true."

The band took a break, and another friend of Jules joined the group. He wore a tight black suit, slicked down hair, and wire-rimmed glasses. As he moved in on Margo and Dierdre, Brencie engaged in a short laughing fit. "I can't help it," she said. "Robert McNamara flirting with a two-headed lady. It's the funniest thing in the world."

Jules looked cross. "Hey, you! McNamara. Bad choice of getup. You resigned, remember? Right before Tet. And the goddamned war rages on."

Lulu's demeanor wilted, and she spoke to the former secretary of defense. "Don't pay any attention. Pagliacci here's angry about everything, especially the war." She turned back to Jules. "Leave it for tonight. Please?"

"OK. OK." Jules embraced Lulu and restored her smile. "That's better." He said. "You go from unhappy to happy in an *Augenblick*. It's a gift."

The band returned to play something with a rock beat. Brencie drained her glass and said, "Come on. Let's hit the floor." When no one moved, she said "OK. I don't think anyone down there has a partner anyway." She elbowed into the frenzy and got lost in the beat, bumping off other dancers, dodging male embraces, loving dancing alone, and willing it to go on and on. When the music stopped, her war bonnet was at her feet, and a man in black jeans and a black turtleneck stood in front of her like a premonition. He wore a simple black mask and a watch cap, and he retrieved her feathers from the floor.

"Is this yours, Miss Friendswood?" The idea he might show up had never left her mind since Lulu mentioned it. It was Chase Dellasera at last.

"Hello," she said. "Um. I was dancing."

"I was watching. I think you were born dancing." He looked up to the mezzanine, and Lulu waved, her impish smile visible even from a distance. Brencie started back to the mezzanine with Chase following. He removed his mask, shook hands with Jules, hugged Lulu, and nodded to the others.

Before they could sit down, the band struck up a march, and Lulu clapped her hands. "Yay! The *Mainzer Narhalla-Marsch*. Conga time!" She grabbed the tail end of a long line with Jules holding on behind her. When Brencie latched on to Jules's wide middle, Chase followed, his hands on Brencie's hips. The line swung across the mezzanine, down the steps, and across the ballroom, breaking into pieces, reattaching, and timing their movements to the merry march.

The line snaked into the main hallway and in and out of a rabbit warren of rooms, each with a different décor, a haunted house with a rock band, Heaven with an old man stroking a harp. The music bled from room to room, carrying the conga line with it. The costumes, the music, the kaleidoscope of decors, all engendered a sense of freedom, excitement, and a signal that anything could happen. When the march ended, Lulu started toward the mezzanine, but Chase held Brencie back. "We'll meet you in a while," he said as the others moved away.

They stood in a book-lined room, probably a small library most of the year, transformed into a French café for *Fasching*, with baskets of baguettes, cloth wall hangings of the Eiffel Tower, and a platform with an accordion on a stand, but no musician. A waiter passed. Chase put some *Deutschmarks* on the tray and took two glasses and a bottle of champagne. He had hardly filled her glass before she drained it. "You're drinking too fast," he observed.

She held out her glass for more. "What are you supposed to be, anyway?"

"Cat burglar. Are you an Indian princess or a *Lutzelfrau*, a witch?"

"I'm more witch than princess, if I have to be one or the other. Lulu says a costume's supposed to turn you into someone else."

He hesitated. "I guess she told you we had a couple of dates, but there was nothing to it."

"She told me."

"What did she say?"

"I don't know," Brencie said. "Something about your unit getting deployed during the Six Day War." *And that you didn't sleep together,* she thought.

"Anything else?"

"She said you're gone a lot."

"It's best not to talk about military operations."

Her war bonnet slipped over her eyes, and he laughed. "You look ten years old." He lifted the headpiece, and she pushed his hand away.

"You don't like me at all, do you? I'm not sure why."

"I do like you. Maybe that's the trouble." She instantly wished she hadn't said it.

The accordionist returned and began to play "*La Vie en Rose*." Chase took her glass, put it down, and pulled her close. As if her own heartbeat gave him permission, he kissed her, and it was incredibly pleasurable, his warmth, the music, the whole ecstatic night. He moved to her ear and neck and whispered something she didn't hear, something about the first time they met, and he looked at her again. "Just as I remembered. Green eyes."

She wanted the moment never to stop, as the warmth spread through her, lit her up from inside, kept building until she felt dizzy and happy, until the feeling oozed over into something else. The bad feeling went away, but came right back, more unpleasant than before. She was way too warm. Her forehead felt sweaty, and moisture ran down from her armpits. The bad feeling rotated to her stomach and stayed there, getting worse with every breath.

No, no, no. Not going to happen, she thought. *It will not happen.* Whatever had settled in her stomach rose up higher, lingering in her chest but still climbing. "I have to go." She broke away. "I . . . I have to go!"

"Brencie, calm down."

"I am calm. I have to go."

She lurched across the room, looking for a sign saying *WC*, but she saw none. The crowds slowed Chase down, but her insides fluttered again. She swallowed a cucumber burp and the nausea increased. A mirrored ball overhead cast shards of light over everything and made her more unsteady. When she reached their table on the mezzanine, there were new critters present, a demon and a fish, and Margo and Dierdre sat in their pink bikinis. Lulu and Jules were now enclosed in the big sequined dress.

"Lulu, I have to go. I'll get a taxi." Brencie gathered her things and made a run for it, with Chase closing in.

"And the *chase* is on," Jules mumbled. "This isn't good for Nolan."

Brencie pushed through the crowd, and when she escaped through the rotunda and outside onto the portico, she felt slightly better in the cold air. Maybe she would be OK.

Chase caught up with her. "I'll drive you home." Taxis were lined up a few feet away, but he held her back. "You've had too much champagne."

"I'm not drunk. I've never been drunk. Stop talking." She didn't know why he laughed. "There's nothing funny about it," she said.

"Wait here. I'll get my car." He hurried away, and not a second too soon. She rushed down the steps to the sidewalk, where she threw up, all over a holly bush and a hot ground light. When the mess hit the light, it sizzled, and the smell caused Brencie to throw up again. She steadied herself, fished in her bag for a tissue to wipe her mouth, and got in a taxi, hoping she could make it home before she was sick again.

———

In her apartment she shed the war bonnet and purged twice more in the cold arms of the toilet. If this was drunk, she resolved never to be drunk again. When she was sure it was over, she washed her face and brushed her teeth, feeling physically normal but emotionally foolish.

Twenty minutes later, a knock, and Chase stood in the hall with tendrils of hothouse freesia, dozens of them, wriggling in his arms, alive as puppies. She had hoped he wouldn't follow, but now she felt better and was pleased he had.

"I was worried," he said. "I wanted to be sure you got home in one piece."

She laughed as he filled her arms with flowers. "Where did you get these?"

"At the Bahnhof. I bought all they had. You laugh with a Texas drawl. It's almost as good as throwing yourself in my arms."

"Or puking on your cat burglar jeans? Or worse. In your car."

"You were sick? Are you better?"

"Yes. I can proudly report I barfed in the bushes at the most glamorous party in the world."

He laughed. "Have a glass of water and take some aspirin. You're going to feel lousy tomorrow." He looked at his watch. "It's already tomorrow. Wednesday's Valentine's Day. I'll pick you up at eight o'clock. For dinner."

"You're kidding. You want to take Puke-ahontas to dinner?"

"I wanted to see you again the first time we met, and I'm not wasting any more time. See you Wednesday." And he was gone.

Chapter 6

Dear Brencie,

Fasching sounds wild! Did Nolan make it? There's a football team? Are you sure you're not in the U.S.A.?

Thanks for the maps I asked for and labeling your stomping grounds. The cold war map is scary. The bad guys are breathing down on Europe. Did you know that when you signed up?

Skip (the kid who cuts the grass now your gone) ran over a nest of baby rabbits and went home crying. I had to shovel them into a trash bag. I like to never found the shovel.

Honey, you signed a contract to stay 3 years but will you? And will you ever forgive me?

Love your Agnes-Rose

p.s. I sent a bones-eye (sp?). They said instructions would be in the box.

S he had stopped using the more affectionate Bee Bee, in subtle acknowledgment of Brencie's coolness. Even so, her stepmother's unwavering affection had restored some of their old intimacy. The debacle was seven months ago, after all. Agnes-Rose's letter arrived on Valentine's Day, as did a bonsai tree, a little green juniper, something Brencie would never have expected from her stepmother. She reminded herself. When it came to Agnes-Rose, the unexpected was to be expected.

There were a dozen yellow roses from Nolan with a card. "Sorry I'm missing Valentine's Day. Love, Nolan."

If it hadn't been for a car wreck in Friendswood, followed by a wrecked engagement, Brencie would be married and living in Texas. Nolan almost made it to the Fasching ball, but he didn't, and Chase Dellasera did, so she had a date with Chase. The domino effect. Or the ripple effect? Was falling down the same as spreading out from the center?

She was about to get in the shower when the phone rang. It was Nolan. "Hi. Happy Valentine's Day. Did you get the roses?"

"I did, and they're gorgeous. Thank you."

"I'm sorry I didn't get back, and now there's a giant scheduling cock-up. I have to stick around and smooth some feathers. I'll be back for the next home game . . . *Oh, hell no*. . . Sorry, Brencie, not you. Gotta go. The detail's leaving. See you soon."

Brencie let out a long breath, relieved he hadn't asked if she was doing anything special tonight. She wouldn't have lied, though she wasn't sure what she would have said.

Chase's bouquet from Fasching was on the coffee table, and now there were roses too. She placed them on the shelf above the radiator, next to the bonsai tree, then she showered and put on a black jersey dress. Thick silver loop earrings, a touch of Shalimar perfume, spicy and exotic, and she was ready when Chase arrived, as attractive in a sportscoat as he was in uniform. "Hey, is that a bonsai tree?" he said. "And roses. Who are they from?"

"Not from you, obviously. I'll get my coat."

He looked amused, but he said no more about it as they left the apartment. His car was in temporary parking in front of the hotel, a sleek red thing that had the leathery new-car smell. She read the initials on the gearshift. "BMW? What does it stand for?"

"*Bayerische Motoren Werke.* Bavarian Motor Works. Do you like it?"

"The car? Do guys think girls care about that?"

He smiled. "Some do."

The restaurant was a short distance away, and Chase led her down a flight of steps to the basement level. An illuminated glass case by the door contained a menu and a sign that said *Patrizier-Keller.* He entered the restaurant in front of her in the European manner, and they followed a waiter to a booth. He removed the *reservieren* sign and said, *"Willkommen, Herr Kapitän. Und Fräulein."*

Flames danced in a fireplace a man could stand in, and all ten wood-paneled booths were occupied, as were ten tables with pink cloths, each adorned by a single red rose. Copper pots hanging from the ceiling beams reflected the light, and every person in the room had the look of love, at least for the night.

"I requested a booth," Chase said. "More private."

"You've been here before?"

"I've been here, but not with anyone special. If you want me to live up to the fighter jock reputation, I warn you, my swash is still OK, but my buckle's rusty."

She was relieved when he smiled, and despite herself, charmed. "How long have you been in Wiesbaden?" she said. "Oh. I'm not supposed to say that. Lulu says it's the same as asking 'Should I waste my time on you if you're leaving soon?'"

"There's something to that. I'll be around for two or three more years. If nothing changes." The menus were in gothic script, difficult to read by candlelight, even with the English subtitles. "Fondue's the specialty," he said, "but they make a great steak *au poivre*. Let's start with *Schnecken*. That's escargots. Snails."

"I know escargots and *au poivre*. I took French in high school. I dreamed of living in Paris, but I never heard of Wiesbaden until six months ago. Let's have the fondue, but no snails, please."

"Great," he said. "but I'm ordering *Schnecken*. You'll try it."

"Will I? I'm stronger than I look, and not afraid to make a scene."

After Chase placed their order, the waiter made a ritual of pouring the wine.

"Here's to you, Miss Jessup," Chase said, "but that's all the wine you get. After the Fasching ball I'm not sure you should have any. How old are you, Brencie? Am I cradle-robbing?"

"I'll be twenty-two soon, so old enough to drink. Just have to learn my limits. How old are you? Where did you grow up? Give me the first-date lowdown."

"You're very direct. I'm twenty-eight. Grew up in Memphis. I'm the youngest of three. The only boy. My mom's a housewife, and my dad's a partner in a CPA firm. The men in my family served the country going back to the Civil War. After graduating from Vanderbilt, I kept up the tradition and joined the Air Force. That's the basics."

"Ah. Tennessee. You don't have that Deep South accent, but I heard something southern."

"You get razzed about it in the military, so I tamp it down. It comes back now and then."

"You're the baby and the only son? I'll bet you were spoiled."

"Doted on, for sure. You're from Texas. Can you ride a horse?"

"You're from Memphis. Do you know Elvis? I did have a boyfriend who owned a quarter horse. One was Johnny and the other was Billy. I can't remember which, but one of them taught me to ride. I sketch a bit. I play tennis. I water ski and hope to learn to snow ski."

He smiled. "Is Friendswood on the coast? I bet you had a boyfriend who had a boat."

"I did. Now I need a boyfriend who owns a mountain resort. Friendswood's thirty minutes from Houston, forty minutes from Galveston, so water all around."

"Go on. The first date lowdown."

"My mother died when I was a baby, and my stepmother raised me. She sent the bonsai thing. I scanned the instructions. I'm supposed to shape it. I like music. I read a lot. College didn't work out, so I went to work for NASA until I ended up here."

"You didn't mention your father."

"Long gone by the time I was ten. Not a story for Valentine's Day."

"OK. Then tell me something about Brencie Jessup no one else knows."

She almost accused him of asking game-show questions, but decided against any more challenging remarks. "OK. I'm five foot ten inches and I weigh ninety-eight pounds."

He laughed. "I'd say around five six. I'm not dumb enough to guess your weight, but I'm pretty sure it's more than ninety-eight pounds. You're funny and good at ignoring what you don't want to talk about, like who the roses came from, or telling me something about yourself."

She sighed. "I couldn't think of anything unusual, that's all, but there is something embarrassing. I like to sing. Colonel Foss and I sang 'Be kind to your fine feathered friends,' you know, the Sousa thing, watching a marching band on the parade ground." Best not to mention the hymn at Schierstein, with Nolan, Lulu, and Jules.

"Wow! How 'bout you sing something now." He glanced around the room. "Maybe singing can wait, but I want you to laugh. There's something about it."

"So I've been told. All it takes to make me laugh is for something to be funny, which almost everything is."

"Here's something embarrassing about me. I'm a Leo. In junior high, I went around humming 'The Lion Sleeps,' like it was my theme song. I thought it might get me a girlfriend, or at least a date. Turned out to be a girl-repellent, but I found other ways."

I'll bet you did, she thought.

The Schnecken arrived, bubbling in butter, herbs, and garlic, and Chase speared a snail with his fork. "Come on. Try it."

It smelled good, so she worked the piece into her mouth. "Oh, that's the best thing in the world. I want them all."

"Don't be greedy." He impaled the next snail and held it near her mouth. She ate it and licked the butter off her lips. He tried to give her another piece. "I love to see a girl with appetites."

She raised her eyes. "Are we still talking about food?"

"Ah. I caught you flirting. I wondered if you could. You've got some sharp edges."

"I can flirt when I have to." She put a snail onto her plate.

The main course arrived just after the appetizer was cleared away. Chase skewered a piece of raw beef and dipped it into the oil. She did the same and let the meat sizzle. Bite by bite, hints and insinuations, savoring every morsel, dinner took a long time. When they finally left the restaurant, a delicate sprinkling of new snow had covered the night in diamond dust. "It's beautiful," said Brencie. "Let's walk home."

"Why not? It's only a few blocks. I'll come back for the car." They strolled under soft streetlights, sated from the sensuous meal and the nourishing beauty of the night.

Brencie looked at the baroque balconies of the apartment buildings. "This must be the best walking city in the world."

"It wasn't heavily bombed," he said. "The Americans picked it to be headquarters before the war ended. No need to destroy the house before you move in." They stopped at a crosswalk, though there was little traffic, and Chase gently removed her glove and raised her hand to his lips. "What would you sing now?"

She could hardly breathe, but she tried to think of a song. "I like the Righteous Brothers. 'Unchained Melody.'"

"That's a good one." He recited the words and didn't let go of her hand. "'Oh, my love, my darling . . .' Now will you sing? I'll start. 'Time goes by so slowly, and . . .'"

"That's not singing. That's croaking," she said.

"Are you still miiineee?" His attempt at the high note caused a dog-walker to stare, so he let go of her hand, and they walked on.

"We're almost home," she said. "Too late for more singing."

The Amelia Earhart rose in front of them, aloof on its hill like a castle, light shining from its many windows. People came and went, laughing, happy, and every time the front doors opened, a moment of music escaped. It was closing time on Valentine's day, and "Let Me Call You Sweetheart" announced the end of the evening. Brencie never imagined this town, or the candlelight and copper of the Patrizier-Keller, but she had conjured Chase from old movies, tall tales, and promises of princes.

When they stopped at the corner, he kissed her, and she was breathless again. Whatever happened tonight, no one would know or judge her. They walked inside and directly to the elevator.

"You're flushed," he said. "I don't think it's from the cold."

They were alone in the small space. The attraction between them was so palpable she was surprised she couldn't see it in the elevator mirror, and then she remembered. This was a first date, not a magic carpet ride.

He took her key and unlocked the door. When he leaned close, she knew what he was going to say. "Can I stay?" he whispered.

She almost said, "What kind of girl do you think I am?" It sounded fatuous, even in her head. "No."

"Just no?" He pulled her close, but the spell was broken. "Do you mean it?"

"I do mean it."

He smiled, almost like he was relieved. "OK. I'll be flying tomorrow, so I'll see you the day after, and every night from then on. And if you still doubt my intentions, let me be clear. We aren't going to be casual, Brencie. If you've been seeing someone, you'll have to cut him loose."

He left without touching her again, and she went to the balcony. When he emerged from the hotel, before he got in a taxi, he looked up, stood at attention, and sent her a salute.

They had been together night after night, sometimes talking until predawn, but for Brencie, the next step was fearsome. "Fear scares the hell out of everyone," Agnes-Rose said, and she was right. Brencie reminded herself not to get in too deep, too fast, with anyone. She expected Chase to pressure her to go to bed with him, but he didn't, and there was Nolan. She owed him something. Two weeks had dragged into three, but he would be back soon.

The Saturday morning before he was due back, Chase picked her up wearing his orange flight suit."

She laughed. "Love the color. Are you a pilot or a runway marker?"

"Whatever my country needs me to be, ma'am, plastic cone or conqueror. See all these zippered pockets? It's tradition for the pilot's lady to find the prize hidden in one of them. Would you like to try?"

"Nope," she said. "Not even tempted."

"You're no fun," he said.

"As a matter of fact, I am, but still no. Let's go."

Chase took her to the base and walked her to the flight line, where four jets, F-4 Phantoms, sleek, comely, dangerous, were parked on the edge of the runway, canopies lifted in a kind of salute. "There's going to be an open house. We love to show off our birds," he said. "I'll be on duty, but we're not open yet. Come on. Up you go."

"What? Climb the stairs?"

"Back when it was still the Army Air Corps, girlfriends got taken up sometimes, but even then, it had to be on the QT. I can show you the cockpit, though."

She climbed the portable stairway abutting the plane, and he followed closely, his breath warm on her neck. "You can get in," he said. "If you promise not to fire it up. The jet, I mean." He helped her into the cockpit, and when her skirt rode up, he put his hand on her thigh to steady her. As she lowered herself into the seat, she wondered what it would be like to soar over the world. The thought excited her, made her want to do it, so she gingerly poked a button that said "press to test." An array of red lights blinked on and off quickly, and when she held it down, the lights stayed on. He leaned in and removed her hand. "I told you not to touch anything."

"Which is all but daring me. That was fun. Think of actually flying it."

"Flying it is fun, but I think of you too much. It's distracting."

"Be careful then. Doesn't flying one of these require concentration?"

"Concentration and strength in the arms and legs. Especially the legs." When she didn't reply, he said, "Is that learned or instinctive? That non-answer? It's like a secret weapon."

She looked at the instrumentation. "Do you really know what all these dials and gauges are? What's this one?"

"Radar on/off."

She pointed to another dial. "And this?"

"Total fuel remaining."

She put her hand on a shaft at the left side of the plane. "Is this the throttle?" She rolled her hand around the knob at the top. "What's this part?"

"It's called the stick, and the knob is the trim switch," he said.

"What's this one?"

"Tailhook." He placed his index finger on a specific spot near the stick. "This controls the afterburners. Imagine what all that thrust feels like."

She flushed. "Some things have to be experienced. Can you make that happen?"

They stared at each other.

"Maybe, but not in the airplane," he said. "You're getting excited, aren't you?"

"I don't know. Maybe. Get in here and we'll find out." She laughed, delighted to be exactly where she was at this exact time in this amazing world.

"Now you capitulate? That's provocative. And impossible." He checked his watch. "Almost time for the crowd." He helped her out of the cockpit, climbed down, and waited for her at the bottom of the stairs.

She stopped midway down. "Are you looking up my dress?"

"Taking the fifth on that," he said. "But that skirt is stylishly short."

Just before she stepped off the stairs, he put his arms around her and lifted her down, lingering until it became an embrace. "I have to stand here and answer questions, so I'll be a while. You can wait if you like. There's refreshments over there."

She got a cup of coffee and found a place to sit where she could watch as people surrounded Chase. The ladies seemed the most interested. Brencie decided not to wait. She walked to the back of the crowd, signaled Chase with a wave, and got the shuttle back to the Amelia.

A while after she got home, Chase knocked softly, and she opened the door. He leaned against the door frame. "Why did you leave? Seems you like to stay just out of reach."

"You were busy with a lot of girls clustering around you and your airplane. It reminded me of Joseph O'Barry. Cute, popular. He lived down the block, and I knew him all my life. I took a ballroom dance class in sixth grade. Eleven girls and one boy, Joe. The girls clustered around, asking him to dance. Except for me. I didn't."

"You didn't. Did it work?"

"Did it *work?* It wasn't supposed to *work.* I just wasn't interested in clustering."

"And eventually he fell madly in love with you."

"No, but he asked me to dance, and we became friends. Nothing complicated."

He laughed. "I'm standing in the hall. Are you going to invite me in?"

"I don't know. What time is it? I'm meeting Lulu for drinks."

"It's sixteen thirty. Why don't you get a watch?"

"I don't want one. And I have a clock."

"Aren't you late sometimes?"

"Never. Clocks are everywhere. I had a watch, but I was always looking at it, measuring time when I didn't need to. I don't have to meet Lulu until fifteen thirty, so you can come in for a while."

He grinned. "Sorry. I can't. I have to debrief the open house. There. I made you laugh. The truth is, I wanted to ask you something in person. How about we go to Garmisch?"

"Is that some kind of cheese?"

"Very funny. Garmisch-Partenkirchen. In Bavaria," he said. "It's late in the year, but there's skiing on the glacier. You want to learn, and there's an armed forces rec center there."

"A recreation center? Do we own most of Germany?"

"The occupation ended in 1952, but we still strut around. We spend a lot of money, so the locals tolerate it. Think about Garmisch, but don't wait too long. The hotel fills up on weekends, so I should make the arrangements soon."

Chapter 7

Freezing rain fit Brencie's mood. Ice was accumulating on the tree branches, and cars fishtailed on the street in front of the Amelia. Staring out at the gray day, she gave up hope of improving weather. At least it meant she wouldn't be going to Nolan's game in Mainz. Jules and Lulu canceled as soon as they saw the conditions, but Nolan had called and scoffed at the idea the game might be off. "It's football," he said. "Football ain't for sissies, but you should stay home. Roads are slippery. I'll be over after the game."

She dreaded it. His business with the team had kept him an extra week, another week she spent with Chase. Still, breaking up with Nolan was much harder because she wasn't letting him go because she didn't care for him. It was because she met someone who bowled her over with feelings so strong she didn't altogether trust them. Still, she had thought it to death, and she couldn't lead Nolan on.

She went downstairs to the arcade to pick up her dry cleaning and to the deli for instant coffee and cereal. She ran into Lulu in the deli. "Jules sent me for bagels," Lulu said. "He can't live without them, and today there aren't any. Bread truck doesn't deliver when the roads are bad. What's the matter with you? You look gloomier than the weather." They left the deli and were on the way back upstairs.

"I have to break it off with Nolan," said Brencie. "Tonight."

"Ah. After Valentine's day you got the full court press. Where's Chase tonight? Does he know?"

"I don't know. I made excuses for this evening, but he knows I've been seeing someone. I think he even knows it's Nolan. He saw us together.

Lulu shrugged. "Did Chase show you his shiny jets?"

"Yes, he did. I might be in love already, but I feel terrible about Nolan. Did you get the jet treatment?"

"Not even close," said Lulu. The elevator stopped on Brencie's floor, but Lulu held the door open. "Look, you're right not to lead Nolan on. He's not the *guten* howdy *wieder* bye-bye type. You know, don't forget to forget. A word of caution. Chase turns a girl's head by walking into the room. I mean he's the most beautiful man I ever saw, but in case you haven't figured it out, jet jocks have a reputation. You took it slow with Nolan. Take it slow with Chase."

"He wants to take me skiing, and you know what that means. We've been close, but when I let him know I wasn't ready, he didn't pressure me."

"Because he's figured out pressuring you wouldn't work." The elevator alarm started ringing, and the doors slid shut when Lulu removed her hand.

Brencie waited for Nolan in the bar, and he arrived in an ebullient mood. "Sorry I'm late. We won, but it was a tough game and then Grindel's Mother threatened to slide off the road. Twice. Where's Jules and Lulu?"

"Not coming. There's something on TV they want to watch. Peggy Fleming. She won again."

"Jules likes ice skating?"

THE SECOND LIFE OF BRENCIE JESSUP

"Lulu likes the costumes. He like the legs."

He smiled his quick smile. "I'm glad they aren't coming. I've missed you." He scanned the room. "No tables." He lifted a heavy bar stool with one hand, moving it closer to her. He talked about the game, the team, and an injury to one of the players. "It's Bob, the running back? You met him. Broken ribs. They want him in the hospital for a day or two."

"Can you make the playoffs without him?"

"Oh, you betcha, baby. Might be a little harder, is all." He ordered a beer. "I told Bob I'd bring his mail. We can take in the flick. It's a spaghetti western." He checked his watch. "You're quiet. Are you tired? Do you mind? About the movie?"

Brencie had planned to tell him about Chase at once, but there hadn't been the right moment. "No, I'm fine. It's fine."

They walked to the American hospital, no more than a block away, where there was a small theater for inpatients, but open to anyone with a U.S. military or civilian ID. The theater smelled like antiseptic instead of popcorn, and it slowly filled with GIs in light blue pajamas and dark blue bathrobes, some on crutches. Margo, in her nurse's uniform, waved at Brencie and directed gurney traffic at the back of the theater. The starched efficiency of Nurse Margo contrasted comically with the image of Fasching Margo in a pink bikini, and the click click of wheelchairs tapped on Brencie's nerves. The scene was surreal. An audience in pajamas, her own dread, hurt people gathering to watch violence and death, and Clint Eastwood having the time of his life.

Nolan took her hand. "Your palms are sweaty. Are you warm?"

"I'm fine." She repeated the lie. "I'm fine."

He left to deliver Bob's letters but was back by the time the house lights dimmed. A scratchy film flickered on, a black-and-white image of the American flag waving in slow motion to the tinny sounds of "The Star-Spangled Banner." Everyone who could stand got to their feet with a groan and a shuffle, a sound repeated when the anthem ended.

The picture began, and with no change in expression, Clint Eastwood smoked cigars and shot countless bad guys to a foreboding soundtrack, a perfect accompaniment to Brencie's thoughts. She wished the evening was over, but it felt like it never would be. It took time to exit the theater because of the slow-moving patients, and Brencie suggested a nightcap, knowing the bar at the Amelia would be fairly empty.

Nolan ordered their drinks. "We got a TWX last week. That big plane, the C-5 Galaxy? They may land one at the base this summer. Making plans for it, anyway. The thing's huge. We can go see it at the air show in July."

Brencie remained silent, but after the drinks were delivered, she couldn't stall any more. "Look. There's no good way to say this. I've met someone else."

His face remained blank until he realized it wasn't a joke. "What? Since when?"

"I met him at the Fasching ball."

"A couple weeks ago?"

"Three weeks, almost, but we met before that, and I've seen him every night since Valentine's Day. We—"

"Valentine's Day? I called you, for hell's sake. Was he there? Are you telling me you met someone at a Fasching party and that's it for me? Did you sleep with him?"

"Why do men always ask that?"

"Because it's important. Maybe more so, because you haven't slept with me. Did I get you all primed for him?"

"That's disgusting!"

"Maybe, or maybe you should think about that."

"OK, if it makes you feel better, I haven't slept with him."

"I'm sure he gave it his best shot."

"You don't know him."

"In three weeks? Neither do you. I thought Jules and Lulu didn't come because you wanted us to be alone. I thought you were going to let me spend the night." When he understood that for her, the conversation was over, he said, "Brencie, I'm in love with you."

"You never said that before. Are you trying to make this harder?"

"I was going to tell you on Valentine's Day, but I was away. I'm telling you now in case it might make a difference. It's Chase Dellasera, isn't it? When we passed him at the American Arms that one time, he looked at you like he owned you. I was invisible. I don't know why, but I made it a point to find out who he was."

"You *investigated* him?"

"I asked around. Only one officer named Chase living at the Open Arms. God damned officers. They take what they want. Maybe I *should* investigate him." He motioned for the waiter and paid the bill, glancing around as if he expected Chase to appear and claim her.

"I'm sorry. I like you, Nolan, I do, but you can't explain feelings. Listen, I hope—"

"You hope we can be friends? Not possible." When he stood up, he knocked his chair over, and it caused a clatter. He left it where it fell and walked out.

The last time he left in a temper, on New Year's Eve, Brencie knew he would be back. This time he would not, and the thought made her want to follow him, to stop him. She considered what her stepmother once said, as they watched a weepy Saturday soap opera. "One Life, One Love? That's a fat slice of spoiled baloney. One at a time, maybe."

Nolan had been a romantic possibility and would still be, if Chase didn't exist and if she wasn't a "normal young woman," as Lulu put it. Brencie had to choose. She was normal, but she couldn't sleep with them both.

She waited until she was sure Nolan had left the hotel, and then she stood the chair back up and went to her apartment. The phone was ringing when she unlocked the door, and although she didn't want to talk to anyone, she answered anyway.

"I'm just checking," Chase said. "Have you decided? About Garmisch?"

Chapter 8

Dear Brencie,

You'll be 22 this month. Most girls don't have a lick of sense, but you do, so go slowly. Nolan is out? Chase is in? Dellasera? Is that made up? I knew an Italian named Bart Della Salda. I couldn't stand him.

I hired the private eye to find your dad. He said see a lawyer. Declare Anson dead. I can't make myself kill him off.

Developers (so-called) want to buy The Swank and build a feed store. They want the land, I mean. I'm thinking about it.

Your letters are full of fun things. Maybe your over it? Or at least you don't hate me?

Love your Agnes-Rose

PS – You mentioned Oktoberfest. Why do they call it Oktoberfest if it's mostly in September? Weird. You must be in a foreign country after all – sort of.

B rencie didn't know what she would need, so Lulu went with her to shop for ski clothes. "Ski pants. Black or dark blue for your curves," she said. "Turtlenecks. At least one heavy sweater and a parka. Lucky they carry this stuff at the BX. It's way more expensive in town."

"Chase wanted to buy the clothes, but he's paying for the trip," Brencie said. "That's enough."

Lulu shrugged. "It's an armed forces rec center. The trip probably cost less than the clothes."

"I've worked full-time since I was eighteen. I had my own apartment. I can buy my own clothes."

"You had an apartment? When you were eighteen? I thought you lived with Agnes-Rose."

"My lease ran out, and I got engaged, so I moved back to the house. It was temporary."

"Are you all atwitter about Garmisch? How stinkin' romantic. Not that tall-blond-and-drives-sexy-jets hasn't seduced you already."

Brencie gave her a stern look, "Lulu, in spite of your encouragement, I didn't sleep with Nolan, and I'm glad, because of Chase."

"Or maybe if you'd slept with Nolan, there would be no need for Chase. And don't let on like you don't miss Nolan."

Brencie sighed. "You're right. I do miss him. I think about him. But I can't have them both."

"As a moral matter? Or a practical one?

"Agnes-Rose would say a practical one, but I say it's both. Now, can you help me decide between the black or the white parka?"

When they got back to the Amelia, Chase was waiting in the lobby, so they put Brencie's ski clothes into his car and then went upstairs for her suitcases. She glanced outside. The weather had been foul, spitting cold rain again, but Nolan trained relentlessly, and he ran by on the street below. Seeing him all the time, even at a distance, kept him in her thoughts.

They got on the road, and by the time they stopped for a late lunch, the rain had stopped. They spent a pleasant hour in Hohenschwangau at a Gasthaus with a view of *Schloss Neuschwanstein*, and Brencie thumbed through her battered copy of *Europe on $5 A Day*.

"Brencie. We need to talk. Can you put the book down?" said Chase.

She looked up. "Sorry. Bavaria's fascinating. This says *Neuschwanstein* was the model for the castle at Disneyland. Let me check one more thing." She flipped the page. "Yes. 'Other Attractions. Hitler's Eagles Nest and Dachau.'"

"War as entertainment," he said. "See where Adolph ate lunch. Peek at the ovens where they burned the bodies." It was as though he wasn't speaking to her. A moodiness had settled on him, and it diluted her own good spirits.

"I see your point. What did you want to talk about?"

"Nothing. Forget it for now. Maybe we can tour the castle on the way back."

Chase felt sleepy after lunch, so he asked her to drive while he took a short nap. He woke up with a start. "Hell, Bren. What are you doing? When I went to sleep the car was going mmmm. I woke up because it's going eeeeee. You're hitting a hundred."

"Everyone was passing me."

"No speed limit. It's Germany."

"It's amazing how often I forget that. Should I pull over?"

"Yes, as soon as you can. You're going way too fast." He smiled. "Said the fighter pilot to the Texan."

At the hotel in Garmisch an attendant in lederhosen brought a cart for their luggage and Chase's ski equipment, but as they started toward the reception desk, Brencie held back. She had made two overnight trips with her ex-fiancé. They checked in as Mr. and Mrs. Rick Smith, so it sounded phony, though it was his real name. European hotels required passports, and Chase's and hers had different names. She glanced at the lobby, the hunting lodge theme, elk heads, chintz, and framed photos of skiers frozen in impossible grace.

"Chase, I don't think . . . um, I mean, you know. I'm sorry. The truth is I'm embarrassed to check in together. It's plain we aren't married."

"Not yet," he said, but he looked away. She couldn't adjust to this moody version of Chase. It would be their first time together. Performance anxiety? She doubted that, but something was bothering him. "Brencie. We're grownups. It's Europe. No one cares, but give me your passport and wait here. I'll check us in."

Fifteen minutes later he put a filigreed brass key into the lock and opened the door. European charm dripped from the faded floral rugs and slightly mismatched furniture. A huge bed with a billowing white comforter dominated the room, and Brencie wondered how many girls Chase had brought into rooms like this. She scolded herself for the thought.

A bottle of red wine and two green-stemmed glasses sat on a table. "As I requested," he said. He uncorked the wine as she explored the room, parting the heavy drapes to a stunning view of the *Zugspitze*, highest mountain in Germany. She looked into the bathroom. A sink, tub, and shower stall. The toilet was in a separate cubicle marked WC.

"Cuckoo. Cuckoo. Cuckoo. Cuckoo."

Brencie jumped when the little bird stepped onto his tiny stage and warbled out the hour. "He seems nervous." She giggled.

He looked up in surprise. "You never giggle. Are you nervous? Crap. Now I'm nervous." He took her hand. "Look, you're young, but you're not a teenager. I assume . . ."

A blush spread to her face. He knew about her engagement, but not in detail. "Don't worry. I've done this before, but only . . ."

"No explanation. And no numbers."

Because you don't want to know? Or because you don't want to tell, she wondered. There it was again, that seed of doubt, perhaps sewn by Lulu's remark: *Jet jocks have a reputation.*

Brencie put her arms around Chase and kissed him gently. "I'm a little nervous, but the wine will help. It was amazing of you to think of that, and to make this special, but something's bothering you. What is it?"

He broke the embrace. "I'm going to the bar while you freshen up."

Before she could say anything, he left. Was he being thoughtful, allowing her privacy to use the toilet and wash up? She went to the bathroom and ran water in the sink, but the immaculate porcelain tub looked inviting. She turned on the taps, and to take the chill from the room, she switched on the space heater on the wall.

The deep tub filled slowly, so she explored the bottles and toiletries lined up along the sink. Something with a German label produced foam when she tested it, so she sprinkled more into the tub. A wave of bubbles replicated madly and danced on the surface of the water. The ceramic elements of the heater glowed red, so she switched off the overhead light, and the bubbles turned pink in the rosy radiance. She undressed, watching herself in the mirror. She liked the tone of her skin in the delicate light. She fluffed her curls, and when she lifted her arms, the movement raised her breasts. She imagined herself through Chase's eyes, and then she climbed into the high-sided tub and settled up to her chin in lavender-scented bubbles.

When Chase returned, he knocked on the bathroom door and opened it a crack. "I'm back." He opened the door wider. "You look . . . breathtaking." He stood there making up his mind, and then he came in, bringing a slight draft and the sweet smell of bourbon.

With his back to her, he undressed in the soft illumination, taking his time, like he understood the beauty of his own form. His shoulders flared and tapered to his waist. The Vietnam tan had faded, but the hint of it remained in the slightly darker tone of his long shanks compared to the whiteness of his buttocks.

When he turned around, the gleam of blond hair on his chest, along with the male contours of his abdominal muscles, aroused her. She felt giddy, and it made her giggle and slide under the water. She surfaced and said, "I'm sorry. I didn't mean to laugh."

He smiled. "You giggled. Again. I admit, the male member isn't impressive until it gets angry. I laughed the first time I saw mine in the mirror when I was a little boy."

He put his hand on her back and moved her forward in the tub, so he could get in behind her. When she was positioned between his legs with her back against his chest, they settled in, warm and comfortable, with no sense of urgency. She sighed.

"Yogis call that a cleansing breath," he said. "Very relaxing. Are you thinking this is the best thing in the world?"

"I'm thinking the bathroom's more romantic without a toilet."

He lowered his voice, and the Deep South surfaced in his timbre, smooth like honey. "Let's see if I can take your mind off the bathroom fixtures."

He lathered his hands and washed her neck, then massaged her earlobes. Brencie was astonished that such a small motion could be so erotic. He moved to her shoulders and her back, spreading the sweet-smelling soap in a thin layer and rinsing it away with water cupped in his hand. As he moved to her collarbones and upper chest, she felt him growing hard against her lower back. He caressed her breasts slowly, lifting them in his hands, brushing the nipples until they were hard, and then he slid his hands to her belly. When he moved his fingers farther down, touched her inside, she felt a gathering need, then something happened that didn't usually happen until later in this dance—if at all. She burst, had an experience that was all new. He pressed harder, until her shuddering increased and slowly faded, leaving her limp against him.

"There," he said as he stroked her belly. "That will do for now."

He eased her forward so he could step out of the tub. After he dried himself, he extended his hand to steady her out of the tub and dried her with a fresh towel from the heated rack. By the time he led her to the bed, Brencie felt flawless, transformed, like she had never been so perfect. He explored her body, carefully and slowly. "Let me make you happy," he said. And he did, and in a way she had never been before.

In the morning, they made love again, and Chase rolled Brencie unto her back and nuzzled her neck. "Wow," he said. "That was fun."

"I didn't know a girl could do that twice in a row."

He laughed. "Some can."

"Speaking from experience?"

"Come on, Brencie. I'm older than you, and I'm a man. Of course I'm more experienced. You were engaged to a prick, and I don't mean that in a good way." He got out of bed and parted the curtains. This palpable change in his mood made Brencie uneasy.

But will he respect you in the morning? She hated that line, but it was inculcated and reinforced by everyone, from Ann Landers to high school PE teachers. Brencie couldn't remember Agnes-Rose ever saying it, though. All that came to mind from *The Book of Agnes-Rose* was "Sex can mean everything or nothing or something in between."

The cuckoo chirped once and someone rapped sharply on the door. "It's oh nine thirty. Right on time," Chase said. He barely stepped into his briefs before the waiter came in. Brencie, still naked in bed, pulled the sheets over her head. After greeting them cheerily and remarking on snow conditions, the waiter put a tray down, wished them good skiing, and left.

She peered over the top of the sheets. "He just came in. Wasn't the door locked?"

"The staff has keys. They're trained not to notice a thing."

"Including the condom wrappers all over the floor?"

"If he tripped over them, he might manage a bow and *entschuldigen sie bitte*. Come have some breakfast. Skiing's hard work."

She donned a red silk robe and went to the table. Prettily arranged on the tray were hard rolls, black bread, butter, jam, a pot of steaming milk, and a pot of black coffee. To her delight, Chase added a package wrapped in white paper with a sprig of evergreen.

"I know it's not until next week, but happy birthday," he said.

"I love surprises, and I love little presents." She held the box to her ear, shook the package, then kissed the sprig of evergreen and tucked it behind her ear. She didn't open the wrapping. She shredded it.

"God, Brencie. You're like a cross between a French poodle and a bulldog. I might have to marry you for the entertainment value."

She looked at him, but he looked away. "Forget I said that. It was a bad joke."

Not knowing what part was the joke, or why his moods were so mercurial, she focused on the jewelry box in her hand. The shape indicated a bracelet or a watch. She lifted the lid to see a watch with diamonds, one on either side. "Chase, it's lovely, but too extravagant."

"Now you won't be late to meet me ever."

But I never was, she thought. *And I told you I don't like to wear a watch.* She didn't say any of that, barely allowed herself to think it. She put on the watch and enjoyed the sparkle against her pale wrist. "It's gorgeous. Thank you."

"You're welcome." He stood up and pulled a purple cotton turtle-neck over his head. "I'm going to see the concierge about lift tickets."

⸎

Chase walked beside her in ski boots, skis and poles on his shoulder, and Brencie enjoyed the fabulous colors all around. "It's like plumage," she said. "Male birds are much more colorful than females. It's the best thing in the world." She didn't stand out at all in her black pants, white jacket, and red hat. The common male neutrals were replaced by red pants, chartreuse sweaters, and striped hats. Chase wore a light blue sweater over his purple turtleneck, but he had left his ski cap behind. The spring sunshine had turned the snow to slush in the village, so he left his parka behind too.

They went to a small chalet to arrange for ski rental and lessons for Brencie, but it was late morning, so all instructors were booked, and Chase's surly reaction didn't faze the scheduler. The amazing night and morning elevated Brencie's outlook on the universe, but it didn't seem to have the same effect on Chase.

"Look, I'm sorry," he said to the scheduler. "Not your fault we got up late. Let's book a lesson for tomorrow morning and rent her equipment now."

Chase helped her with the boots and skis.

"You think high heels are uncomfortable?" she said. "These boots are the most uncomfortable thing I've ever had on my feet. Chinese foot-binding can't be worse."

"You'll get used to them. I'll show you a few basics and how to

— 99 —

use the lifts. Even you can manage that." He walked ahead of her, so she couldn't see his expression. She wanted the day to go well, but she was beginning to think it might not, although she was confident skiing would be manageable. She had always been athletic, water skied on the bayous near Friendswood, roller skated, and excelled in intramural sports, especially tennis.

She made it to a short rope-tow, falling only once along the way. Holding the bar and letting the rope pull her along wasn't so different from water skiing. It was only about a hundred yards up an almost invisible slope, a bunny hill, Chase called it.

"OK. The snowplow," he said. He turned his skis in until the tips touched in front, then he pushed his heels outward, forming a V. "It's a beginner's way to control your speed or stop."

She got the theory of the snowplow he tried to teach her, but it was counterintuitive, not a bit like water skiing. Still, she liked the feel of it, the smooth, quiet motion. They went down and back up a couple of times, and her progress satisfied Chase.

"Now we'll take the chair lift." He indicated a line some distance away. As their turn approached, he explained. "Get ready. It slows down, but it doesn't stop. Both poles in one hand and then line up in front of the chair and sit down when it touches the back of your legs."

Brencie managed to get onto the lift. As they ascended, the beauty overwhelmed her, the way the mountains challenged the sky for dominance. The silence engendered by the snow, the dark green fir trees along the trails, and the bright punctuation of skiers passing underneath the lift. Muffled laughter. Crisp air. Sunshine. It would make anyone believe in God.

Chase smiled. "It's something, isn't it?"

She had nothing to say that came close to what she felt.

When they neared the top, he said, "Here we go. It won't stop unless there's a pileup."

"A pileup?" She hadn't heard anything so ominous since Nolan said something about "tanks on the Wilhelmstrasse."

"If someone falls and doesn't get up quick, the next person falls, and the next. There can be a tangle of skis and poles. OK. Here we go. Poles in your right hand. Drop your skis to the snow, glide along in the ruts, then stand up and push off." He lifted the safety bar.

Drop and glide went all right, but when she tried to stand up and push off, it went wrong. Chase got her on her feet and out of the way quickly, so at least there was no pileup. When they stood at the top of a steep downhill run, Chase said, "Are you scared?"

"Scared? I'm excited. I can't wait to try it."

"Watch for now," he said. "I'll come back up, and we'll practice the snowplow."

His dismissive tone annoyed her, but she thought teasing him might help. "You just want to show off."

"Nothing wrong with that." He barked at her then started down.

Brencie focused on the bright blue of his sweater and the glint of the sun on his gilt hair, the swing of his shoulders, the rhythmic bend and release in his knees. By the time he got back on the lift at the bottom of the hill, she decided skiing looked easy. She edged forward, tempted to give it a try, and then she couldn't resist. She leaned forward and started down, gaining momentum, laughing at the thrill of it, until her knees started to shake. She tried to swing her heels into the snowplow, but it didn't work. She couldn't slow down. When her skis got ahead of her, she overcorrected, which sent her tumbling, coming to rest next to a snow bank as Chase arrived and stopped short, sending up a rooster tail of snow.

"What's the matter with you?" Only the acoustics of the packed snow kept his voice from echoing over the valley. "You could've broken your own neck, or worse. See those kids over there? You were heading right at them. You could've plowed into them, hurt them, even killed one. Kids you don't even know." He said it twice, and the phrase resonated. *Kids you don't even know.*

He was scolding her like a child. This wasn't about skiing. Chase had dropped bombs on targets, but there were people in that abstraction. She wasn't ignorant of what war can do, and every day Vietnam seemed to close in like a headache that might signal a change in the weather or a brain tumor. The light came from behind him as he stood over her, so she couldn't see his face. He might be a stranger holding out his hand.

"Alright," she said. "I'm sorry." *I'm not the lion, but I have to give the lion's roar.* Chase said something like that to Lulu a long time ago. Did he do what he was asked to do, but not what he was cut out to do? Did the children trigger something? But his moodiness started before that.

"Let's get something to eat," he suggested. They made it to a lodge midway down the mountain, where hamburgers and bratwursts sizzled on an outdoor grill, making Brencie's mouth water from the aroma. Beach chairs were scattered on the snow-packed hillside, and skiers rested in the sun, some of the men shirtless, their sweaters and gloves littering the snow.

After they ate, they rested, and again Chase brought up her foolishness. "You easily could have broken your leg. Tomorrow you'll have a lesson, and you don't move until you can snowplow well enough to stay under control. You have to learn to be less impulsive."

"Do I? Maybe I'd rather be myself and take the consequences."

His face softened. "I don't know if that's infuriating or admirable. Or just surprising."

"OK, look. Skiing is harder than I thought, but I understand what you're saying about staying in control."

"Good. That's progress." He took their trays, deposited the trash, and sat back down. "Brencie, you know what? There's something else ..."

She was finding the conversation tiresome. "I'm sure there is, Chase, but I'm enjoying myself at this moment, for the first time since I put on skis. Can you save whatever it is?"

He looked at the mountains, and there it was, the thousand-yard stare, that vacant look, empty-eyed, searching, knowing whatever's there, he didn't want to see it. "Sure, Bren. It can wait." He kept her on the bunny hill the rest of the afternoon.

———⟨●⟩———

They were settled in at the hotel bar sipping coffee with brandy, strong and hot. She savored hers, but he downed his and asked for another, and another. Huge windows faced the slopes, and skiers could be seen making their final runs while the light held. "Talk to me, Chase. What's on your mind?"

"Why don't you go have a shower?" he suggested. "I'll be up soon."

"Chase. Something's bothering you." Besides the war, she had one possible thought, and she forced herself to ask. "Is it me? Are you disappointed?" If he looked away, or hedged, she would know how he felt, no matter what he said.

"What? No. You're incredible. Last night and this morning." He smiled and took her hands. "And it will only get better."

The server came, and he ordered another drink. "Now go up-stairs. I'll be along in twenty minutes."

To appease him, maybe get back on the right foot, she looked at the watch, ticking away the time on her wrist. "My exquisite time piece tells me that would be about sixteen forty-five."

He smiled, and Brencie left him to finish his drink. She showered and put on dusty pink pants and matching sweater, *après ski*, Lulu called it, perfect for a sleigh ride and dinner. Chase came back and took his turn in the shower, while Brencie applied fresh makeup, and then she sat down and leaned her head against the sensuous velvet of the chair. Because of the blips in Chase's mood, the day had been uneven. She stretched, shifted a bit, and saw a newspaper in the wastebasket. He probably got it when he went to check about lift tickets. The room had been made up, but the paper was balled so tightly it was almost invisible in the bottom of the basket.

She fished it out and spread the front page of the *Paris Herald* across her lap. The English language publication was popular with Americans, especially, but was widely read by Europeans too. The headline was huge. *Largest Number of American Casualties in Vietnam since the Beginning of the War.*

Chase's agitation was about the war, probably set off by the article. The war was going badly, and he knew more than what was in the newspaper. Still, her instinct said that wasn't it, that there was more to it, and it was about her.

He came out of the bathroom in a white terrycloth robe and took the paper from her. "And that's just the American casualties. They don't bother with the others, though they're just as dead. War isn't fun. People die." He threw it back in the trash. "People have no idea what's happening, stuff that won't be in the news, but it's only a matter of time. I feel guilty because I put the war in a dusty place in the back of my mind and leave it there. Most of the time."

So maybe it was about the war after all. "I'm sorry. I don't know what to say."

"Don't say anything. I have you now, and that changes everything."

It wasn't the time to question the remark, but Brencie didn't know how she could change anything, and what did *having* her mean?

Chapter 9

The clock radio clicked on.

"It's oh seven hundred, and this is Donnie Ray the DJ for Armed Forces Radio. Welcome to April 1 in the Rheingau. Look out for mine fields, you fools! Now here's a favorite from last summer."

"If you're going to San Francisco. . ."

Brencie snuggled deeper under the covers. "San Francisco." Chase's favorite pop song, though he laughed at the hippies, saying they looked unsanitary and stoned. She agreed about the lack of sanitation. The so-called summer of love, only last year, intrigued her at the time, but now it seemed far away and irrelevant.

Chase had gone back to his apartment when they got home from Garmisch, because he had a training exercise all week, but thinking of him made her so happy she laughed out loud. She pushed away the covers, showered, and dressed for work. The bonsai on the window sill needed attention, so she gave it a little water and then picked up the tiny scissors and snipped off a small piece. The view outside changed from week to week, even day to day. Golden fall, snowy winter, now tight spring buds dotted the trees below, and nest-building birds scrambled and twittered.

She wondered if Nolan had already run by. She admired his persistence, and he was a touchstone, nothing more. Every morning she checked Agnes-Rose's bonsai and Nolan ran by.

The announcer switched to the morning news. "Good morning. Our top story today is President Johnson's speech last night, announcing that, and I quote, "I shall not seek, and I will not accept, the nomination of my party for another term as your president.""

Brencie switched off the radio. She detested April Fool's Day.

It was Mexican night in the Café Amelia, so Brencie and Lulu indulged in excellent margaritas, soggy tacos, and a good deal of conversation about President Johnson. Leah Crum came in, still in uniform, and Brencie introduced her to Lulu. "Leah's the admin officer in Materiel. We've started playing tennis one day a week, when it isn't raining, and she always wins."

"You're getting better," Leah said. "Nice to meet you, Lulu. What do you guys think about Johnson?"

"A stunner, according to my boyfriend," said Lulu. "He listened to a rebroadcast of the speech, and it's all about the war. I thought it was a stinkin' April Fool's joke."

"Me too," Leah said. "It clears the field for Bobby Kennedy, and probably Nixon will be the other candidate."

Brencie invited Leah to sit down. "Thank you, but I'm joining my friends. Nice to meet you, Lulu."

"She seems nice," Lulu said as Leah walked away. "Not many lady officers. Jules hates Nixon. Well, he hates them all. Except Bobby. He loves Bobby." She leaned in with mischief in her blue eyes. "I'd rather hear about your ski trip."

Brencie recounted lift mishaps, sleigh rides, good meals, and weather conditions. "I didn't have much style, but by the end of the last day I could do the blue trails."

"Was it the best thing in the world?" Lulu said. "And you know exactly what I mean."

"Oh, my god, Lulu. Do you want me to sing the chorus of 'Wunderbar?'"

"Yes! Yes, I do." Lulu waited for more. "Is that all I'm going to get?"

"It is. Now, about the party." Chase's unit was having something called a dining-out. It was formal, and Brencie had nothing to wear and no idea of the protocol.

They went to Lulu's apartment, and she began pulling dresses out of her closet. "There's the dining-in and the dining-out," she said. "*In* is officers only. *Out* includes guests, and inviting you is like declaring his intentions. Try this."

Brencie slipped the slim-fitting, wine-colored gown over her head and worked it down over her body. "Wasn't there a grade school story about a porridge pot that was never empty? Your closet reminds me of that." The bodice was cut so low it would have been in bad taste, except for the sheer organdy panel across the chest.

"Suits you," said Lulu. "Silk cut on the bias clings to the lady curves. I'll have to hem it. Don't want you tripping all evening, especially during the twist contest. There's always a twist contest. Makes them think they're cool."

"Twist contest? I'll win. I always win the twist contest."

"Of course you do," said Lulu. "Now put these heels on so I can get the right length." Brencie stood patiently while Lulu sat cross-legged on the floor, pinning the hem in place. "There. An inch shorter. How do you like it?"

Brencie looked in the full-length mirror. "Wow! At least I'll be confident about what I'm wearing. It sounds like a fancy party. Oh, Lulu. Am I out of my depth? I like military razzle-dazzle, but I'm a Texas girl from a blue-collar town."

"My dad's enlisted and says officers are only special because they *say* they're special. Repeat that in your head when they put on airs. Oh, shit! I stuck myself." Lulu looked at her finger. "No blood. The four of us should do something together. Jules thinks Chase won't go for it. You know Jules. The whole world performs for his personal observation. Ornithology. Or some kind of ology."

"Ornithology is birds, which makes it right," Brencie said. "Birds of a feather . . ."

Lulu laughed. "Flock together. Officers with officers, enlisted with enlisted."

When Brencie modeled the dress for Chase, he said, "You look beautiful. Someone might try to steal you, and you're all mine." He peeled the dress from her shoulders, and they made love like they had been apart for weeks, not days, then they drifted into love-soaked sleep. After midnight the telephone jolted them awake, and the caller asked for Chase.

He took the phone. "Captain Dellasera. Roger that. I'm on my way." He hung up. "I have to go to the base. They've initiated the call tree." He pulled a list out of his billfold and made two calls, saying little more than "Report to the base ASAP."

"What's happened? How did he know where you were?"

"They have to know how to reach me at all times. I put your name on my contact list as soon as we got back from Garmisch. It's just a briefing." He got dressed and started to the door.

"When will you be back?"

"I don't know, but it would be better if you moved in with me."

She sat up and wrapped the sheet around herself. "How would that be better?"

"I wouldn't have to go to the Arms and change, for one thing."

He walked back to the bed. "Damn. You look tempting. Besides being more convenient, I'm six foot one. The sofa bed's too small." He kissed her and left.

By the time she was ready for work, he was back. He sat down and put his head in hands. "Martin Luther King was shot in Memphis. My hometown. He's dead."

"Dr. King? Dead? I watched that dream speech on TV. He can't be dead. Why did . . . I mean how are you involved? Us. Here?"

"We're not. We get briefed when something big happens. By the time we're assembled, it's usually determined there's no threat. There's sure to be plenty of trouble at home, though."

⸺⸻«◉»⸻⸺

The dining-out was postponed because of Dr. King's death, which left the community deeply unsettled and brought tension to the atmosphere at work. Half the high-ranking enlisted men, senior master sergeants, and chiefs, were black, and all the officers were white. Hostility surfaced where there had been none, or at least none that showed. Colonel Foss was called to a meeting of division chiefs, and when he returned, he assembled the entire division.

"I believe the way to squelch rumors is to be open about what's happening. So here it is. Dr. King was shot by a single gunman, according to what they know, but no one has been arrested. Riots have started, the worst in Baltimore and Washington, D.C. It's expected to spread. You'll see pictures in *Stars and Stripes*, but photos in the *Frankfurter Zeitung* and *Paris Herald* will be worse. There's going to be violence."

He paused and looked at the group. "Right here, in this division, yesterday we walked around this office color blind. Today I sensed something I don't like. That stops now. We're a team. We keep the planes in the air, and we work together. Any questions?"

Senior Master Sergeant Whittington, a black man from Ohio, spoke first. "No questions, sir. The men in my section support the mission. Period."

One by one the branch chiefs weighed in positively, and the tension eased. Brencie was relieved and proud of Colonel Foss.

"Good," he said. "If anyone has anything to discuss, see Captain Crum. She's discreet, and she has a list of resources for anyone who needs to talk. You're dismissed."

When the others were gone, Colonel Foss looked world weary and shook his head. "If anyone understood all this, maybe it wouldn't be happening. But that's locking the barn door after the cows are out. President Johnson's doing his best, but . . . well. Vietnam's the main reason he isn't running again. Dr. King's death will make things worse."

The unrest spread across the U.S. and Europe too. Pictures of barricaded Paris streets appeared in *Stars and Stripes*. Angry students dug up the cobblestones on the left bank and tossed them at police. Labor strikes. Students against the war. Protesting racism around the globe. Twice more Chase was called to the base in the middle of the night, both times for briefings. Brencie asked what it meant, what he knew.

"There are things I can't tell you, but I could get deployed. I might have time for a phone call, but if I can't reach you, you'll only know I'm gone because I'm gone. If you move in with me, we could stay in closer touch, instead of bouncing back and forth from your place to mine."

"I don't understand why that would be better. I'd be alone over there without my friends, and you'd be gone." *Besides, I love my apartment. I love the balcony and the view, and I don't want to give it up.*

He read her thoughts. "You could keep your apartment, but you'd mostly be with me. I want to be with you all the time, and I thought you wanted the same thing." He embraced her. "And remember my big, wide, fluffy double bed. I could make you very happy."

Make you happy was their personal code for making love.

Brencie saw no reason to move in with him, except he wanted it that way. Unmarried couples living together was mostly confined to Hollywood types and New York beatniks, although it was becoming more acceptable. Still, the arrangement made Brencie uneasy. It was neither married nor single. Her intuition whispered *Good for the man. Bad for the woman.*

⸻ «◈» ⸻

By late May the American community had adjusted to bad news every day, but a little of the carefree spirit returned with the beautiful spring. On Sunday morning Brencie walked into the Café Amelia and spotted Lulu and Jules. She sat down as their breakfast was delivered. Jules folded his newspaper and dug into his pancakes.

"We're going up to the Opelbad. Wanna come?" Lulu said. "It's probably too cold for swimming, but that won't stop the Germans, as long as the sun stays out. Where's Chase?"

"Another briefing. The sky's falling again."

Jules polished off his pancakes. "The sky's falling? Look around. No one's pulling their hair out. They're eating scrambled eggs. That's the thing. It's not just the big ol' human brain. It's our adaptability. Whatever happens, we survive."

Lulu, as usual, tried to lighten his mood. "What about plague? Or famine? What if the hippies burn San Francisco to the ground?"

"What about the Donner party? They got snowed in and ate each other. Then there's the camps right here in *Deutschland*. Everyone should have given up and died, but some survived. Let the hippies burn down San Francisco. It might be an improvement."

"God, Jules, you're so cynical. People are feeling better because of Bobby Kennedy. He's electric and sure to win."

"Right," said Jules. "Another glamorous Kennedy will find a way out of the war. He'll feed the poor from loaves and fishes and magically make everyone the same color, ending racism for all time. Can't wait." He belched and grinned. "Call me crazy, but I almost believe he will."

"Uh-oh. Your cynic is slipping. The Opelbad calls, and there's the rest of our fun seekers," said Lulu. Margo and Dierdre stood in the doorway next to a tall, blond young man with a haircut that gave him away."

"Jesus. Who the hell's that?" Jules asked. "He's right off a Nazi recruiting poster."

"His name's Jürgen," said Lulu. "They met him, I don't know, somewhere, and please don't say that Nazi thing when you're introduced. Are you coming, Brencie?"

"No, thanks. They rescheduled the dining-out for tonight. Beauty processing to do."

⸻ ⦿ ⸻

Even though things had normalized, something was still eating Chase. Did he know worse things than Brencie imagined? She tried to talk to him about his occasional surliness, but he denied it, and he made it clear he didn't want to talk about Vietnam.

He was in good spirits when they drove to town and handsome in his dress uniform. The event was held in the mirror-lined ballroom of the Schwartzerboch, the best hotel in Wiesbaden. Chase checked their coats, and Brencie watched the officers and their ladies reflected around the room, the men in elegant mess dress, their ladies in chiffon and satin. She remembered something from high school science. Mercury, quicksilver, mirror lining, messenger of the gods. Military bearing and evening clothes made them all look like gods, or at least like they owned the room, and maybe the whole Rheingau.

Chase escorted her to the bar and handed her a glass of champagne. He drank Chivas straight up, and as they were moving from one group to another, a captain intercepted them. His slimy expression put Brencie on guard.

"Hello, Dellasera." He didn't take his eyes off Brencie. "Is this your latest flame? You had a thing for blondes in the old days." He swayed almost imperceptibly. "Yup. One particular blonde in the old days."

Chase stiffened. "Brencie, this is Brad Clark. We went through part of our training together a million years ago."

"Riiiight. Brencie. I hear you're a friend of Little Lulu, or as we call her, Loose Lulu."

Anger grabbed Brencie, quick and mean. "What do they call officers with bad manners? Pricks?" she said.

Clark sneered and started to say something. Chase interrupted him. "Be careful, Captain Clark."

Brencie continued to glare at Clark as she spoke to Chase. "I can handle a drunk, Chase. I learned before I was ten years old. It's not that hard."

"Wow," Clark said. "She's a lot scarier than you, Dellasera. I have had too much to drink."

"As usual," said Chase. "Now if you'll excuse us . . ."

Chase led Brencie away, but Clark took a parting shot. "Bout time for the ol' deployment disappearing act, isn't it? It's so *convenient*. Deployment. Reassignment. The ol' easy kiss-off."

Chase steered her to the only other person in the room she knew, Captain Leah Crum, wearing an unbecoming outfit. "Will you excuse me for a moment?" Chase said.

"What's that about?" Leah asked as he walked away. "And no remarks about the female officer formal wear. I can't decide if I look like a nun or a man in a long skirt. Or a waiter."

"Well. The jewelry's nice," Brencie said.

"Oh. The medals. They make noise, but at least they're shiny. I have a fighter jock date somewhere in the room. Otherwise I'd be tucked up with a book. They resurfaced the courts last week. Are we on for Wednesday?"

Brencie watched Chase and Brad Clark exchange words. Chase took a step closer, and Clark held up his hands, fingers spread. Chase stared at him, and then turned away. "What? Oh, tennis," said Brencie. "Sure. I could use the exercise."

After stopping at the bar for another drink, Chase came back as though nothing had happened, and the maître d' announced dinner. As they went in, Chase said, "I wish I had a picture of Clark's face when you called him a prick. I bet you've never said the word out loud in your life."

"I didn't exactly call him that, and I have said it out loud. When no one was in the room and I was talking to a cactus." It didn't make him laugh.

When all were seated, the presiding officer invited a chaplain to deliver the invocation. The special guests were introduced and toasts were offered. They enjoyed an excellent meal, but Chase was drinking too much, which Brencie could no longer chalk up to the general amount of heavy drinking where booze was cheap and parties were frequent.

The drinking agitated Brencie, and Clark's remark didn't help. *The deployment disappearing act.* What did that mean? As for blondes, Chase would soon be twenty-nine years old. Blonde, brunette, or redhead, there were women in his past. There were men in hers.

By the time the evening ended, it was sprinkling outside, so they dashed to the car, and Brencie offered to drive. Chase declined in a surly voice. He started the car and pulled away. "Damn. It will probably rain all week," he said.

"Might be a good time to get together with Lulu and Jules. Just dinner in her apartment. She likes to cook." She had mentioned this before and gotten a cool reception.

"You could cook for me sometimes. Why don't you?"

She wasn't sure if it was the alcohol or being among his own tribe, but his demeanor seemed aggressive. He had asked the question before. "Sure, Chase. My specialty is TV dinner al dente. I don't like to cook. I told you that. What about Lulu and Jules?"

"Look, I like Lulu. I like Jules too. He's like a lot of enlisted guys, especially the medics. Smart, halfway through college. Going back when he gets out. It's about fraternization. Rank's a part of military life."

"Yes, but I don't have to swallow it whole," she said.

"Well, I do."

They were arguing, and she wasn't sure how they got to that point. She stared at him, puzzled by his hard expression and the edge in his voice, and when she looked back at the road, she screamed, "Chase!"

It was too late. The dark, wet street curved to the left, but they kept going straight, and the BMW careened over yards of muddy ground into a ditch. When the car stopped she felt warm liquid trickling down her face, and Chase pulled her from the car.

"Oh, my God, Brencie. I'm sorry. I didn't see the curve, I . . . Do you want to go to the hospital?" He dabbed at her eyebrow with a handkerchief. "There's a cut, but it isn't deep. I don't think it needs stitches."

"I hit my head. Are you OK?" she asked.

"I'm fine. I might have a bruised knee."

They struggled back to the street and hailed a taxi, feeling lucky it stopped, given the late hour and their disheveled state. They went to the American Arms, which was closer than the Amelia.

"But shouldn't we call the MPs or something?" she asked, once they were in his apartment.

"No! I got picked up for drinking and driving in college and once in flight school. I was just over the limit. Tomorrow I'll see to the car, but no official report or insurance claims. If anyone asks, anyone official, you can't say anything."

She was in the bathroom washing the blood off her forehead, and she suspected her eye would be black by morning. She went back into the living room. "Can't say anything about what?"

"About how much I had to drink."

She sat down. What was he asking her to do? "I won't be a party to that, Chase."

"To what? To protecting me?"

"To lying."

"Oh, please. Everybody lies. I've heard you do it."

"White lies. Maybe lies of omission. I don't lie when it counts," she said. "You know what. I'm going back to the Amelia."

"Your dress is all muddy. Stay here."

"A girl strolled in naked last weekend. I saw her myself. She went straight to the elevator. Arriving in a muddy dress won't rate a second glance."

The prickliness drained out of him. "I'm sorry, Bren. I shouldn't have said that, about not talking to anyone. It's not likely anything will happen. If you moved in, you wouldn't have to worry about stuff like that."

"Stuff like what?" He wasn't making sense. He nuzzled her neck, and she caught sight of herself in the mirror. "I'll bring over some clothes and a toothbrush, and we'll stay here on weekends, but right now, you're going to bed, and I'm going home."

In the morning she felt off her feed, but she dabbed the eye with makeup, got dressed, and caught the bus to Lindsey. Steps before she reached the door to Materiel, she felt worse. There was no bench nearby, so she lowered herself to the curb as Wolfgang Ritter pulled up in one of the fancier motor pool cars. He got out and ran to her. "*Zuckerschnecke*! What happened? You have a black eye. And a cut."

"A car accident last night. I'm a little dizzy, that's all."

The general's secretary approached on her way in. "Erika, call another car for General Novak," said Wolfgang. "I'm taking Brencie to the hospital. She was in a car accident last night. Just a precaution. Go on, now."

Once they were at the hospital, Brencie told the doctor only as much as she needed to, and after checking her over, he decided to admit her for observation. Her protests didn't move him, and satisfied she was in good hands, Wolfgang said, "Don't worry. I'll go see Colonel Foss and tell him what's happened."

Once she was tucked up in a sterile white bed with nurses and corpsmen fussing over her, Brencie decided to take advantage of the consequences. She was in the hospital, like it or not. Might as well enjoy it. She called Lulu. "Hi. Guess where I am. The hospital. No, it's nothing. I'll explain when I see you. Bring me something to read. And a Snickers bar."

Lulu-no-doubt called everyone. Jules, on duty in another part of the hospital, stopped by, followed by Margo and Dierdre, starched and white. Colonel Foss came by, and Brencie was enjoying herself. She had great friends, and Wolfgang and Foss the Boss looked after her. There was so much foot traffic the floor nurse shooed everyone out. "This isn't the *Maifest*. It's a hospital. Come back during visiting hours."

Lulu arrived after work. "Here's *Stars and Stripes* and *Cosmo*. And a Snickers and your Betty Boop PJs. Cuter than that shroud you're wearing."

When Lulu left, Brencie drifted into a light sleep and woke to see Nolan standing by the bed with a bouquet of daisies. Except from her balcony, she hadn't seen him since she told him about Chase.

"How are you, Brencie? What happened?"

"Nothing, really. An overreaction by the doctor to a bump on the head."

"Lulu told me Dellasera put the car in a ditch. Was he drinking?"

"It's Disneyland on the Rhine. Everybody's drinking."

"I don't have any right to make this my business, but are you going to sort this out with your boyfriend?"

"You're right. It's my business. It's good to see you, Nolan." She meant it; she had missed him.

As he picked up a yellow plastic water pitcher and thrust the daisies into it, Brencie recognized the signs of anger, the red around his collar, the tightness around his mouth. He looked like that when the prissy lieutenant dressed him down for missing a salute. "Good to see you too, Brencie." He left. The daisies looked natural and appealing, and they were the first thing Chase saw when he arrived half an hour later.

"From Hanik? Was he here?" When she didn't answer, he gave her a look, but he let it go.

"Did you see to the car?" she asked.

"I did. Not much damage, but it won't be ready before the weekend."

"We need to talk, Chase. You're drinking too much. You could have killed us. What's it about? Is it about the war? Will you talk to a counselor? They're available right here in the hospital."

"I can't. They say it's anonymous, but no one believes that. Someone sees you coming and going or a corpsman talks too much.

I have to consider my future in the military. I'll get counseling as soon as we get home, when I can be sure of privacy."

"When *we* get home? But fraternization is about *your* future? My father was an alcoholic. I never told you that. If there's a *we*, meaning you and me, you've got to stop drinking."

"Listen to me. I love you. I won't let anything come between us. Or anyone."

Chapter 10

Dear Brencie,

Are you upset about MLK? Everyone is.

Every time I say no to selling The Swank, they raise the offer. I didn't know I was such a good horse trader. It's tempting, cuz I'm tired of explaining to customers I can make them not so scary, but I can't make them look like that Julie Cristie.

I'm thinking about selling the house, but the agent says she can't list it without clear title. She said I should have Anson declared legally dead. Well, I can't kill him, even on paper.

The bluebonnets are blooming. How's the bones-eye? Haha. I know it's bonsai.

Love your Agnes-Rose

Although the blue bonnets were a seven-day sapphire miracle, when they disappeared, spring in Texas was barely discernable from summer. In Wiesbaden June felt like early May, and the *Rheingau* was glorious. Chase and Brencie sat on her balcony sipping wine and smelling the sweetness of rain sweeping over the Taunus mountains in silver sheets. "Where did the porch chairs come from?" said Chase as he refused a refill.

"They were here when I got home yesterday, stored for the winter in the sub-basement, which is the size of Rhode Island. Full of luggage, Christmas decorations, and droppings of long-gone residents. They say the Arc of the Covenant's there."

Though it was hard to make him laugh these days, he chuckled, and since the car accident, he had kept his promise to cut down on the drinking. He leaned back in his chair and stretched his long legs in front of him. "We're going to be spoiled when we go back home. It's idyllic as long as the balloon doesn't go up. Then we go from having a great time to high on the nuke 'em list."

"You don't really think that will happen, do you?"

"Seeing that it doesn't is why we're here. It's easy to forget that."

"Sometimes I wonder if I'll have more culture shock when I go back home than I did coming here. I read somewhere that the past is a foreign country. Maybe when it's in our past this will feel like a foreign country, but right now the Air Force does it's best to make us forget that."

The rain reached them along with the wind, and they went inside as the phone rang. The official voice Brencie dreaded asked for Captain Dellasera. She checked her watch. Lulu and Jules were coming for drinks, which Chase accepted as a compromise, despite his reservations.

The usual routine followed. He made two calls. After the first time he was called away, she suggested he leave a clean uniform at her place, so he changed clothes and said, "Make my apologies to Lulu and Jules." He left.

When Lulu and Jules arrived, Brencie explained Chase's absence as she took a cheese plate out of the fridge, gave Jules a beer, and poured wine for Lulu.

Lulu shrugged. "It can't be helped."

Jules quaffed his beer and launched into his usual enthusiastic conversation. He was in good form, and Brencie was sorry Chase wasn't there to appreciate the smart, funny, irreverent Jules.

"Did you read about Andy Warhol?" he asked. "The girl who shot him is called Valerie Solanas. She's *SCUM*. Shot his business partner too. Warhol was pronounced dead, but they revived him, no doubt irritating the shit out of his collectors. The value of his soup cans would skyrocket if he died."

"I'm not impressed with pop art," said Lulu, "but anyone who shoots anyone for no reason should be called scum or worse."

"Not scum lowercase. Uppercase. Society for Cutting Up Men. She's a crackpot women's libber and sole member of SCUM."

"It's kinda funny, though," said Lulu. "The SCUM part, not getting shot."

"Speaking of shooting, there's a rifle drill at the base this weekend in honor of D-Day," said Jules. "If you can skip the shopping trip. What do you buy, anyway?"

"Well, I encouraged Brencie to buy an Italian leather purse the right size for her sketch pad, and I wouldn't let her buy a flowery print raincoat. Bad taste," said Lulu.

They finished their drinks. "Come to the dining room with Jules and me," Lulu suggested. "It's fried chicken tonight."

"OK, sure," Brencie replied. "I'll put things away and meet you in a few minutes."

———— ((◉)) ————

As soon as the elevator doors opened, Brencie knew something was wrong. The lobby was the beating heart of the Amelia, and the rhythm never stopped. Night or day, people made trouble, greeted friends, argued with a desk clerk, bought a paper, and exchanged dollars for marks. It was never quiet or deserted. It wasn't deserted now, which made the silence ominous.

Lulu and Jules huddled on a couch, and Brencie went directly to them. "What's happened?" She whispered, not daring to interrupt the silence.

Lulu sobbed and choked on her words, so Brencie looked at Jules. "It's Bobby Kennedy," he said. "He's dead. Shot in L.A."

Brencie sat down next to Lulu. "It's not possible," she whispered. "How do you know?"

Lulu found her voice. "It was on German TV first, then on Armed Forces Radio. Details are unclear. Maybe it's not true."

"That's why Chase was called," Brencie said. "He'll be briefed."

Lulu suggested they all go to her apartment, but Brencie shook her head. "I'll go to my place and wait for Chase."

⸺ «◎» ⸺

Chase called the next morning, but by then the details were all over the radio. Robert F. Kennedy had been shot at the Ambassador Hotel in Los Angeles after being declared the winner in the South Dakota and California presidential primaries. He was pronounced dead at 1:44 a.m. Pacific time, on June 6. D-Day. Chase had nothing to add, except he would be deployed for a couple of days. Brencie knew by then not to ask questions.

She stepped out onto the balcony. It was a clear morning, yet something was wrong, something about the whole world. How could the beauty of the valley be the same? The cheerful petunias were the same; her coffee smelled good. But Bobby Kennedy was dead. That couldn't be. Either the valley was ugly, deforested, church spirals removed, bells silenced, the gold scraped from the dome of St.

⸺ 123 ⸺

Elizabeth's, or Kennedy would be the next President of the United States. But the beauty remained unchanged, Bobby was dead, and Nolan Hanik ran by.

When she arrived at work the same silence dominated the Materiel building, broken only by the tapping of typewriters rolling from office to office like an echo and the occasional ring of a telephone. Brencie ran into Wolfgang in the hall. He held her hand for a moment, and his face said it all. In her office Colonel Foss hugged her and asked if she was OK. When she distributed the overnight cable traffic, there were no cheerful greetings, and no one had brought in the Friday morning doughnuts.

Leah Crum came to Brencie's office with a bouquet of daffodils. "Hi, Brencie. These look so wrong now, but they were meant to say thank you for staying late last week to help with that Congressional inquiry."

"I was glad to do it," Brencie said, and Leah left. Brencie put the daffodils in water and sleepwalked through the rest of the day, leaving well ahead of Retreat. It would be unbearable to watch the flag come down. She walked past the guard station and off the base, and when she passed the flower stand on the corner, the florist was in tears. "*Schade, schade,*" she said, as she took Brencie's hand. The man at the newsstand also spoke to her. "*Ach, Fräulein. Herr* Kennedy. *Das tut mir leid.*"

She went directly to her apartment, and the phone rang. "We're going to the bar," said Lulu. "Come join us. Company might help."

Brencie agreed to come, but when she stepped off the elevator, she regretted it. Friday usually meant the happiest of happy hours, music and the merry ting and rattle of slot machines from the bar. Today, from desk clerks to waiters to residents, no one spoke above a whisper. The bouquets of seasonal flowers that usually adorned both ends of the reception desk were gone, replaced by white lilies bound with black satin ribbon. The lilies were not in water, but laid flat, as though they were encouraged to wilt.

Brencie was about to go back upstairs just as Lulu and Jules stepped off the other elevator. "Oh no, you don't," said Lulu. "It won't do any good to brood. Where's Chase?"

"Deployed."

"All the more reason," Lulu said.

The tables were occupied, bar stools too. The community wanted to be together, and the murmured conversation sounded like a wake. The slot machines remained shrouded, and the juke box was dark. Leah Crum sat with a group of friends, and Dierdre and Margo were at a table, hunched over their drinks. Brencie was glad their new friend Jürgen wasn't there. It was a time for Americans only.

Nolan was at the bar wearing gray slacks and a white dress shirt, and when Brencie stopped to say hello, he gently traced the thin line above her left eye with his thumb. His touch almost made her weep. "Just a small scar from the accident," he said. "It will fade."

Dierdre and Margo made room for them all, Brencie, Lulu, Jules, and Nolan. Even after drinks were brought, there was little conversation, no music, no good cheer. Martin Luther King was dead. Bobby Kennedy was dead. The riots in the United States signaled something, but no one knew what. Hopelessness had come to the party dressed in mourning.

"I hope he didn't suffer," said Dierdre.

"God. Andy Warhol got shot too," said Lulu. "No one will remember that now."

"Shut up, both of you," said Jules. "You wouldn't know 'Babalu' from Babi Yar." He got up and slammed into a waiter, who dropped a tray of drinks, creating an explosion in the silence. Jules left without looking back.

There were tears in Lulu's eyes. "He let himself care about Bobby."

"He's not mad at you, Lulu," said Brencie.

Lulu said, "During the Six Day War it was like this, but more anxious than sad. It's like a film that runs over and over. Someone storms out, a waiter drops a tray, someone starts to cry. Same script, different people. I'd go home if I had one. I've lived in Germany since I was fourteen."

They drank until the lights flickered. Someone had dictated the bar close early. Margo and Dierdre left, and Brencie and Lulu stood up, both a little wobbly. "I'd better see you two get where you're going," Nolan said.

They went to Lulu's door first and then to Brencie's. She leaned against him, putting her forehead on his chest. He smelled like the starch in his clean shirt. "What will we go home to, if we go home?" Brencie asked.

"We will go home. We're Americans. The country's going through something, but it will pass." He kissed her cheek and resurrected the ghost of what they almost had. She knew he felt it, and that he wouldn't act on it. He left as soon as she unlocked her door.

━━━◉━━━

Dr. King's death followed by Bobby's infected the summer like a virus, but the festivals along the Rhine continued, the parties, the easy way of life, all the same on the surface, but there was a collective holding of breath. The community had a case of nerves. At home riots continued to rip through the major cities.

Chase was more restless and angry than ever. Although his desire for Brencie remained intense and they made love often, it felt less intimate.

One night in the afterglow, Brencie went to the bathroom for a cloth. She dampened it with warm water and went back to the bed to wipe the perspiration from Chase's face. She brought Perrier from the refrigerator, which she kept because he liked it. Taking advantage of the moment, she mentioned their summer plans. "I need a vacation, and so do you. Let's go somewhere we can think about nothing. What about Paris?"

"We aren't going. Don't ask again." His tone was hurtful, especially considering they had just had sex. "Bren, I'm sorry. I didn't mean it. It's just that ..."

"What's bothering you? Is it the assassinations? Is it the war? Or is it me?"

"No! You're all I want. It's partly the war. It's turning into a parlor game at the Pentagon. I did my duty, and I stand by that. I'm proud of it."

"Then let's go somewhere. There's so many places to choose from. Lulu says Majorca's nice."

<hr />

They flew over the Mediterranean to an island off the coast of Spain, and when they stepped into the balmy air of Palma de Majorca, the geographic cure seemed to work at once. Their hotel room was painted azure and so near the shoreline, the sunlight cast watery reflections against the walls. When they lay in bed, it felt like they were floating in the sea.

Even so, in the morning Chase grew distant after they made love. Brencie suggested they wear their bathing suits under their clothes, hoping the prospect of sea and sun would cheer him up. She wondered if she would ever piece together the puzzle of his shifting moods, the turning away, the silence.

She hoped this place would make those things go away for a while, and at least the morning began with a laugh. The breakfast room featured six blue wooden tables with a bowl of fresh fruit—oranges, lemons, and bananas—on each table, and when they walked in a parrot on a perch screeched, "Awk! Awk! Birds can't talk!"

They were still laughing when they took a table with a view of the Mediterranean.

"Chase, I know something's bothering you."

He reached for her hand. "Just looking at you cheers me up."

"Really? Watch this then." She selected three of the smaller oranges from the bowl, deftly tossed one in the air and then another. Soon she juggled all three in an orange arc.

He laughed. "Where did you learn to do that?"

"Waiting for a tennis court in Friendswood, Texas. Nothing to do but sit there, which I hated, and too noisy to read, to crowded to sketch. I learned to juggle with the tennis balls. Marginally." She allowed the oranges to fall back into her hands. "But that's it. Nothing fancy. Just the three."

"Something tells me you could surprise me for a lifetime." The implication seemed clear, but instead of the soulful look she expected, he looked around for the waiter and ordered coffee.

After the usual continental breakfast of bread, fruit, and cheese, they walked to the water and rented a purple paddle boat with *Titanic* stenciled on the side. They paddled farther and farther away from shore, but the water was so clear it never looked deep. "The boat guy said it's about fifteen meters this far offshore," Chase said. "Almost fifty feet."

"I don't believe it." She removed her coverup and dove in, deeper and deeper, and Chase followed. When she thought her lungs would burst, she touched the bottom and shot back up. They broke the surface together and clung to the side of the boat.

When he caught his breath, he said, "I thought I might drown. Let me ask you a question."

It wasn't a romantic moment, but his words called to mind what Lulu had said about their getaway. "Oh, my god. Majorca! Sunshine and everyone almost naked all day long. I'll bet he's going to pop the question."

He ran his fingers through his wet hair and hoisted himself onto the *Titanic*. After he helped her aboard he said, "How come you coastal people aren't afraid of the water?"

"That's the question? That's easy. We respect the water. Non-swimmers don't drown, because they don't go in deep water. Swimmers who forget to be respectful are the ones who drown."

After they docked the little boat and laughed at the name one last time, they enjoyed lunch under a coral-colored awning, flat pans of golden paella that reminded Brencie of Dierdre and Margo and how much they loved Spain. The restaurant was so pleasant Brencie and Chase returned every day. Chase grew less and less preoccupied, and he wasn't drinking, beyond a little wine. They made love every morning. At night they danced on the terrace at a club across from their hotel and then went to their room and made love again. The band always closed with "*Guantanamera*," and the music drifted in on the jasmine-scented breeze.

Chase whispered in her ear as they lay naked in bed. "It means 'Girl from Guantanamo Bay.' 'I am a truthful man, from the land of the palms. Before dying, I want to share these poems of my soul.' It's on the juke box at the Arms. I asked a guest worker from Spain. Of course, I'm never sure they don't give us bad information."

She turned in his arms and propped herself up on her elbow. "*They? Us?*"

"*They* foreigners. *Us*, Americans. A friend bought a shirt in Moscow with something on the pocket in Cyrillic. They said it meant Follow Your Dream. She found out it meant Capitalism Equals Death. The shirt fell apart the first time she washed it."

"Maybe it should have said Communism Equals Crappy Shirts."

He laughed. "You're funny, Bren, and I love you so much. Someday . . ."

She held her breath, unsure of what she hoped for, but he said no more. Maybe living together was as far as he wanted to go. He snuggled against her and began breathing deeply, but she sensed he was pretending to sleep. As for marriage, was that what she wanted? Would the reality live up to the fantasy?

On their last night in Palma, they drank enough wine to loosen all inhibitions, and he took her in his arms as soon as they stepped into their room. "Let me make you happier than you've ever been."

The gentle beat of "*Guantanamera*" covered them like a cocoon, protected them from all but the moment. Chase kept his promise, and Brencie wondered if she would ever again be as happy as she was right then. She knew the answer, and it made her sad.

A week after they got back from Majorca, Brencie went to work expecting Chase to meet her at five o'clock. When he wasn't there, she assumed he would call later, unless he had been deployed again. He warned her it could happen.

Captain Clark's remark at the dining-out refused to leave her head. *'Bout time for the deployment disappearing act. The ol' easy kiss-off.* It was irrational, but when he hadn't called after a week, Brencie confided her anxiety to Lulu, mentioning Chase's persistent moodiness.

"Brencie, he's in love with you. I don't know why you're so anxious. I hope it's not because of anything I said. He's a fighter jock, sure, and I didn't really think he would propose. Maybe it's because of your broken engagement. Or your father. Girls don't get over being abandoned. He's deployed, that's all. You'll get used to it."

"I'm not sure I want to. I'm not even sure I want to marry him." But waiting got more difficult as weeks passed. She scoured the news for events that might account for his absence. He had never been gone this long. When she went to the lobby to meet Lulu for their Saturday shopping, "That's What You Get for Lovin' Me" came from the juke box in the bar. It was a Gordon Lightfoot tune she last heard at the Sand Mountain coffee house in Houston, a million years ago, a million miles away. Just after her engagement fell apart.

Lulu was at the desk holding the dull yellow paper of a telegram in her hand, and her face told Brencie something awful had happened. Even the unflappable desk clerks looked anxious. Lulu gave the telegram to Brencie, and when she read it, her brain could cope only by flipping its toggle switch to the Off position. She fainted for the first time in her life.

⸻ ((◉)) ⸻

It took most of the night, but with Lulu's help, by morning Brencie was booked on a flight to Houston via New York. It was an agonizing process, after which Brencie got a two-striper in the communications center on the phone. She bullied him into patching a call through to the hospital in Friendswood. It was a bad connection, all echo and static, and it was cut off before the end. Brencie still knew nothing about Agnes-Rose's condition, except she was alive. Brencie broke down, unable to control her sobs.

Lulu put her arms around her friend. "Brencie. It's probably going to be all right, but you won't know for sure until you get home."

"Oh, Lulu. There's something I haven't told you."

"What? For hell's sake, tell me."

"All right, but you have to promise not to tell anyone. It's humiliating."

"I swear on the life of the Queen of England. You know I love her."

"I broke my engagement because Rick was unfaithful, but I didn't tell you who with. I caught him with Agnes-Rose."

Lulu's mouth dropped open, and Brencie managed a smile. "Lulu, if you open your mouth any wider, I'll see what's in your stomach."

"Oh, my god! You caught your fiancé screwing your stepmother? What a prick! Rick the prick! With your stepmother? At his apartment? I thought I'd heard everything, and now I have. No wonder you weren't looking for a relationship."

"Not at his apartment. At the house."

"Way worse if they were at his place. No heat of the moment explanation for that!"

Brencie shook her head. "I should have forgiven her."

"Damn! That's a big forgive."

"Agnes-Rose loves me, and I love her. I haven't spoken to her face to face since then. I wouldn't hear a word of explanation, and she tried and tried. Now we might not get the chance to make things right."

Lulu's silence was unusual.

"I can hear you thinking," Brencie said.

"It ought to sound like a tuba. I'm pondering. Agnes-Rose sleeps with your fiancé who looks like your father who was her husband. Which naturally ends your engagement, but you didn't care about Rick, even if you didn't know it, and you never saw who he looked like. Which means you were looking for your father all along. You didn't love Rick, but you do love Agnes-Rose. Am I leaving anything out?"

"I know. It sounds like The *Twilight Zone*," she answered, "And I think she loves my father to this day. Gone twelve years, and she still can't bring herself to declare him legally dead."

"Right. You thought Peter Pan flying off the roof of the American Arms was preposterous? Disneyland on the Rhine has nothing on Freaky Friendswood."

Lulu arranged for Nolan to take Brencie to the airport in Frankfurt. He arrived right on time, parked in the circular drive out front, and put Brencie's suitcase in the back seat. Lulu gave Brencie a hug and then stood back. When she looked over the top of the VW, she drew in her breath. "Oh, no," she said. "Not now."

Chase's red BMW pulled in behind the Volkswagen. He went directly to Brencie, ignoring the others. "Bren, I just got back. I called your apartment over and over. You weren't in."

"I was at Lulu's most of the night."

"Chase, something's happened," Lulu said. "Brencie has to go home to Texas."

Nolan materialized like a shadow between Chase and Brencie. "We're ready to go," he said.

"Get out of my way." Chase said it as though he were speaking to a subordinate. "Bren, I'll take you to the airport. We can talk on the way."

"No," said Nolan. "You've been drinking. I can smell it. You put her in the hospital once. That's not going to happen again."

"Move aside, Sergeant," said Chase.

"If you take another step, you won't remember taking it," replied Nolan. "We're not in uniform now."

"Roger that, but I don't answer to you." Chase turned back to Brencie. "I had a couple of post-mission drinks on the base. I'm fine to drive."

Brencie was too exhausted to react, but Lulu put a hand on Chase's arm. "She has a flight at noon, and five minutes later she would have been gone. Chase, you can wait."

Nolan opened the car door. When Brencie got in, Chase knew it was a done deal. As Nolan walked around to the driver's side, Brencie rolled down the window and spoke to Chase. "I'll see you when I get back."

"Alright. I don't want to be part of the problem, but at least tell me what's happened."

Seconds before Nolan put the car in gear and pulled away, Brencie fished the telegram out of her purse and handed it to Chase.

Agnes-Rose tried to kill herself. Stop. Condition uncertain. Stop. Come ASAP. Stop. Signed: Your Neighbor Hazel

Chapter 11

F reeway construction, heat, and football. *Yup*, Brencie thought, *I'm back in Texas.*

The never-ending mess on the Gulf Freeway caused the taxi to creep toward Friendswood, and the forecast called for ninety-five degrees. A radio segment reported on a football game between the Houston Cougars and the Texas Longhorns as though the losers were on the verge of ritual suicide. When she finally arrived at the house, Brencie collected her things and paid the fare. "I could taxi to Paris for that much money," she grumbled.

"Yeah? Never driven that far." As he backed out of the drive, she realized he thought she meant Paris, Texas.

Brencie fumbled under the porch, hoping the key would be in the Cheez Whiz jar, where it always was. She found it, then forced herself to go inside.

The rattling window air conditioner hadn't been turned off, and cold air hit her so hard she closed her eyes. The artificial cold, the smell of the house, even the creak of the loose floorboard on the threshold – the time machine of memory transported her back to the three-minute event that changed her life.

She parks her car on the street, because Rick's turquoise Mustang is in the driveway. He had promised to drop off his mother's list of wedding guests.

She enters the house and starts to the kitchen where Agnes-Rose and Rick probably will be, but the route takes her past the bathroom. The door is open. Her fiancé sits on the toilet, his pants around his ankles. Agnes-Rose straddles him. Their eyes are closed tight, and they're both dressed from the waist up, she in a pink wrapper with a map of Texas on the back; he in a blue knit shirt with the NASA logo on the pocket. Then he passes wind. Toot-toot.

Brencie laughs out loud, and in cosmic choreography, Rick and Agnes-Rose look at Brencie, who says, "We won't be needing the guest list."

The scene dissolved when the telephone rang. Brencie opened her eyes. Now that she had revisited the ugly event, she resolved to let it go. It was in the past.

Brencie had moved back home to prepare for the wedding that wouldn't happen. She had left the house without a word and lived with a friend until she found a new job far, far away. Although she had spoken to her stepmother on the phone, she left the country without seeing Agnes-Rose or Rick again.

It felt odd to be back and to see that not much had changed in the house. Ignoring the phone, she pulled a book from a shelf, a Disney classic from her childhood. *Cinderella.* The junior high summers were there, the Jack London June, the July of Laura Ingalls Wilder, and on to the hot August days of Thomas Hardy.

The phone rang again, and again she didn't answer it. She wanted to get to the hospital. All the way across the Atlantic, she had been awake with worry. She called the hospital from New York to be told her stepmother was resting comfortably and had never been critical. Brencie had dozed on the plane from New York to Houston, but she wouldn't feel comfortable until she saw Agnes-Rose. The old pickup was in the garage, keys in the ignition as usual, so she drove the temperamental Ford directly to the hospital, grinding the gears all the way.

Her stepmother, asleep in the high bed, looked tiny in a faded print gown. She hated prints; they made her look dowdy, she said, but her features in repose seemed young. Brencie's heart exploded with emotion. What if Agnes-Rose had died? What if she had died not knowing the forgiveness she craved had been granted. Brencie sighed, long and deep.

"Brencie." Agnes-Rose didn't open her eyes. "I'd know that sigh if I was blind." When she opened her eyes, her pleasure at the sight of her stepdaughter was better than words. Brencie went to the bed for a long embrace, a moment unto itself, unguarded, spontaneous.

"Bee Bee," Brencie said.

"You haven't called me that in a long time, not even in a letter."

"I know. Now tell me what happened."

Agnes-Rose's smile crumpled. "I've thought about it over and over. Rick came by and . . ."

"I wasn't talking about that. How did you manage to shoot yourself?" Anson Jessup had been a salesman, gone every week. He worried about his women folk being alone, so he bought a shotgun and showed his wife and eight-year-old daughter how to use it. When Anson left for good, the gun stayed loaded, propped against the wall.

"I heard a noise. I got the shotgun. I shot and missed."

"You missed? You didn't miss. You shot yourself."

"That wasn't what I meant to shoot, so I missed. I did hear a noise outside. I thought it might be Mr. Nelson's mean old tomcat, the one that murdered our hamster, but I wasn't sure, so I kept my eye on the window and backed up to get the gun. I nudged it. It bounced off the rubber plant and hit the floor. That's all I remember."

"Why wasn't the safety on? How many times did I check it? How many times did I show you how to check it? Who else has been in the house?"

Agnes-Rose looked sheepish. "Lupe still comes to help me clean once a month. Sometimes she brings her boy. He's twelve or thirteen."

"Oh, my god," Brencie said.

"I know. He could have killed himself or his mother. Hazel heard the shot and came over. She called for help. Now here I sit in a butt-ugly granny print, the food isn't fit to eat, and the TV doesn't work." She squeezed Brencie's hand. "But I'm so glad to see you."

A woman in a white coat and wire-rimmed glasses entered the room. "I'm Dr. Shellenberger. Are you the next of kin? Can I see you outside?" Brencie followed her into the hall. "Your mother was lucky," the doctor said. "Any closer to the gun, and she might not be alive. We pulled some buckshot out of her arm and backside. However, we don't have her on the psyche ward, because after I talked to her, I figured it was an accident, even though your neighbor said she tried to commit suicide. What do you think?"

"Hazel loves drama. As worried as I was, I never thought it was a suicide attempt. Besides, if she wanted to kill herself, wouldn't she shoot herself in the head or something?"

"You wouldn't believe what people do. They don't want it to look like suicide for the sake of their family or the insurance. According to Mrs. Jessup, she was shot by a rubber plant."

"She didn't try to kill herself. No one enjoys life more than Agnes-Rose. It was an accident."

The doctor nodded. "That was my conclusion, but I wanted to know what you thought. You're living in Germany, right? And you'll be going back?"

"I have to." *And I want to*, she thought.

"She shouldn't work for a while, especially not on her feet. If you can stay in town for now, I'll release her to your care tomorrow." She walked away.

The word *accident* had peppered the conversation, and that's how Brencie had re-labeled the event between Agnes-Rose and Rick. Her stepmother was without malice, yet she ended up *in flagrante delicto* with her own stepdaughter's fiancé. How did that happen? Brencie went back to the bedside.

"What did she say?" Agnes-Rose asked.

"She wanted to know if I thought you tried to kill yourself."

"By shooting myself in the butt? What is she, a moron?"

"She had to ask. That's what Hazel implied."

"That nosy Witch Hazel. Wait till I get home. I'm going to pull up all her tomato plants."

Brencie laughed out loud. She had missed Agnes-Rose's wacky way of expressing herself. And something else. "Agnes-Rose! You cut your hair!"

"Every time I see Witch Hazel she asks two questions. Why did Brencie leave the country and why did I cut my hair." Agnes-Rose's eyes filled with tears. "Brencie, I've had plenty of time to think about what happened. I—"

"Never mind for now. We—"

"Please let me say this. I've rehearsed it for months. I have to go back to when I met Anson. I was eighteen, my parents were dead, and I was going to beauty school, working in a drug store, and living at the YWCA. Anson came in for a cherry Coke. We made a date. We got married and scraped together enough to buy The Swank. It was perfect."

Brencie looked down at the floor. "Until it wasn't."

"But the main thing is, Anson brought you into my life. I loved you from the first time I saw you. In a year or two he started drinking, but I wouldn't let him sell The Swank. I knew I might need it to take care of myself and you. Need's a powerful thing, honey."

Brencie walked to the window. It was a double room, but the other bed was empty, and she was grateful for the privacy. "You raised me and ran your own business, young as you were. You did what you needed to do."

"And it was worth it. You know, when all that bra-burning

silliness started, I thought they were weird, but I've thought about it, and those gals may be onto something. I couldn't sell the house. I couldn't get a loan."

The idea of fluffy, gaudy, sparkly Agnes-Rose practically declaring herself a feminist didn't surprise Brencie as much as she thought it would. "They are onto something. And Anson's a shiftless alcoholic who didn't give a damn."

"No, Brencie, he was broken. You're like him in all the good ways, smart and thoughtful, fearless. He could draw. Did you know that? And he taught himself Spanish so he could talk to his Mexican customers. The war happened to him. Your mother died. The drinking got worse, and he couldn't hold it together, and I wasn't enough."

And neither was I, Brencie thought. The expression on Agnes-Rose's face broke Brencie's heart. "You still love him."

"Part of me always will, but if he walked in the door, I wouldn't take him back."

A nurse came in. "Time for a shot, Mrs. Jessup."

"A shot? I hope it's bourbon," said Agnes-Rose.

When the nurse left, Agnes-Rose picked up where she left off. "So that day you were supposed to be shopping at Gulfgate. I don't know why you weren't, but—"

"I had a car accident."

"You did? I never knew that. Was it bad?"

"A guy with naked-lady mud flaps on his truck backed into me at the gas station. I didn't want to take the car out on the highway, so I came home."

"Wow," said Agnes-Rose. "Another piece of the puzzle. Did you know it was our anniversary week, Anson's and mine? I was thinking of him all day, and then he was there. Oh, I knew it was Rick, I won't say I didn't, but I needed something so bad. I hadn't had that kind of fun in a long time. My brain stopped working. It was all my fault. I love you more than anyone in the world, and I let it happen. I wanted you to kill me. I wanted to kill Rick."

Brencie remembered the doppelganger in the officers' club and the shock of seeing her father and her ex-fiancé in the same face. "You called and called. I wouldn't even talk to you. You tried to tell me Rick looked like Anson. If it hadn't happened, I would be married to Rick, so maybe I should thank you. I'm not entitled to judge anyone, but if I were, I'd forgive you with all my heart, and I have."

Agnes-Rose's face lit up, and then she started to cry. Brencie held her until she stopped sobbing. Their hearts had been broken by the same man, and it wasn't Richard Paul Smith.

<hr/>

On the way back to the house Brencie relished the sights of Friendswood, the high school, the library that smelled of old books. The suggestion of a sea breeze from Galveston mixed with the oily smell from the refineries in Pasadena. She missed her hometown. It was a good place, and she appreciated the raw energy of Texas, now that she could compare it to the moss-covered softness of Europe.

At home she showered and changed, and after eating a freezer-burned TV dinner, she called a few friends, reaching only one, who couldn't talk because of a crying baby. Brencie decided to walk down the street to visit with Mrs. O'Barry. Her son, Joe, was Brencie's friend from sixth grade. He was away in the Army, but Mrs. O'Barry said he would be back between assignments in a few weeks. Brencie would miss him. With no one to see and no one left to call, fatigue caught up with her. She went to the house and stretched out on the couch. Hours later, the phone woke her. This time, she answered.

"Hey. It's me, Rick. I heard about Agnes-Rose. I figured you'd come home. I've been calling for two days. How is she?"

"She's going to be fine."

"Can I come see you?"

"Is that a joke?"

"Aw, come on, Brencie. What can it hurt? We can drive to Galveston. I'll take you to Guido's."

All at once it seemed like a good idea. Agnes-Rose blamed herself for what happened, but Brencie wondered if there was more to the story. "Tomorrow. Six o'clock." She hung up.

—◦((�))◦—

Brencie arrived at the hospital the next morning expecting to take Agnes-Rose home, but Dr. Shellenberger explained it wasn't going to be that day after all. "She has a low-grade fever. We'll wait until it's at ninety point five."

"What? Ninety point five? I'd be dead," Agnes-Rose said.

"That was a joke," the doctor said.

Agnes-Rose crossed her arms over her chest. "Doctors never joke."

"Yes, we do. We're just not very funny. Your temp's one hundred point one. I expect it won't develop into anything, but we want to monitor it."

"This is a concentration camp. I can't stand it."

The doctor grinned. "It's a good sign when patients get crabby. We'll take your temp at regular intervals, and if you have no fever tomorrow, we'll liberate you from Auschwitz-on-the-Bayou."

She left, and Brencie pulled a chair close to the bed. "It's only one day."

Agnes-Rose pouted. "It means I have to tell you something I wanted to tell you at home. It can't wait. You could see some paperwork I didn't get a chance to put away. Harley found Anson."

"What? Who's Harley? When?"

"Harley Rosales. You remember. The private investigator."

"Mr. Rosales. I remember, but—"

"Let me tell you, and then you can ask questions. With all that black-Irish charm, naturally Anson found a woman in Tijuana to take care of him. She works. He drinks. I worked, but I wouldn't let him do whatever he wanted. I nagged and threatened. I said you deserved better—"

"Oh, Bee Bee. You deserved better."

"I said that too. That's why he took off, because you and I deserved better. That's what he told Harley. The good news is, Harley met with a lawyer before he went to Mexico. He confronted Anson with the right paperwork. Anson signed everything. Divorce papers, title to the house and the shop. I'm free." She looked away. "Whether I like it or not."

Brencie sighed. Now the most wistful thinking couldn't turn her father into a martyr. As a kid she imagined he had gotten amnesia, the favorite device of children and soap operas. If he had amnesia, he couldn't abandon his wife and child, because he didn't remember he had them.

When Brencie fished for the car keys, preparing to leave, she found a packet of photos Lulu had slipped into her purse. She opened the envelope and thumbed through them, pictures of this and that, parties, her friends, even the first picnic at Schierstein. She handed the photos to her stepmother.

"Wow," said Agnes-Rose. "So that's Chase. I mean, wow. Who's the other one? Nolan? He's not as pretty, but there's something about him."

Brencie realized her heart was in two places. She missed Chase and Lulu and Jules. Dierdre and Margo. Her work friends too, Colonel Foss and Leah Crum. Wolfgang. She missed Nolan too. In fact she had missed Nolan since the day they broke up.

Agnes-Rose studied Brencie. "It's possible to love two men at one time, you know."

"Maybe, but you have to choose."

"You chose pretty quick. Be careful there in Fantasy-baden, or whatever you call it. Imagine living with Chase in a knucklehead town in Alabama. Do you remember Hazel's nephew? The army guy? Major Something? He said military life was two parts glamour, ninety-eight parts ugly base housing and boring cocktail parties."

<hr />

At the house Brencie took another nap and then tackled the problem of what to wear to dinner that would make Rick eat his heart out. She checked the closet in her old room and found a bridesmaid's dress the color of baby poop. No to that. She had another look in her suitcase and found a black dress she didn't remember packing. Perhaps Lulu put it in, fearing the worst. Brencie pulled the well-cut jersey over her head. As for shoes, she had sporty ones and a pair of un-sexy medium-heeled black pumps.

She had ignored the door to Agnes-Rose's room, but if there were sexy shoes in the house, that's where they would be. She went in. The gun was gone, but the overturned plant was there, dirt spilled on the carpet, thick leaves bent against a chair. The domino effect? The ripple effect? She walked around a dark pool of blood. She shuddered and resolved to have the carpet cleaned or removed.

In the messy closet she found a pair of backless hot-pink high heels with rhinestone buckles. She removed the buckles, walked around to be sure she could manage such absurd footwear, and decided the shoes would do. She heard a car, so she peeked out and saw her erstwhile fiancé get out of a white Corvette. He rang the bell, and when she opened the door, he gave her the flick. Face to chest, chest to legs, and then back up again. The lack of any attempt at subtlety made her laugh.

"I missed your laugh. You look fabulous. How do you like my new car? White isn't girly."

Among the insults Brencie had hurled at him on the telephone post-bathroom porn show, she included one for his turquoise Mustang, calling the color girly.

As they drove across the causeway to Galveston, she hoped he had replaced the Mustang at great expense.

"We'll get back together," he mused, "when you come home for good."

"That will never happen. I don't love you. I never did."

"I can change your mind. You'll see."

He was nice looking, gainfully employed, and reasonably well-mannered. And he looked like Anson Jessup. That's all he ever had to offer. She looked at the Gulf of Mexico and the high bowl of sky. When she could count the drops of water in the Gulf, she might make Rick get it. She didn't waste another word.

At Guido's he gunned the engine three times before putting the 'vette in the hands of the valet. After they ordered dinner, he bragged about his recent NASA promotion while she wondered how such a jackass could have any part of putting a man on the moon. When they finished the meal, they crossed the street out front and walked along Seawall Boulevard, where the surf sounds reminded her of high school summers.

"You get a great view of the crab from here," he said.

She stared across the street at the crab that was a fixture on the roof of Guido's for years. It was the size of a small car, and it was painted in the iridescent colors of the Mediterranean Sea, which looked nothing like the sandy waters of the Gulf of Mexico. Rick lifted her chin. "Brencie, look at me."

"Why? The crab's more interesting." She laughed because it was true.

He laughed because he thought she was kidding.

She allowed him to kiss her.

"There. Wasn't that like it used to be?" he said.

"It was like a science experiment." She resisted the impulse to mention how clumsy he was in bed, now that she had a sound basis for comparison. "Let's go home," she said.

———◦((◦))◦———

When he pulled into the driveway and turned off the engine, she waited, wanting him to broach the subject, to argue his case, and he did. "Look, Brencie. I've learned my lesson. I want you back. Chasing women is second nature to guys. I went after Agnes-Rose because she was there."

"Boys will be boys? That's your excuse? And *you* chased *her?*" She remained calm to serve her own ends. "Tell me from the beginning, not just from when I caught you."

"Well, there was only the one time. I always thought she was cute. She's not that much older than me. I made a move on her right after you and I started dating, but she told me to cut it out. I figured she didn't mean it."

Brencie knew Agnes-Rose. When she said cut it out, she meant it. "Go on."

"I came by the house and knocked, but she didn't answer, so I went in. She was in the bathroom using one of those blower things, in that little thin robe. Super sexy. Hmm." He practically smacked his lips. "When she turned off the dryer, I stroked her hair. It was warm and long. I wrapped it around my fingers. It felt alive. I put my face in her neck, and then I kissed her. Pretty soon she kissed back."

He paused to savor the recollection of seducing his fiancé's step-mother, and Brencie understood. Agnes-Rose cut her long, lovely hair in penance.

"She's something." He finished his fantasy with a far-away stare and returned to the present. "Neither of us was thinking at all, and then you were standing there. You laughed."

Brencie focused on the jigsaw puzzle of Rick's face and the face of her father. She wanted to smash it, and she was afraid she might. She got out of the Corvette and hurried up the steps, locking the door behind her. She had never experienced "seeing red," looking through a red fog, or like the light you see in a darkroom. Red. It was a good thing the shotgun was gone.

Then she remembered. She rummaged in her closet as Rick banged on the front door, and she found what she was looking for. A gun. A rifle, to be precise, once carried by Cowboy Number Three in *Annie Get Your Gun*. The firing mechanism had been removed and the barrel filled with glue, but Rick wouldn't know that. She walked down the hall, rifle butt nestled in her shoulder, barrel pointed down when she opened the door. His smile vanished when she raised the gun.

"What the hell? Is that a gun? Is it loaded?"

"Would you like to find out? Be here when I get to three. One…"

He backed up. "What's the matter with you? Are you crazy?"

"I'm not, but I'd love to shoot you all same. Two…"

He scrambled back to his stud car and turned on the engine. He yelled as he drove away. "This isn't over."

He's right, Brencie thought. *It isn't over, because it never was.*

Chapter 12

Brencie waited in the baggage claim area at the Frankfurt airport, catching a glimpse of herself in the shiny surface of the carousel. Gray pants, black blazer, and black silk blouse, still fresh-looking after the long flight. This time she arrived on a Lufthansa flight at the main terminal, not the U.S. military annex, and long gone was the gingham dress with the chocolate stain. She didn't expect or need anyone to meet her. She had been in touch with Lulu, so her friends knew she would be coming back this week, but she hadn't let anyone know her specific plans.

She followed a sign to *Bahnhof Frankfurt am Main Flughafen*, where trains departed for downtown Frankfurt or outlying villages. She was proficient enough *auf Deutsch* to ask questions as needed and get a local train to Wiesbaden. Her timing was good. Within the hour she welcomed the familiar smells, sounds, and sights at the station in Wiesbaden, the steam and grease, the scattered flap of pigeons under the open canopy. She stopped in the terminal to buy flowers and wondered if it was the shop where Chase bought the freesia after the Fasching ball. What an extraordinary evening. She smiled to herself. *Until I threw up in the bushes.*

Taxis were lined up in front of the Bahnhof, and in twenty minutes Brencie entered the lobby of the Amelia Earhart Hotel. She couldn't wait to be in Chase's arms again, and she had missed her apartment, her job, and her friends. Lulu was one of a kind. Margo and Dierdre were like salt and pepper, spicing up every gathering, as Jules pontificated.

Several people spoke to Brencie as she retrieved her accumulation of mail, and Chris Holloway, the manager, waved from her office. As soon as Brencie let herself into her place, she dropped the stack of mail onto the coffee table, stepped out onto the balcony, and breathed in the scent of being back where she belonged. She went inside, eager to call Chase and then Lulu. Chase didn't answer, and she didn't leave a message with the operator. She called Lulu, who insisted on coming right down. Brencie looked through her mail. There was a note from Chase.

Dear Brencie,

I'm gone again, not sure for how long. I hope to be back in Wies. before you are, but if you make it this week, I probably won't. I'll be there soon. Can't wait to see you.

I love you, Chase

Lulu arrived and locked Brencie in a Chanel-scented hug. "Why didn't you let us know your plans?" she asked. "Are you glad to be home? How's Agnes-Rose?"

"She's fine. She's coming to visit in a few weeks."

"Oh boy. I'll get to meet Agnes-Rose at last. Brencie, can I ask you something? Do you forgive her? I mean really? It must have been hard."

"It should have been easier. I was dropped in her lap by my father, and she loved me as much as anyone ever has. She gave up things for me I never even guessed about. I asked her why I never met her boyfriends, and she said she never got to know a man well enough to trust him around a young girl. When you meet her, you'll understand what a good soul she is."

"I do believe that's true. 'Life isn't easy; that's the hard part,'" Lulu said, and they both laughed. "From the Book of Agnes-Rose."

"One more thing, Lulu. Everyone knows my ex was a cheater, but don't tell anyone with who. You're the only one who will ever know, and I don't want people to judge Agnes-Rose. She doesn't deserve it."

"Cross my heart and hope to die. Have you talked to Chase yet?"

Brencie looked away. "He's gone again. He left a note. Two whole lines."

"He's deployed," said Lulu. "It's his job. Don't look so worried."

"I am worried, and I can't put my finger on why. Maybe it's nothing, or just that fighter pilot stuff. Even when I left, he seemed . . . what? Detached, maybe."

"From what you've told me, I agree. Something's not right between you and Chase. If it's not money or sex, then what? The war? It sure eats away at Jules."

"Maybe. Money doesn't seem to be a problem, and sex is better than ever, since I got the pill."

"You got the pill? You said that without blushing."

"He was super careful, but you know, that kind of protection isn't . . . convenient. He asked me to get the pill. It wasn't as embarrassing as I expected."

"I told you," Lulu said. "Now what about your trip to Texas?"

Brencie related the details of Agnes-Rose's mishap and then told her about Rick. "I saw him, and you're going to love this." She spun up the tale of Rick, the trip to Galveston, his seduction of Agnes-Rose.

On hearing the end of the story, the gun, the threats, Lulu laughed until tears ran down her cheeks. "It should be the chorus of a country song. 'The Death of Rick the Prick on the Mean Streets of Friendswood.'"

"He skedaddled in a cloud of squealing tires," Brencie said. "Not a shot was fired."

"Too bad. But you're tired, and I'm leaving. I'm glad you're back. Oh. I almost forgot. Promise you'll come with me to my voice lesson on Saturday. I have a surprise for you."

———※《◎》※———

On Saturday Brencie waited in the lobby, and when the elevator opened, Lulu paused as though the doors were velvet curtains on a private stage. She made her entrance wearing wide-legged pants, tiger-striped boots, and a short leather vest with long fringe. The fringe danced around her knees every time she took a step.

"Where did you get that vest?" Brencie said.

"Galeries Lafayette, when Jules and I were in Paris. What a store!"

When there were no taxis at the curb, Lulu motioned to a desk clerk to call for one, and they went outside to wait in the September sunshine. Lulu lit a cigarette and then crushed it under foot. "Angelika says smoking is terrible for my voice. I've got to quit." She glanced toward the street. "There's Nolan. You were looking for him, weren't you."

"He's a friend." Brencie ran her fingers through her curls.

He saw them and ran up the driveway, "Hi, Lulu. Is this yours?" He picked up the cigarette butt and threw it in a receptacle a few feet away.

Lulu rolled her eyes. "Thanks. I'm a bad girl."

"But we love you all the same," Nolan said. "Welcome home, Brencie. I hear your stepmother's doing well. How are you?" He kept moving, lightly running in place.

"I'm jet lagged. Agnes-Rose is good. She's coming for a visit soon."

"That should be fun. Where are you off to?"

"Shopping after my voice lesson," said Lulu. "Sale at Hertie's. We'll be crushed by packages."

"Can I pick you up and drive you back from town?" Nolan asked.

"That would be lovely," Lulu said. "We should be at the Park Café by fourteen hundred."

Nolan nodded and ran on his way.

"You set that up perfectly. I wish you hadn't," Brencie said.

Lulu cocked her head. "Really? Maybe there's something wrong between you and Chase that has nothing to do with money, sex, or war."

A taxi arrived, and soon they were dropped off at the *Mauritziousplatz*, a short walk from the apartment of Lulu's voice teacher. Lulu rang the bell and nudged Brencie. "Look across the street. That's the Crazy Sexy. It's a whore house."

"What? In the middle of town?"

"When I have a lesson after work, I see the *ladies* standing in the doorway. Angelika says it's a nuisance. You'll enjoy meeting her. She had a career as a solo soprano, but she stopped performing when she turned 70." They were buzzed up, and Lulu introduced a stout woman, expensively dressed and coiffed. A Lhasa Apso wagged his entire body and jumped into Brencie's arms.

"Happy to meet you, Brencie. Ah. Buddha likes you," said Angelika. "Lulu? Do I smell smoke?"

"I put it out. I'm stopping. Ask Brencie."

Angelika took the dog to another room, and he howled all the way down the hall. "*Meine Gott*," they heard her say. "*Du bist ein schlechter Hund.*"

"She called him a bad dog," Lulu said.

"I know. My German classes are paying off."

"Time for the surprise," Lulu said. "The theater group's doing *Camelot*. In Act I the character of Nimue lures Merlin away from

King Arthur. She has a solo called 'Follow Me.' I tried out for the part. I got it. Angelika's helping me."

"Lulu, that's wonderful. Why didn't you tell me?"

"You've been gone. But I am excited. Even the Germans come out for the musicals. Our set designer's an architect when he isn't in the Air Force. You should see his blueprints. The director did off-Broadway. A lot of talent. I've only done tech support and a couple of walk-ons. Jules talked me into trying out. He said if I work hard with Angelika and practice, I can overcome my stage fright." She walked to the window, and with her back toward Brencie, put her hands on the window frame and gripped until her knuckles turned white.

Angelika returned, and after a few warm-up scales, she suggested they practice Lulu's solo. Nestled in the curve of the grand piano, Lulu sang the song straight through as Brencie sketched.

"That was amazing," Brencie said. "You'll steal the show."

"Thank you." Lulu beamed as she looked at the drawing. "That's pretty good."

Brencie shook her head. "It's not bad. I wish I could sketch the song."

Angelika struck a chord. "It was good, Lulu, the voice is there, but the expression needs work, especially the decrescendo at the end. 'Follow me.' Then lower. Then lower, until it's a whisper. 'Follow me.'"

Lulu smiled. "That's why I have you, dear Angelika. To give me help and courage."

The lesson ran long, and it was too late for shopping. *Ladenschlussgesetz*, draconian laws about business hours, dictated the stores close at 2:00 p.m. on Saturday, so the pair went directly to the Park Café. It was warm enough to sit outside under the pink and white awning.

"I have another surprise, about Jules," Lulu said. "He told me he loves me. Not while we were having sex, either. He said it in the cold light of an upright position."

"Lulu, a solo, and a declaration of love!"

"Yes, but he's scared now. Maybe he thinks he ought to do something about it. I certainly do. He can start by staying out of the pokey, as you call it. He's locked up again, same reason as before. Off-limits clubbing."

Brencie sighed. "Oh, Lulu, we're a pair. Your boyfriend can't stay out of jail and mine can't stay in town. Chase avoids talking about the future, maybe because he isn't ready. I don't know, but I admit, I don't quite trust him."

"You don't trust him? Or you don't trust the relationship? It's two different things."

"I know, but Chase . . ." Even as she had the thought, she felt a presence. As if she had conjured him, Chase was standing there, and her heart beat increased as it did every time she saw him.

"Chase! What are you doing here?" Lulu said. "And still in uniform. Sit down. You're conspicuous. Did you know Brencie was back?"

"I just got back myself. Literally. Two hours ago." He sat down and took Brencie's hand. "Hello, Miss Friendswood. When you didn't answer the phone, I got the switchboard. Heidi's a friend. She told me you got back on Thursday. You two come here every Saturday, so I took a chance."

The switchboard operators at the Amelia were young local girls, and Heidi was a beauty. Chase could probably talk her into telling him anything he wanted to know. In order not to make a hostile remark, Brencie said nothing.

Lulu stood up. "You guys don't need me. Chase, you've got the check." She was gone.

"We can't talk here." He motioned for the bill. "Let's walk across to the park." She followed him across the street, where the scent of freshly turned soil filled the air, and newly planted chrysanthemums, yellow and white, made half circles around the bench where they sat down. "Is your stepmother OK?" he asked.

"She's fine. She's coming for a visit, but she has to get someone to run The Swank. She's devoted to her beehive blue hairs." A silence fell, the kind that has to come apart gradually, like tape being removed from a wall slowly, so the paint doesn't come off. She refused to look at him, even though her anger was irrational.

"Brencie, you can't be mad at me for doing my job. I wasn't cavorting with naked ladies in Amsterdam. I was gone longer than usual. When I got back, you were on your way to Texas. I was gone again, but I'm back. Now we can talk."

"Chase, you've got to tell me something about where you go. I'm not a Russian spy. Something's eating you all the time, and your constant comings and goings don't help."

He bent forward on the bench and put his elbows on his knees, the thinking position. "All right," he said. "The long deployment was about Czechoslovakia. Intelligence knew the invasion in August was going to happen. They moved us up and kept us there to see if the Russians made any more moves. There's Soviet-manned facilities northeast of Prague. They're huge, big enough to house unknown thousands of troops, and we don't know what else. Things you don't want to think about, trust me."

"You don't mean nukes?"

"We know there's warhead storage facilities in East Germany, Poland, Bulgaria too. The Warsaw pact conducted an exercise a few years back, just a simulation, but the bottom line was a lot of nukes fired and millions dead. You civilians seem to forget we have a reason for being here, and it isn't so you can have a good time."

"Are you trying to scare me?"

"Yes. The Soviets will do what they can. They wanted Berlin badly, and they tried in 1949. They didn't succeed because of the Berlin Airlift.

But that's history. Right now the assassinations and turmoil at home makes us look distracted and vulnerable. To understand my comings and goings, you have to know this isn't a game. I have a job to do."

At work Brencie had seen references to certain fighter squadrons, Chase's among them. When those aircraft were grounded, getting them back in the air had a high priority. Colonel Foss would know more. Every crisis would be in the Top Secret read-out, which Brencie didn't see. What she did see when she looked across the street was Nolan weaving among the tables at the Park Café, looking for Lulu and her.

"I've got to go," she said.

Chase followed her gaze. "Him. What's he doing here? Have you been seeing him again?"

"Of course not. We ran into him at the Amelia. He offered to pick us up after shopping. I've got to sort this out." She stood up.

He took her by the arm. "No! He can wait. You're coming back to the Arms with me."

"That tone brings out the worst in me."

They stared at each other. "I'm sorry. Let me come with you then," he said.

"No, thank you. I'm tired from the trip. I'll call you in a day or two."

By the time Brencie was back at the café, Nolan was gone. She walked down the block and got a taxi to the Amelia, angry and puzzled. She longed to be with Chase, but his attempts to manage her didn't sit well.

On Monday Brencie surprised Colonel Foss by inviting him to lunch. As they walked to the canteen he said, "What's on your mind, Brencie? Is it about your stepmother?"

"Oh, no. She's almost fully recovered. I wanted to ask you something." She told her boss almost word for word what Chase said about his deployments.

Colonel Foss took his time to answer. "I can't confirm the story for any particular person, but the circumstances and details are true. The rotational squads deploy regularly, especially when there's a crisis, and there have been some you wouldn't know about." It was enough, and as soon as she got home from work, she called Chase but didn't reach him. By the time he called back, it was late.

"I'm sorry, Brencie. There was a *guten* howdy party for my group. I just picked up your message at the desk. Can I come over now?"

"It's almost midnight. I'll see you tomorrow."

———※◈※———

The next day as she entered the lobby at five o'clock, Nolan was waiting. "I need to talk to you," he said. "Can I come up?"

"We can talk here. Look, I'm sorry about Saturday, I—"

"I called Lulu to see what happened. She told me Dellasera's back. You won't want anyone to overhear what I have to say. It won't take long."

"OK, but just for a few minutes." She expected the quick smile, but it didn't happen. When they were upstairs, he walked to the window. "I could never get tired of this view." He turned and walked back to Brencie.

"What is it, Nolan? I have plans later."

"Look. You don't know Chase Dellasera. He's a fighter pilot and a goddamned officer. He's arrogant and used to getting everything he wants."

"Nolan . . ."

"Let me finish. Did you know he comes from money? Oh, not

the yacht and chauffeur kind of money, but the kind that will make life easier for a couple of generations. And one more question. Has he asked you to marry him?" All the answer he needed was in her silence. "He hasn't," said Nolan, "and he won't."

"Why would you say that?"

"Because he's already married."

"What?" It was a desperate attempt to discredit a romantic rival, something out of a Noel Coward comedy. Everyone would laugh, and Chase would pop out from behind an areca palm to gallantly deny it. Silence filled the room like smoke, and Brencie couldn't breathe.

"If you don't believe me, ask him." Nolan walked to the door. "Right or wrong, after he put you in the hospital, I made up my mind to find out everything about him. It took time, but I know people who have access to personnel files, people who owe me a favor. I found out this afternoon. He married Alice Ann Freeman on December 24, 1962. He has taken her off his list of dependents, but there's no record of a divorce."

She hardly noticed when Nolan left; she looked up, and he was gone.

•‹‹•››•

Brencie took a taxi to the American Arms, refusing to believe it. When she stood at Chase's apartment door, she still refused to believe it, yet she couldn't bring herself to knock. She and Chase had been lovers for months. Was everything a lie? Was he deployed, or did he go home to see his wife? It wasn't unusual for a wife to remain in the States, given frequent deployments and kids in school. Did he have kids too?

"Brencie!" He came down the hall carrying a drink. "What's the matter?" He reached for her, but she stepped away.

"Chase. Are you married?"

The color drained from his face. He couldn't speak, and then Brencie knew the answer. Now it would be impossible to believe him about anything, ever again. Her knees gave way as she grasped the horrible betrayal. He moved to steady her, but she stayed on her feet. "Don't you dare touch me."

"I never meant to hurt you. I haven't lived with her in over four years. I don't know where she is, or I would have divorced her. I tried. We were married less than a year. No children."

"And all that flyboy nonsense about classified missions, serving your country in a crisis, was that all lies, too? Do you have a girl in Rota? What about Incirlik? Or Lakenheath?"

"No."

"I don't believe you." She heard the shrillness in her own voice, but she didn't care.

"We met when I was in college and we eloped just before I got commissioned. She was with me in flight school—"

"In flight school? The dining-out. That captain. Clark? That accounts for the smirk on his face. He knew your wife. And that's it. The drinking. The moods. It wasn't about the war. You're a cheat, a garden-variety fighter jock. Did you even have the decency to feel guilty?"

"Constantly. To the point it felt like a physical thing. Her name was Alice. Her only ambition was to own a Mustang and listen to the Beatles. We were about to break up when she got pregnant, and—"

"Already a lie. You said there were no kids."

"She lost the baby before we even told anyone. She hated military life, didn't understand my commitment. She hated the war, said it was illegal." He was speaking rapidly, sounding desperate. "She smoked pot. I was obligated to report her, but I couldn't do it. She said it was immoral to kill, war or not. She demanded I resign my commission, and one day I got home and found a note. It said living among evil people was killing her. She was gone."

"I don't believe you."

"Her parents didn't either, until I showed them the note in her own handwriting. I tried to find her, to get a divorce. Right after I got orders to Vietnam, her mother called me. Alice had called to say she was safe and living far away from toxic people. As far as I know, they never heard another word, and neither did I."

Two people passed them in the hall, and he waited until they were gone. "Brencie, I screwed up. I'm sorry. I kept waiting for the right time to tell you, and I fell in love with you, like I never loved anyone. This place, this time, you. It's magic. I wanted it to go on and on. Even before Garmisch, I contacted the law firm, started trying to find her again . . ."

"The magic didn't interfere with your practical side. You certainly took steps to see I didn't get pregnant."

"Would you rather I got you pregnant? Knowing I wasn't free?"

"I'm going, now, and if you try to stop me, I'll scream. I don't care what kind of scene I make."

"I'm sorry. I planned to tell you right away, but it was Valentine's Day. I didn't want to break the spell." He realized his words weren't working. "All right," he said. "For God's sake, Brencie, this hasn't been easy. You wondered what was wrong? Why I was drinking? It was everything. The war. I don't know who my bombs killed. But mostly it was deceiving you. Loving you and lying to you every day, all the time, only getting in deeper. I allowed you to believe it was all about the war. Just one more layer of wrong."

"We're finished."

He followed her to the elevator. "Brencie, please," he said. "I love you. You can see me as a conniving liar or a guy who was desperate to keep loving you. Scared all the time you would find out."

"And I did."

"Who told you? No one knew except Brad, and he's back in the States. It was Nolan Hanik, wasn't it? I'd like to know how he knew."

"That's what matters to you? How I found out?"

"No! No, of course not. It's—"

She stepped into the elevator, and when the doors closed, she confronted her own sad reflection in the shiny brass panels.

Chapter 13

"Oh, Brencie. I'm so sorry," said Lulu. "And a little shocked, though it's not the first time. The cheating bastards sometimes have a wife back home. What did he say?"

"What could he say? All those months, he didn't tell me."

Lulu shrugged. "There's no defending him, even if I wanted to." She looked at her watch. "Let's go. Jules is meeting us." The Wiesbaden warriors were in town, so Brencie had agreed to go to the game. She enjoyed football. It took her back to Friday night lights in Friendswood.

The crisp weather made them decide to walk the short distance to the field on Lindsey Air Station.

As they entered the front gates, Brencie said, "Remember what you promised, Lulu."

"Yes, yes. Nolan doesn't know you're coming. If he spots you, I can't help that."

The bleacher space was limited, but they found places right behind the volunteer cheerleaders, mostly secretaries from Lindsey or the air base. Jules looked them over. "A little long in the tooth for it," he said, "and a few pounds too many on most."

"They're having fun, Jules," Lulu scolded. "They bought uniforms with their own money, and they practice. I think they look good. Why do you have to be so critical?"

He looked chagrined. "Sorry. I'm brilliant and entertaining, but kind of a jerk."

The warm-up drills ended, and Nolan gathered the Warriors into a huddle. He spoke to them, gestured, and then the huddle broke with a cheer. The game was close. Nolan's form in motion was familiar, but he wasn't just running by the Amelia. He was running at or over, into or around, with purpose. Brencie wanted the Warriors to win, but she wanted the other team to have the ball, so she could watch Nolan.

The Warriors were behind by a field goal at halftime. "I signed up for football in high school," Jules offered. "I mostly observed from the bench. A team needs a guy like Nolan. He's a natural leader, plus he's a beast on defense."

Brencie smiled. She knew perfectly well Jules was promoting the virtues of his friend and thinking he was being subtle about it.

"He knows she's here," said Lulu. "He saw her as we sat down. He's playing to the stands."

In the last five minutes, the Warrior defense stopped a drive, with Nolan making a critical tackle. They got the ball and won with a touchdown. Nolan was on her mind as Brencie walked back to the Amelia with Jules and Lulu. When they went to the bar, Brencie headed to the elevator.

Chase ambushed her. Weeks had passed, and she had ignored his calls and letters. She heard him call her name. "Please, Brencie. Talk to me." The fighter pilot panache had vanished.

"Has anything changed? Did you tell me about your wife, and I forgot? You lied to me every minute we were together." She dropped her voice. "Every time we made love."

"We can't talk here. Let me come up."

"If you don't get out of my way, I'll have the desk call security." She walked around him.

He spoke to her back. "Just let me explain. Is it fair, not to hear me out?"

She turned on him. "Don't you dare talk to me about what's fair."

After a second threat to have him escorted out of the hotel, he left. On the way to her apartment, she reconsidered what he said. She hadn't let Agnes-Rose explain, and she came to regret it.

———————

The shuttle bus pulled up just as Brencie was leaving the Amelia, so instead of taking a taxi, she got on board. Third stop ahead on the route would be the American high school, which in the evenings was the venue for adult continuing education. She read the letter from Agnes-Rose for the second time.

Dear Brencie,

What happened to Chase? He was all you talked about, and now notthing.

News of the day: You remember when I was a Brownie leader for a couple of months until the other mothers ousted me? You were embarrassed. Well, I ran into the brother of one of the other mothers, one who thought I was cool, not crazy. He asked me out. Nothing much, but a little something, anyway. I get lonesome.

Wish Lulu the best with her solo! Send pictures!
Love your Bee Bee

Nolan knew about the breakup, but he didn't call. She appreciated his sensitivity; he had only been the messenger, but she didn't want to see him. She had arrived in Wiesbaden determined to avoid romantic complications, and if she had stuck to that, she wouldn't have engendered the calamity of Chase Dellasera.

To stay busy, she enrolled in a third semester of German classes and often went with Lulu to *Camelot* rehearsals. Seeing the play come together had been fascinating. Now it was only days until the opening, and Lulu's nerves had ratcheted to maximum volume. She was so nervous, she almost convinced Brencie the whole enterprise would be a flop, Lulu's solo and the play itself. The Wiesbaden American Players was among the first amateur groups to stage *Camelot*, and according to Lulu, that fact guaranteed disaster.

Brencie put away Agnes-Rose's letter as the shuttle bus arrived at the school. Her class met twice weekly, and when it ended, she always left in a hurry. There were no taxi stands near the school, so she didn't want to miss the shuttle. She didn't see Nolan until she almost literally ran into him.

"Whoa!" he said. "Well, uh . . . hi. I heard you were taking more German." They hadn't spoken since he told her about Chase. "Uh. I'll have the language out of the way when I re-enroll at the university. I've already applied to law school."

"That's wonderful. Congratulations."

"I haven't been accepted yet. Are you enjoying the class? It gets a lot harder."

"That's for sure. At least all nouns are capitalized *auf Deutsch*. You always know where the nouns are, but nominative, accusative, genitive? I don't know what that is in English."

"Yeah, no one gets that, except the Germans. Sometimes I wonder if they do."

She fell back on a reliable topic. "How goes football? Another winning season?"

He smiled. "I saw you at the game."

"Lulu said you did. She said you were showing off."

"I was. We won't make the playoffs. Four of our best guys went home this summer."

They were out of small talk. "Well. I'd better go. I'll miss the bus," Brencie said.

"Can I give you a lift? It's raining again." He looked out the window. "And there goes the bus. Twenty minutes until the next one."

"Thanks. That would be nice."

Grendel's Mother waited in the parking lot, and they got underway. "I haven't seen you on the base lately," she said.

"I've been traveling, supporting the brass, not that they let me do much. Even when I do, my boss gets credit. Probably not fair to say that. He's a good guy."

"Lulu says you're seeing someone."

"If you call a couple of casual dates seeing someone. A German girl who works at the audio shop. Long tan hair, long blond legs. I mean . . ."

"Blond legs?" They both laughed, and it eased the awkwardness. When he suggested they stop at the Chianti Keller for pizza, she agreed. They had been there when they were dating, and it was still all candlelight, checkered tablecloths, and the smell of garlic and tomatoes. Opera music played in the background.

"That's *Va, Pensiero*," Brencie said.

He smiled. "How do you know stuff like that?"

"Lulu's a Verdi fan. Hanging out with her is an education."

"Lulu and Jules are a good match. He has the same effect on me. I practically speak Latin now."

Nolan told her about his work; she told him about Rick and the useless rifle. She expected him to laugh. Instead he said, "You should have shot him." He relented. "It is sorta funny." The beautiful quick grin came, and he explained. "I'm only venting. In Vietnam it was a way to stay sane. We bitched and did our duty, but we never had to kill anyone."

She remembered Chase's words on the ski slope, about killing

—— 166 ——

children. "Do you hold people who kill in war responsible? Personally, I mean?" she asked.

He thought about it. "I don't know. All I'm saying is, the guys who did crazy things were the ones who had to kill people. No data. Just an observation. Did you vote? People think Nixon will do better, about the war."

"I did vote. My first time. Absentee."

Nolan hadn't tried to renew their relationship after he told her about Chase; he surmised correctly she would have suspected his motives in telling her. When they first met, Nolan seemed uncomplicated, but he was as complex as anyone she knew.

"Has your stepmother recovered? Agnes-Rose. I love that name."

"She has. She enjoys referring to her gunshot wound. I still see you running sometimes."

"Do you? When I run by the Amelia at night, your drapes are closed. I heard the MPs once rousted a bunch of guys with binoculars from the trees in front."

"Lulu told me. Did you know she's in *Camelot*? Opening night's this week."

"I know. Are you and Jules going together? I'd like to come with you."

"And bring your girlfriend?"

He gave her a familiar look, a look that suggested he knew what was in her head. "Don't be coy," he said. "It's not like you. I won't bring anyone. Maybe you and I should start seeing each other again."

Brencie sighed. "I'm not sure I'm ready."

"I can wait, but promise me if you want company, you'll call me."

"I won't promise."

"What if there's a party?" he teased.

"We have mutual friends," she conceded. "I'd expect you to be there."

"What if we run into each other in the canteen?"

"You can buy me a tuna sandwich."

"What if there's another beer fest at Schierstein? I can still polka like a mad dog."

Brencie was laughing, and she remembered why she liked Nolan Anthony Hanik. In this moment she felt like the most fickle yellow rose ever to leave Texas.

———⊙———

The auditorium of the American Community Center was not huge, accommodating about two hundred people, so Brencie, Nolan, and Jules arrived early to get good seats. Soon the room was packed. Several people from Brencie's office were there, including Leah Crum, Colonel Foss with his wife, and Wolfgang in a coat and tie. Opening night is opening night. Nerves, anticipation, chatter, and excitement.

"What the hell? You would think it was Broadway," said Jules. "There's Angelika. Damn! We should have offered to drive her. Well, we can take her home."

Brencie stood up. "I'm going to check on Lulu."

The stage manager, wearing a tuxedo, allowed her to come through, and she found Lulu in the green room, staring blankly into a lighted mirror as the rest of the cast dealt with nerves in their own way. King Arthur, played by an officer from an air base tactical wing, stood in a corner running his lines. Guinevere, played by a school teacher from California, surreptitiously took a long swig from a leather flask. Mordred seemed to be getting into character by shooting evil, glaring looks to one and all, including Brencie.

"Oh, I can't do it," said Lulu. "I'd cry, but my makeup would run. Is there a full house? There always is for the musicals. I'll open my mouth and a toad will jump out." She put her head in her hands and then looked up with a hopeful expression. "I know. You can do it. You know the lyrics. Save me. Please!"

"Even if that were possible," Brencie answered, "I couldn't get into that dress, and no one can do this as perfectly as you. You look stunning."

"Oh, God. I need a cigarette."

"Just pretend the auditorium's empty. You won't be able to see anyone for the lights. Or better, know we're all pulling for you. Dierdre and Margo too, way in the back. Late as usual."

"Angelika? When I think of her, I hear her telling me what to do, and I do it."

"She's down front. Lulu, look in the mirror. You are Nimue."

The stage manager came in. "This is it, everybody. You've rehearsed your asses off. You know the blocking, the songs, the pace. King Arthur, get out there and break a leg!"

"I'd better go," Brencie said. Lulu was shaking when Brencie hugged her and returned to the audience, where Jules looked anxious.

"How the hell is she? She's been a wrecking ball all week." he said.

"Keep your fingers crossed." Brencie looked around the packed house. There was standing room only at the back, and there stood Chase staring at her, looking like Lancelot at the end of *Camelot*, broken and lost. He didn't look away; he didn't wave.

If Brencie hadn't been worried about Lulu, the sight of Chase would have upset her. When the house lights dimmed, she turned back to the stage. Nolan sensed her agitation. "Don't worry," he said. "Under Lulu's *flibberty* there's a strong *gibbet*."

The orchestra, two from the U.S. Air Force band, the others recruited from the rank and file, struck up the music, and King Arthur stepped on stage to "Wonder What the King Is Doing Tonight." He convinced the audience he was counting on Merlin's help, and applause followed. One song down, two to go, and then Lulu would take the stage.

Next Guinevere ran lightly across the stage in a purple gown trimmed with white fur. In song, she begged her patron saint for help.

She looked the part, critical in amateur productions, according to Lulu. Brencie's palms were sweating, too worried about Lulu to enjoy the introduction of the theme song, "Camelot, Camelot." The play was a hit already. Arthur and Guinevere had to be good, and they were.

It was time for Lulu. A spotlight appeared in the middle of the dark stage. Lulu's small foot in a silver boot lingered at the edge of the spotlight. In a brilliant bit of stagecraft there was a pause, then Nimue stepped into the light. She wore a silver wig and a light gray satin dress with a chiffon cape that floated like a cloud. The cape, dusted with loose glitter, sent sparkles into the air around her.

The orchestra struck the introductory chords, and Lulu's mouth opened, but nothing came out, not even a toad. Brencie thought she would stop breathing herself, and Jules grabbed her hand and squeezed it hard. The orchestra began again, and it happened.

Lulu's voice filled the room like something that could be touched. She didn't miss another note. Brencie didn't want it to end, because she knew what it meant to her friend. The last words came out in perfect decrescendo. "Follow me, follow me." Then, barely more than a whisper, seductive, compelling: "Follow me."

When it was over, Lulu stood with her arms raised and then she dropped them, stepped out of the light, and vanished. Merlin would be useless to Arthur now. He would follow the irresistible Nimue. The audience exploded in applause, and tears were rolling down Jules's cheeks.

Now that Lulu had her triumph, her fans could enjoy the rest of the play, and when it ended, Lulu got the loudest applause of all. The director came on stage with pink roses, two dozen for Guinevere and a dozen for Nimue. Brencie looked over her shoulder, but Chase was gone.

Because the entire cast and crew had job obligations at the base or elsewhere, the show was scheduled for only two weekends, Thursday, Friday, Saturday nights and a Sunday matinee. Every performance sold out, and the demand for tickets was so high the director asked the cast if they would be willing to do a third weekend. The unanimous answer was *yes*. Brencie, Nolan, and Jules attended a performance every weekend, meeting Lulu for drinks after the show.

"Lucille, you're fabulous," said Jules one evening. "I can't help it. I love Lucy."

"Why should you help it? I'm a great girl. And don't call me Lucy. It's Lucille or Lulu."

"And you're a good guy, Jules," Brencie teased. "You're failing as a rascal. You haven't been in the brig for days."

Jules, the image of devil-may-care, said, "I've got to get ready for real life."

Lulu invited them to the cast party when the show closed, and again Brencie spent the evening in Nolan's company. The attraction between them felt stronger than ever.

The party was in a banquet room of the Amelia, and when the weary staff flickered the lights to signal the end of the evening, the cast and crew and Jules, Brencie, and Nolan left singing a drunken version of the chorus. "Camel-rot. Camel-rot."

"Why does drinking convince people they can sing?" Nolan grumbled.

"Too bad about the Kennedy's. The former residents of Camel-rot shot dead," said Jules. "Well, Bobby and Ethel had twenty-seven kids. Maybe one of them . . ."

They were instantly quiet. "Leave it to you to spoil a mood," said Lulu. "It's only a mythical place anyway. Never was, never will be, but we can pretend for a while."

"You're right," said Jules. "I hereby rechristen the Amelia as Camel-lotta-rot." The four of them got in the elevator, and Nolan and Brencie got off on her floor, leaving Lulu and Jules in a giggling embrace as they went on up.

"Would you like to come in? I think I've got a little scotch. Or I have coffee, if you don't mind instant."

Nolan hadn't been to her apartment since the conversation about Chase. "Coffee sounds good."

She boiled water, stirred in coffee, and sat the mugs on the table, remembering he took it black.

"I've been wanting to talk to you about something," he said. "I'm being sent to Berlin with a legal team. I'll be there for a couple weeks, so there's a weekend in between. Why don't you come? See the divided city. It's quite an experience, they say."

"Oh, Nolan. I don't know."

"It's a chance you won't get again. I can arrange a seat on the troop train, and I'll book separate rooms. We're friends. You should come."

"You're the one who said we could never be friends."

He smiled. "Looks like I was wrong. A guy from my unit took the troop train a few months ago, and it was right out of a John le Carré novel. It travels through the so-called *Deutsche Demokratische Republik*, but it's operated by the American military. DDR officials come on board and count heads before it crosses into soviet territory and again when it leaves."

Brencie was intrigued. "Why?"

"If there were one hundred people on the train the first time, there better not be one hundred one, the second time. It's possible to hop the train when it slows down and ride it into the western sector. More probable on the trip from Berlin back to Frankfurt. If the numbers don't match, there's a problem. If they can't find the stowaway, they pick someone at random to pull off the train. I can see you want to come. Are you still upset I told you about him?"

"You did the right thing, but I can't thank you for it."

"What about Berlin then?"

The promise of such an adventure was a siren song as compelling as Lulu's solo, but Brencie declined.

"Are you sure?" he said. "If things get worse politically, they may not let civilians take the train any more. Berlin can become a hot spot. USSR leadership's up for grabs. They say it's a troika, but no one believes that. Kosygin's gaining ground. There could be trouble."

"Tempting, but no."

"OK." Nolan finished his coffee and said goodnight, but he made no move to touch her when she walked him to the door. "I'll see you around, Brencie."

She had been spending time with him, but Camelot was over, and she didn't want to stop seeing him. He was almost out the door. "You know what?" she said. "I've changed my mind. I'd love to see Berlin."

Chapter 14

B rencie sat in a roped-off section at the Frankfurt station, an area reserved for Americans waiting to board the special military train to Berlin. Rain pattered on the glass canopy overhead like a sad song: "Killed in Vietnam. Killed in Vietnam." Hoping to make the refrain stop, she opened *The Spy Who Came in From the Cold*, checked out from the Lindsey Air Station library. She couldn't focus; her thoughts returned to Agnes-Rose's letter.

I'm so sorry to tell you, Brencie, but Joe O'Barry got killed in Vietnam. God. I picture you and him dancing around the gym when you were 12 or 13. I don't know any of the details, and his poor mother is so destroyed she couldn't talk. She won't ever get over it.

Joe was woven into the fabric of her life, taken for granted. He lived on her street. He *lived*. He could not be dead. He had no politics, yet he grew up and went to war.

She went to a newsstand for the *Paris Herald*. An article about Nixon's close win suggested nobody liked him, not the Americans or the Europeans, but the Democratic display of venom during the Chicago convention frightened people. The country seemed to be alienated, unmoored. The rain started again, harder. "Killed in Vietnam. Killed in Vietnam."

Nolan had made the arrangements and gathered the forms needed for the trip, but she had to fill them out herself. When she struggled to get the quadruplicates into her Selectric typewriter, she decided a better name than Cold War would be Forms War. If the forms could be bundled up and lobbed on the USSR, Mother Russia would drown in a deluge of paperwork.

The train pulled in on time, and Brencie lined up to have her documents checked by an imposing chief master sergeant in charge. He put a hash mark by her name on a list and said, "You're all set. Have a good trip."

On board, an Army three-striper directed her to her seat. "You can move around when we're underway," he said, "but take your seat at the border crossings. We have to count eyes and divide by two." He chuckled and moved on.

Brencie shared the compartment with one other person, a military wife who had been visiting friends in Frankfurt. Her husband was stationed in Berlin, and she was heading home. They exchanged pleasantries, and after a while, Brencie nestled into her seatback and dozed.

———◈———

A jolt and slight whiplash woke her. The train had stopped. A voice carried along the corridor. "Are you in your assigned places? Return to your places, please." The voice arrived with its owner, a U.S. Army captain dripping officiousness. "I'm the train commander," he said as if in capital letters. "Is this your assigned seat?"

The wife looked out the window. "It's the East German Border," she said. "Hope everything's quiet. My husband was on this train right after Svetlana Stalin defected. The Russians were furious. Delayed the train. The numbers kept coming out wrong on purpose. Just harassment. Diplomatic doodoo."

Two officials of the *Deutsche Demokratische Republik* entered the compartment, a sergeant and a lieutenant with a huge-looking side-arm. Two armed American MPs waited in the corridor. The sergeant had a box suspended on a strap around his neck. The box butted against his paunch to form a flat surface, a kind of portable desk.

"Passports!" The DDR lieutenant possessed the malevolence of a dangerous dog. He mutilated the pronunciation of both their names and then asked, "You stop in Berlin how long? And dese are bags of you?"

They answered politely, as the lieutenant drifted toward Brencie until his booted calf pressed against her knee. When she shifted away, he narrowed his eyes in satisfaction as he handed the passports to the sergeant, who placed them on top of the portable desk. Drawing a metal stamp from his pocket, the sergeant opened the top passport and attacked. *Thwack!* The wife jumped, and then he assaulted the document twice more and slapped it shut. He opened the second passport. Thwack! Thwack! Thwack! Slap!

Brencie couldn't help it. She giggled, and the satisfaction dropped from the lieutenant's eyes. She didn't know what he had the authority to do, though she couldn't imagine the MPs would allow him to drag her off the train. The lieutenant glared, muttered something Brencie didn't understand, and pivoted on his bootheel. He left, and the entourage moved out of earshot.

The wife put a hand to her throat. "I thought he was going to shoot you."

"And get blood on his shiny boots?" Brencie replied with more bravado than she felt.

The outside doors of the train closed with a pneumatic hiss, and the peaked cap of the DDR lieutenant glided past the compartment window like the dorsal fin of a shark. The tension, the strangeness, the news from home, it was too much. Brencie bolted to the WC and let the tears come. Tears and tears and tears for Joe. For everyone. By the time she recovered, the train was underway again. The passport routine was repeated with a less loathsome DDR contingent, and they crossed into the western sector. Nolan stood on the platform, and she resolved to do her best not to ruin the weekend. As she left the train, the ragged bits of the seals around the doors flapped and twisted in the cold air.

She surprised Nolan by stepping into his arms. He said nothing and stroked her hair until she was ready to move on. In the taxi he pointed out the shattered steeple of the bombed-out Kaiser Wilhelm Church, standing like a ghost, storm clouds showing through the skeleton of the tower. When they arrived at the hotel where Nolan had been staying for a week, he walked her to her room. "I'm around the corner, room six oh two, if you need anything."

They agreed to meet for dinner in an hour. Brencie showered and donned a short black skirt, black pantyhose, and a white silk blouse with edelweiss embroidered on the wide collar and the cuffs. She looked in the mirror and thanked Lulu for those shopping trips. She would never have Lulu's style, but confidence could be found in the right clothes.

Nolan stood up when she entered the hotel restaurant. "You're just plain beautiful," he said.

"Thank you, but plain and beautiful are contradictions." She changed the subject as they were seated. "How's the law school application process?"

"One rejection, one acceptance, and the one to Northwestern still outstanding. That's my first choice, but I don't think I have a chance. At least I'll have the GI Bill. I'm proud to serve, but not about 'Nam." He looked away. Brencie knew the pattern. Colonel Foss did the same. So did Jules. And Chase. A mention of Vietnam, a pause, the shifting gaze.

When the succulent Wienerschnitzel arrived, the waiter refilled their wine glasses and withdrew. Nolan said, *"Ein Prosit. Der Gemütlichkeit,* a toast to good times and good cheer."

When Brencie didn't meet his eyes, he reached across the table for her hand. "Are you all right? You aren't eating."

"Sorry. It's just . . . I got a letter from my stepmother. A kid I knew got killed in Vietnam."

Nolan's dark eyes filled with tenderness. "That's hard. Were you good friends?"

"Since we were kids. He lived on my block, and we took dancing lessons in sixth grade. I can't see how he can be dead. Did anyone you know die?"

"A nurse. On a medevac mission. The chopper crashed. Let's talk about something else."

Dinner remained subdued, and they went to the bar afterward. Nolan sat close to her, and they ordered Irish coffee that was prepared at their table by a pretty waitress. The pleasant surroundings and the showy presentation of the coffee lifted the mood. "How about some Berlin night life? I hear it's outrageous," Nolan suggested.

The night life was entertaining and lewd, and when they got back, they went to their separate rooms.

Nolan had arranged a sightseeing tour, so they met early for breakfast and then took a short walk as Berlin came alive. Proprietors unrolled awnings, filled tubs of water with cut flowers, or stacked marzipan in bakery windows. The tables and chairs of outdoor cafés remained stacked close to the buildings because of the misty rain. At ten o'clock they boarded the tour bus. Brencie had her first look at the central issue, the wall that appeared like a broken spine through the city, in and out of view.

The guide explained the Kaiser Wilhelm Church, the *Gedächtniskirche*, had been left as it was as a reminder of the terrible past, and she related a short history of the Brandenburg Gate. The ruins of Hitler's chancellery could still be seen, fenced off and some distance away. Certain questions weren't answered and never would be, the guide said. Were Hitler's ashes part of the dust? Was he cremated with Eva Braun, his bride of only a few hours? "No one knows for sure," she said.

She changed the subject. "Just there, on the horizon, you can see Templehof Airport. Who knows about the Berlin Airlift, which the Germans call the Air Bridge?"

Nolan spoke up. "The Americans called it Operation Vittles."

"Just so, thank you." The guide nodded. "In 1949 the Russians closed all access to the city, trying to force the allies out. It didn't work. For fifteen months the allies supplied Berlin. Four thousand tons a day, planes landing every three minutes, all day, until the Russians gave up. We Berliners don't forget."

The tour was almost over. "And now," said the guide, "a small joke to end our excursion. In Berlin we love the Kennedys, and we were sad when they died. We remember the famous '*Ich Bin Ein Berliner*' speech. He said he was a Berliner, but you have seen the stacks of powdered doughnuts in bakery windows? They're called Berliners. When we say '*Ich Bin Ein Berliner*' we're also saying 'I am a jelly doughnut.'" There was polite laughter as the tour ended.

They bought bratwursts with hard rolls from a street vendor and then walked along Bernauer Strasse, where the wall took on a macabre character. Buildings had been scooped out by bulldozers, their facades left standing and bricked up from behind. The front walls looked like the faces of corpses, lifeless, the window-eyes full of bricks, the doors like mouths nailed shut, rendered speechless. Crude crosses held together by barbed wire punctuated the cracked sidewalk, as though each time someone died, a cross grew out of his blood. Nolan read the name etched on a rusty cross. "Give Georg liberty or give him death."

Scrawled on the wall in white paint were the words *In Tyrannos*, reminding Brencie of the slogan she once saw on an overpass as she left Houston. *Peace in Vietnam.*

"World War II. The Cold War." Nolan kicked a stone and watched it skid over the cobbles and through a shallow puddle. When they caught up to it, he kicked it again. "Kennedy said the Cuban missile crisis was about Berlin, that the Soviets planned to invade the western sector if they got missiles into Cuba."

"Do you think it's true?"

"I don't know. Maybe everything's about everything when it comes to war. I don't even know if it's classified. I can't remember if I read it in the Top Secret read-out or *Stars and Stripes*. Sometimes it's in both." When he spoke again, his voice conveyed resignation. "We're going to lose in Vietnam," he said. "We don't have the resolve. If the Russians blockaded Berlin today, I don't think we would have the will to save it. As for Vietnam, Americans die every day, but more Vietnamese and Cambodians will die than anyone can ever count. No one's telling the truth about that."

Brencie sighed. "But every day the news says things are turning around."

"Turning around? Maybe turning around the wrong way." They caught up to the stone again, and he picked it up. "Something happened in 'Nam, in a village I can't even pronounce. It was Army, but the whole military establishment's trying to track down anyone involved. If it's true, it will come out, and it's horrible."

She could think of nothing to ask, and everything was twice as bad because it was now a world where Joe O'Barry was dead. They passed away from the shored-up buildings, and the wall was a regular wall again, twelve feet high.

"War reminds me of that game, Rock, Paper, Scissors," Nolan said.

"Rock crushes scissors, scissors cut paper, paper wraps rock, and so on." She stopped walking. "I see. No one really wins."

"Exactly," he said, "but everyone gets hit."

There were observation towers along the wall, steep wooden steps leading to a narrow platform near the top. A family crowded onto a platform, a husband and wife, by the looks of them, and a genderless bundle about two years old. The couple waved at someone on the other side and then held the child up, encouraging it to wave. At grandparents? An aunt? The wall was older than the child. "Families arrange a rendezvous through the mail," Nolan said.

When the family left, Nolan and Brencie climbed the steps, and when she shivered, he encircled her in his arms. From the street there appeared to be a single wall, but from the top, a second wall was visible, with a no-man's land forming a buffer zone between the two. Half a dozen angry-looking dogs patrolled the space, tethered to cover a certain area, but just out of reach of each other. The second wall contained watch towers every fifty yards. With machine guns protruding from their shoulders like pikes, guards prowled as restlessly as the dogs.

A bouquet of daisies lay amid the broken glass embedded in the top of the wall. A tear traced the curve of Brencie's cheek and puddled in the divot where her breastbone met her neck. When they were on the sidewalk again, Nolan removed his glove and wiped the tear, tenderly. "It should make us all cry," he said.

"Jules says there's only one war, rotating around the globe like a virus, always mutating so it can't be destroyed. He says our sons will go to war, and their sons too."

❦

All day they had touched in ordinary ways, fingers passing bread, hands crossing the street, side-by-side at dinner, for warmth and comfort in a dark place. Brencie felt undone by the city, so she wanted to turn in early.

Nolan walked her to her door. "Goodnight," he said, turning so quickly she wished him goodnight as he walked away.

She let herself into her room and leaned her back against the door, confused. What did she want? Why did she mind his abruptness? Her nerves were raw, and she was chilled from the rain, from the city, from what Nolan said about Vietnam and war. And Joe was dead. She took a hot shower, but it didn't work. Overwhelmed by sadness and need, still damp, she wrapped herself in red silk and stole down the hallway to Nolan's room.

He opened the door and stepped aside, fresh from the shower himself, wearing a towel around his waist. She had never seen him shirtless in all the time she had known him, and when he closed the door he was breathing hard and his torso rose and fell, emphasizing the contours of his chest. He picked her up and carried her to the bed, and although he laid her down gently, his physical strength was almost brutish. He entered her at once, pushing so hard it was only a decibel short of pain. Be it fear or sorrow, loneliness, need, or the presence of death, Berlin was erotic and immediate. She came as quickly as he did.

Still inside her, he spoke first. "I'm sorry. This isn't how I wanted it to be."

He moved away then, and she said, "There's nothing to be sorry for, but I'm confused. That's as close as I can come to saying something honest." Two more tears fell, tears she hadn't felt coming. "That's for this place, and for Joe," she said. "And for the guilt I feel just for being alive, for being here with you."

"You can't stop living because people die, and there's nothing's more alive than making love." He smiled. "I'd cry too, but not when

I'm in bed with my dream girl." When Brencie laughed, he said, "See? It's simple, but life goes on."

"It does, but I'm nobody's dream girl."

"I know, and I'm nobody's Prince Charming."

She got out of bed and picked up her robe. "I'd better go, or I'll oversleep and miss the train."

He reached for her hand and pulled her to the bed. "Stay," he said. "I'll get you to the station in the morning."

"If I stay . . ."

"If you stay, I'll make love to you again. I'll show you how I wanted it to be." He gave her the quick smile, and it was more persuasive than any long, soulful look.

Chapter 15

B rencie wanted the last leg of Agnes-Rose's trip to be comfortable, so she enlisted Wolfgang to drive her to the airport in
Frankfurt. Happy to help, he shushed her when she offered to gas
up his late-model Citroën. She read Agnes-Rose's latest letter on
the way.

Dear Brencie,

*Just think. I might get there before this letter! I'm soooooo excited. Wait
til you see my great clothes, most of them from the Dallas Cowboys
catalogue. I hope I got the weather right, though. Always trickky in
the fall.*

*I can't wait to meet everyone and see everything. You never know
what's going to happen until it happens! Could be ANYTHING!*

Love, your Bee Bee

Yes, Brencie thought. *Anything.* She couldn't get Berlin off her
mind, but having Agnes-Rose in residence would make it easy to
avoid private time with Nolan. Still, there would be the inevitable
questions about Chase and Nolan. Brencie sighed, and Wolfgang

spoke without taking his eyes off the autobahn. "Are you all right, *Zuckerschnecke*?

"I'm fine," Brencie replied. "I got back from Berlin Monday. I'm not over it."

"*Ach, ja.* Divided *Deutschland.* A tragedy made possible by other tragedies."

By the time they reached the airport, Agnes-Rose's plane had landed. When she emerged from the customs area, ten hours on a plane had taken a toll. The left side of her hair was flat as a west Texas highway, and the right side looked like a freshly dyed tumbleweed.

"Oh, my god, Brencie, am I glad to see you." They embraced for a long moment and then stepped apart to look at each other.

"Ah-hum." Wolfgang cleared his throat.

"Oh, sorry. Agnes-Rose Jessup, this is Wolfgang Ritter."

Wolfgang stared at Agnes-Rose like he had never seen such a woman, and then he spoke shyly, as though to a queen. "Welcome, *Erdbeerchen.*" He brushed his lips against the back of her hand.

Agnes-Rose sucked in, tossed her hair, and bloomed. Brencie had never seen love at first sight, but she imagined it would look like this. She laughed, but neither Wolfgang nor Agnes-Rose noticed. Brencie looked at Wolfgang as Agnes-Rose might see him. He was good-looking, the right age, and lean in his American jeans. Brencie had no way to be objective about Bee Bee, but she had seen men react to her stepmother like this, starting with Anson Jessup, her own father.

Wolfgang led Agnes-Rose to a waiting area, and Brencie followed. When Wolfgang went to get the car, Agnes-Rose turned to Brencie. "*Erdb . . .?*"

"*Erdbeerchen.* Little strawberry. I think it's about your hair. Strawberry blonde, or whatever you call your latest shade of unbelievable." The teasing reference to her hair color, an old joke between them, went unnoticed.

"It sounded like 'I love you.'"

"That would be *Ich liebe dich*." Brencie smiled. "He calls me *Zuckerschnecke*. Sugar snail."

"Oh, is he a piece of strudel? Is he married?"

"He's widowed."

"And I'm divorced."

Brencie spared a thought for her father. She would likely never see him again. Still, she was glad her stepmother was free and over-due to be lucky in love. Wolfgang pulled the car up to the curb and clicked his heels when he opened the doors for his passengers. Agnes-Rose looked at Brencie as if to say *Did he really click his heels?*

"Why don't you get up front where you can see better," Brencie suggested. By the time they arrived at the Amelia, Agnes-Rose and Wolfgang had sorted out the important stuff. Neither was in a re-lationship, both had no living parents, Brencie was the only "child," and Agnes-Rose's visit would be for three weeks. Brencie would take some time off, but Wolfgang volunteered to look after Agnes-Rose when Brencie was at work.

He left the car in front of the Amelia and took Agnes-Rose's bags to the elevator. He didn't get on, but as the doors closed, he winked at Agnes-Rose. "I'll see you soon, *Erdbeerchen*."

When Agnes-Rose stepped into Brencie's apartment and saw the view, the beautiful valley, the mountains, the gold dome of St. Elizabeth's, she said "You told me about this, but I never could imag-ine it. And look! The bonsai. It's thriving!"

"I kept it alive. There's an art to it. Sorry the place is a bit crowded. The folding bed isn't usually here. You must be exhausted." Brencie opened the bed and smoothed the sheets. "Why don't you have a little nap?"

Agnes-Rose kicked off her shoes and stretched out. Staring up at the ceiling as though speaking to a higher power, she said, "After all these years alone, only skirmishes into the dating game, I step off an airplane thousands of miles from home, and there he is. It's a miracle."

———◦«◊»◦———

Two nights later to welcome Agnes-Rose, Lulu arranged a dinner party at the Samovar, a Russian restaurant that allowed no electric lights in the dining room. Candles lined tables and shelves, bookcases, pedestals, and even the windowsills. The place was a fire hazard, but it was lovely, and so small their party had the place to themselves.

They gathered by the bar, and Brencie watched everyone fall in love with Agnes-Rose. Bidding for her attention Dierdre and Margo topped each other's sentences, as Jürgen tried unsuccessfully to interrupt. Jules cut in to offer his take on balalaika music, borscht, and the siege of Stalingrad before he stumbled onto forbidden ground. "May I ask how old you are?" At Agnes-Rose's stern look, he recovered. "I mean, how did you get so smart at such a young age?"

"I learned most things the hard way," she said. "By messing up. Messing up and fixing it. That's the big challenge."

"Is that from *The Book of Agnes-Rose*?" Lulu asked.

Brencie was embarrassed. "She doesn't know I call it that."

"Yes, I do," said Agnes-Rose.

Spotting a waiter, Lulu whirled over in three layers of chiffon animal prints and requested more wine. Brencie joined her to make arrangements for the bill. When the waiter left, Brencie said, "I don't know how you make that outfit work. No one else could. Except maybe Agnes-Rose."

"You've really forgiven her, haven't you?" said Lulu.

"I've learned *forgiveness* has real meaning. Not just something you say."

Lulu took the opportunity. "We've not had a chance to talk since Berlin. How did it go?"

Brencie looked away.

"Oh, my god. You slept with Nolan," Lulu said. "I thought you might."

"Don't read too much into it. It doesn't mean we're a couple."

"Jules invited him to come tonight," said Lulu. "At least you're not claiming to be madly in love because you slept with him. That's progress."

"Is it? He's Jules's friend, but I wish he hadn't been invited."

"No you don't," said Lulu.

"You're right. I want to see him, but it scares me. What's wrong with me? I can't wait to be with him again. And there's still Chase."

"Nothing's wrong with you, except now you know Chase isn't the only man who knows his way around the bedroom. I'll bet Nolan does too." As they rejoined their friends, she said, "Blink twice for yes."

Brencie rolled her eyes but obligingly blinked. Jürgen said, "*Ach.* Who's about blinking speaking?"

"*Speaking* about *blinking*. English," said Margo.

"*Ja.* Who cares? My English better than your German always will be," he teased.

Dierdre had the floor. "So being from St. Louis, we made it our mission to meet Augie Busch at a gallery opening, but he didn't show, and we had to look at some paintings my four-year-old niece could have done."

"I know Augie Busch," Jürgen offered.

"You know Augie Busch?" Dierdre and Margo said in unison. "Really?"

"*Naturlich*," said Jürgen. "Americans think *Deutschers* only make sex on Friday night and carry a briefcase with bratwurst inside. I know Augie. Our fathers since 1947 friends have been."

Jules had warmed to Jürgen in recent weeks. "Good for you, Jürgen. Put your objects where you want them. Sex on Friday and briefcase bratwurst? That's what Americans think about Germans. What do Germans think about Americans? In four words."

Jürgen thought about it. "Crazy. Wasteful. Toothy. Clean." Combined with good company and plenty of wine, the line got a bigger laugh than it should have.

Agnes-Rose needed the ladies' room, so Brencie accompanied her, in case there was an old lady knitting socks and collecting *Pfennings*, which there was. "You have to pay to pee?" Agnes-Rose asked. On their way back, she said, "It's a great party, honey. You have fun friends."

"Lulu put it together. She's hostess to the universe." Brencie observed Dierdre and Margo standing with their arms around each other, and Jürgen beside them. "I can't figure out if Jürgen's with Margo or Dierdre."

Agnes-Rose smiled. "Margo and Dierdre are a couple, honey. Jürgen's their friend."

As they rejoined the group, Lulu said, "You look weird. Is something wrong?"

"Margo and Dierdre are a couple."

Lulu laughed. "How did you not know that?"

"I don't know, and I'm trying not to feel dumb. Maybe I'm not as interested in other people's sex lives. Maybe that's it."

"Oh, please. Everyone's interested in everyone else's sex lives."

The restaurant doors opened and the candles flickered. They all looked toward the door. "Well, well," muttered Jules. "Dracula's here."

Nolan Hanik's broad shoulders filled the doorway. He spotted Brencie and flashed the grin, which caused her to shiver and then grow very warm.

"Oh my god," whispered Agnes-Rose. "If that isn't virility incorporated, I don't know what is."

—«(◦)»—

Brencie took some vacation time to accompany Agnes-Rose and Wolfgang on short excursions, including a cruise on the Rhine, the Frankfurt Zoo, and across the river to Mainz to see the fifteenth-century Gutenberg Bible. As always, Agnes-Rose was content to be exactly where she was, from Friendswood to The Swank to Disneyland on the Rhine. When Brencie had to go to work, Wolfgang announced he would take time off for the rest of Agnes-Rose's stay. "I have so much leave saved up," he explained, "I can't use it all before I retire or die."

They had drinks and dinner together almost every night, sometimes with Jules, Lulu, and the others. One evening toward the end of her visit, Agnes-Rose said she wanted to turn in early, but she encouraged the others to stay. "I haven't had this much fun since we got ourselves banned from the Galveston roller coaster, but all this partying's taking its toll."

Wolfgang stood up. "A lady can't walk home alone," he said. "You can tell me the roller coaster story upstairs."

"Roller coaster?" said Lulu as Wolfgang and Agnes-Rose left.

"It was no big deal. Roller coaster attendants have no sense of humor. You know what, Lulu? Agnes-Rose is happier than I've ever seen her."

—«(◦)»—

A day later Brencie entered the Amelia by the side door as Chase left through the front. She tried not to wonder who he might be visiting, but the sight of him caused her heart to thump, and it was still beating hard when she stopped for her mail. There was a white business envelope in Chase's handwriting and a thick manila envelope with a Tennessee law firm as the return address. It was registered mail, so Brencie signed by her name. As she started to the elevators, Agnes-Rose came from the bar. "Brencie! You'll never guess. I met Chase. I was coming from the deli, and there he was. He introduced himself. I don't know how, but he knew exactly who I was."

"It could be the Dallas Cowboys motorcycle jacket."

Agnes-Rose glanced at the State of Texas on her right sleeve. "I forgot about that. Anyway, he bought me a drink, and we visited. He just left. He wanted to be gone before you got home, but he dropped something at the desk. Looks like you have it. He told me everything. No wonder you fell in love with him. I almost fell in love with him myself."

"You mean he turned you on. At least I didn't catch you in the act with the beautiful Captain Charming."

"I would be crushed if I thought you meant that."

Brencie hung her head. "I didn't mean it. I'm upset. Forgive me."

"Of course I do. You forgave me for worse. People need to forgive as much as they need forgiveness. Maybe more."

"I told you! He's married and he lied about it. Are you saying I should forgive him?"

"I'm saying you should read the letters."

"Come on, Bee Bee," she said. "I'll buy you another drink. I could use one myself."

As they sat down Agnes-Rose said, "You're torn between Noland and Chase. Maybe I know it better than you do."

Brencie wasn't eager to return to the subject of Nolan or Chase. Instead, she said, "Guess what. Jules is going to propose. He thinks it will be a surprise, but Lulu suspects. She's already asked me to stand up with her if they decide to get married here."

"That's wonderful. It's best to fall in love when you're young. It gets much harder. Brencie, you're in love with them both. Nolan and Chase."

And just like that, it was clear. Agnes-Rose had it right. "If it hadn't been for what he did, I'd swear it could only be Chase. You don't know what being with him was like. But Nolan's . . . I don't know. He's Nolan."

"He's as Nolan as it gets. After meeting Chase, I have some idea of his appeal. Combined with this place; well, you can't imagine. I wonder if you'll ever adjust to a house in the suburbs and a couple of kids."

"Maybe I don't want that. There are options. A woman manages the Amelia. Margo's decided to go to medical school. She says after knowing a few doctors, it must not be that hard. I'm friendly with a female officer at work. I'm thinking about college when I come home."

Agnes-Rose didn't hesitate. "I'll sell The Swank. You can have the money."

"I couldn't take your money. If I stay the full three years of my contract, I'll save enough for at least a year's tuition. I'll work and attend school at night."

"And you'll have time to sort out your love life, and speaking of love life, I won't be home tonight."

Brencie laughed. "Really? And where might you be?" Brencie reached across the table and touched her stepmother's arm. "You know what? I could use a little alone time. And here's your man."

"Goodnight, honey," said Agnes-Rose. "I can't wait till tomorrow."

"What about tomorrow?" Wolfgang asked. "Do we have plans?"

"Oh, you know me. I always can't wait until tomorrow."

※

Alone in her apartment, Brencie put the two envelopes side by side on the coffee table. She opened the white one first. It contained a handwritten note from Chase.

Dear Brencie,

You'll get a registered packet today. If you choose not to read it, or if it doesn't change anything, I've done all I can. Not telling you the truth from the start is the biggest mistake of my life, and I'll always be sorry, whether you forgive me or not. I love you.

Chase

She barely finished the note when the phone rang. "It's Nolan. I'm in the lobby. I'm part of Jules's proposal plot, and tonight's the night. The ring had to be sized, and he couldn't get off to pick it up, so I did, but I have to get to football practice. Can I leave it with you?"

"Sure, bring it up." She turned the correspondence over and placed a heavy book on top of it. She was ready when he knocked.

"Where's Agnes-Rose, with Wolfgang? That's been fun to watch." He glanced at the coffee table. "You're reading *The Rise and Fall of the Third Reich*. Everybody tries, but it's too long for most people, including me."

"I used to pick library books by the size of their spines. The bigger, the better."

He grinned. "I expect you'll get through it." He handed her a black velvet pouch with a ring box inside, and looked at his watch. "Did you eat? I have time for a burger."

"No, thanks. I'm not feeling well."

"Oh. Sorry. Jules will come for the ring before he takes Lulu to that expensive French place she likes, the one he calls Cash Money."

"*Caché Monet*. OK. I'll be here."

He flashed the smile, but it disappeared quickly. "I have the pictures from Berlin. Can I bring them by next week? Not that I need the pictures to remember everything." It was the first reference he had made to the trip. "Brencie, Berlin happened. I understand you need time, but we'll have to talk about it, and soon." He hesitated, but she didn't answer, so he left.

She removed the book from the letters, reread Chase's note, and opened the registered packet. There was a cover page with a string of names across the top, all lawyers.

"Dear Miss Jessup," it began. Before she could go on, there was a knock at the door. "Brencie? It's Nolan."

She turned the pages over again and went to the door. "Forget something?"

"No," he said, "I just don't want you to be alone if you're really sick."

"It's girl trouble." It was as facile as "The dog ate my homework," but it always worked. To men, *girl trouble* explained everything from howling at the moon to eating seventeen milkshakes to not wanting sex.

"Oh. Make sure you eat something, then. I'm going, but you can't put me off forever." He left.

She peeked at the ring and snapped the box shut. She didn't want to think about Lulu's engagement. It would change things. She opened a desk drawer and put the ring out of sight.

Lulu would soon be Mrs. Jules Pasternak. Brencie had almost been Mrs. Richard Paul Smith. She had once thought she would be Mrs. Captain Chase Dellasera. Someday she would almost certainly be Mrs. Somebody.

Would that be *Auf Wiedersehen*, Brencie Jessup?

Chapter 16

Dear Miss Jessup,

On behalf of Winston, Winston, Durham, and Flack, I'm writing at the request of Captain (Major-elect) William Chase Dellasera, USAF, and with the permission of Mr. and Mrs. Alonzo Freeman, parents of Alice Ann Freeman Dellasera.

H e had been promoted. He told her it was a long shot, but it might be possible because of his combat record. In spite of herself, she was happy for him.

Captain Dellasera felt it was important to mention the Freemans, as testimony to the veracity and accuracy of this letter and the enclosed report.

To provide background, Captain Dellasera first contacted this firm in December of 1964. At that time he sought our advice on how to initiate divorce proceedings against Mrs. Dellasera. However, Mrs. Dellasera had broken all contact with her husband, her parents, and all known associates. Our private investigator, formerly of U.S. Army Intelligence, followed every avenue, to no avail.

Brencie put the letter down. Mrs. Dellasera. Chase's wife. She stood up to close the drapes and saw the spotlights illuminating the gold dome of St. Elizabeth's. Was it a bad omen to look too long at a church dedicated to lost love?

Seeing the name *Mrs. Dellasera* broke Brencie's heart, but she was ready to read the rest.

Captain Dellasera was under military orders to Udorn, Thailand. After back-to-back tours in Southeast Asia, he received orders to Wiesbaden, Germany. While home on leave, he contacted our firm again regarding divorce proceedings, and we informed him that with the passage of time, the laws regarding spousal desertion would apply, and he could obtain a divorce in absentia.

In late February of this year, Captain Dellasera contacted me personally with renewed urgency, and this firm reopened the matter, although we felt all efforts to locate Mrs. Dellasera had been exhausted. However, we uncovered new information.

It was known that Mrs. Dellasera left the base residence she shared with Captain Dellasera in the company of Miss Melanie Schwartz, the daughter of the base commander. The girls were traced to Washington, D.C., where they participated in antiwar protests. After that the trail went cold.

However, Miss Schwartz recently returned home. Her mother learned that her daughter and Mrs. Dellasera had hitchhiked to California, ending up in the Haight-Ashbury district of San Francisco. After several months the two girls parted company. Miss Schwartz knew nothing about the location or status of Mrs. Dellasera, except that she had begun using the name Peaceful Jones. That information was relayed to this firm, so our investigator had a new starting point.

THE SECOND LIFE OF BRENCIE JESSUP

Forgive the abrupt segue into the most important information I wish to give you. The fact is that Mrs. Dellasera, aka Peaceful Jones, died in June of 1966. At the time she was living in a commune 50 miles north of San Francisco, where she accidentally drowned in a reservoir on the property. We located several people who lived there at the time, but no one had known her real name. She had no identifying papers and no known next of kin. Thus she was buried in a pauper's grave, and her personal effects were stored in the usual manner, along with fingerprints and photographs.

This was enough to identify the person buried as Peaceful Jones to be Mrs. Alice Ann Freeman Dellasera. For detailed information, names, dates, and the unfortunate circumstances of Mrs. Dellasera's death, please refer to the enclosed report.

Feel free to contact me or any member of this firm if you have any questions.

Yours sincerely,
Joshua P. Winston
Senior Partner

Brencie put the contents of the letter back into the envelope. By the time she met Chase, his wife was already in her grave, but he hadn't known that. The room had grown dark, so she switched on a lamp and called Chase.

"You got the report. Can I see you?" he said. "I can be there in twenty minutes."

"No, I'll come to the Arms." She wanted to be certain of privacy. No interruptions from Lulu, Agnes-Rose, and especially not from Nolan, whose steady presence had sustained her, and then came Berlin. Should she tell Chase about Berlin? From *The Book of Agnes*

Rose: Never confess if it's just to make yourself feel better, especially if it makes someone else feel worse.

She taxied across town, and when she arrived, the door to Chase's apartment was ajar. His back was to her, and he turned and opened his arms. He had Mozart on the stereo, and the room smelled like the freshly laundered shirts hanging on a hook behind the door. She wanted to remember everything—the murmur of voices in the hall, the sound of car doors on the street, even the messy stack of books and papers he never had time to put away. She stepped into his embrace, like a homecoming.

He stepped away and sat down on the couch. "I'm over the shock of knowing Alice died, but there's an ache there. We loved each other once."

She sat close to him and touched his arm. "I understand. You would be less than human if you didn't mourn for a girl who died so young, a girl you cared enough for to marry."

He seemed to gather his thoughts. "It was wrong not to tell you. There's no question about that. Very wrong. I'm so sorry. I can't change that, but I can tell you the truth now."

He talked about the beginning, how he met Alice at Vanderbilt, she a psychology major, he in ROTC. "Politics didn't matter. In college everyone's liberal. Then it did matter. She became vehemently antiwar, and I was committed to serving my country. We were about to break up when she got pregnant. We got married, and she lost the baby before we even told anyone about it.

By the time I was in flight school, Vietnam was an argument every morning and every evening when I came home. I thought maybe it was hormones or something, after the miscarriage. I'm not downplaying her objections to the war, but she seemed unhinged. She was doing drugs too. I don't know what.

I started hanging around the officers' club more. I drank, and when I got home she accused me of things, from cheating to war mongering. Then one night when I came home she was gone. She left a note and her ring. One last jab."

"Oh, Chase. I'm sorry."

"Just like that. Gone. At first it felt like walking off a cliff, but the worst part? Soon all I felt was relief."

"So you came here and pretended to be single?"

"I know how that sounds, but it was two years later, and I had stopped feeling married way before that. I dated, but nothing serious. I slept with a couple of girls, but I told them about Alice first."

"You told them? And it didn't matter?" Brencie had a horrible thought. "Did Lulu know?"

"No! No doubt she would have told you."

"And then you ran me down at Fasching and lied to me for months."

"I meant to tell you on our first date, but it was Valentine's Day. The meal, the walk back to the Amelia, all of it. 'Unchained Melody.' When was I supposed to bring up my wife? I thought you might let me stay, and I promised myself I would tell you before anything happened. By the time we had one or two more dates, I knew you would bolt if I told you, and I was in neck-deep already."

He was right. She would never have continued to see a married man, no matter how long he had been separated. Agnes-Rose said there were way too many men in the sea to waste time on the married ones.

"Then Garmisch. I knew I should tell you. I planned to, but I couldn't. I almost came apart. We live in a small world, and I never knew when someone who knew Alice would turn up, and it happened. Brad Clark, a troublemaker all his life, at the dining-out. We had locked horns before, and although I threatened him, I couldn't be sure what he would do.

The war news was worse. We have a purpose in 'Nam, but things aren't clear about how the war's being run. I let you think my moods were about that. I had contacted the lawyers again, hoping every day I'd get things sorted out, even push the divorce through. You found out about Alice before I knew she was dead." His voice caught. "I've been tormented, drinking too much, angry with you when you didn't deserve it. Even cruel. Can you forgive me? If I promise never to lie to you again, and no secrets, ever?"

No secrets, ever? What about Berlin? she wondered. The quiet in the room amplified the traffic noise outside, the sounds in the hallway, the ticking clock on the table. Right or wrong, if she told Chase about Nolan, she could never untell it. She had been unforgiving to Agnes-Rose, and judging her had been a mistake; forgiving her had made everything right again. Forgiveness was a gift to both parties.

They curled up together, emotionally spent, and fell asleep with no more conversation and no further confessions, and in the morning they made love. Chase held her, and she knew he thought everything was resolved. She wasn't so sure. Did forgiveness feel like love? The trust had been broken, and pieces of Brencie's own heart drifted in her bloodstream. Did she love him, or was he just a spell she couldn't break?

———•《◐》•———

Chase had a dining-in to attend in the evening, which did not include guests, so Brencie went back to the Amelia. She wasn't hungry, but coffee would be welcome. She went to the café, and Lulu was there with Jules, who finished his omelet and said, "I'll see you tonight, ladies. Gotta go back to the barracks and clean up and call the restaurant. I've reserved a table for this evening, but two more people are coming, now that it's an engagement party."

What table? What people? Brencie thought. Then she remembered. Agnes-Rose's going away party, of course. Then the word *engagement* ran through her head. *Oh, no!* "Oh, my god, Lulu. The ring." Jules must have proposed without the ring. Should she offer congratulations? Was she upset when there was no ring? Jules hadn't seemed angry, and Lulu remained inscrutable.

Lulu burst out laughing. "I wish you could see your face," she said. "I don't think I've ever seen such a deer in the headlights expression in my whole life."

Brencie let out the longest of long sighs. "You should kill me. I forgot about the ring. What happened?"

"He popped the question and then took your name in vain a few million times, but you know Jules. He's over it. I never expected a stinkin' ring. I thought that would come later, but Jürgen helped him get a good price for a big rock 'n roll, as Jules put it. Can't wait to see it, but it won't be as good as the look on your face."

"I'm beside myself with sorry. And happy it worked out. And happy for you. Congratulations!" She got up and went around the table to hug Lulu.

"Oh, well, thanks, but that's not the end of it." Lulu enjoyed a pause. "Where the hell were you? Jules called you, and when you didn't answer, he called Nolan, who said you had the ring. Nolan called you over and over all night. Were you at the Open Arms with a married man?"

"Chase isn't married. His wife died."

"Holy crap! When? What happened?"

Brencie explained. "Come up later, and I'll let you read the report from the investigator. It's much more detailed, but that's the gist of it. Now I need a nap."

"OK, but Nolan knows you didn't come home last night, and he has an idea where you were. Get a good nap. The going-away party's still on, and Nolan's invited, because it's also an engagement party. He's to be best man. The entertainment portion of the evening will commence when Nolan meets Chase again."

"He won't. There's a dining-in."

"Thank God for small favors. *Ciao*, Bella. See you tonight."

Agnes-Rose arrived home at midmorning, and Brencie told her Jules had proposed without the ring and why. Agnes-Rose also read the lawyer letters. To Brencie's surprise, her stepmother refused to offer either criticism or opinion, about the ring debacle or Brencie's reconciliation with Chase.

———— ⊰◉⊱ ————

The combination engagement party and going away party was at *Atlekronen*, a small restaurant specializing in *Goulashsuppe* served in small copper skillets, beaten up with the charm of age and frequent use. Jules dipped his bread in the gravy. "God, that's good." He passed a basket of hard rolls to Nolan, who took one and handed the basket to Lulu. She hesitated and then took a second roll. "What the hell. It's a celebration."

Because the group included Wolfgang and Agnes-Rose, Margo and Dierdre, and the ubiquitous Jürgen, plus several other of Lulu's friends, Brencie managed to sit well away from Nolan.

Even Wolfgang's blue mood at Agnes-Rose's pending departure was partially lifted by cheerful talk of Lulu's engagement. "Jules has another year on his tour," said Lulu. "I don't want to wait, so we'll get married in Switzerland."

"In Basel," Jules explained. "It's easier. All in English, and no heavy tax. I checked it out. It's close to two month's salary in Germany. Mail your documents to Switzerland, arrange a date, and it's almost done. Get on the train, go see a magistrate, and come home with a life sentence, ha-ha. Well, I've been to war. Marriage can't be worse."

"If you put it that way," Lulu teased, "it's not too late to back out."

Jules took her hand. "I'd be a fool to do that, Lucille."

At the end of the evening, when Brencie stood up to make a toast, the room tilted. Too much champagne. She managed the words of congratulations, then Nolan said, "Come on, Brencie. I'm taking you home."

"I'll get a taxi," she said. "You can drive the others."

"They aren't ready to go, and I can't get everyone in the car anyway. They can get taxis. I'll drive you."

Not a word was spoken until they pulled into the parking lot at the Amelia. She hoped to escape his questions, but as usual, he tackled everything head on and full out. He killed the engine but made no move to get out of the car. "What the hell's wrong with you? It was the goddamned engagement ring. How could you just forget about it?"

"I've apologized to Lulu and Jules."

"They should have disowned you. You spent the night with him, didn't you?"

"Which is what this is really about."

"If you hadn't forgot about the ring, no one would know anything, so it's your own fault. I'm trying to look out for you. You aren't the type to be with a married man."

"He isn't married. His wife's dead."

"Did he kill her?" He wasn't joking.

"For God's sakes, Nolan. It's complicated. She was antiwar, so she left him. She drowned in California. I have proof."

"So does he consider her a casualty of war or something? Collateral damage? When did he find out?"

"Just recently."

"Recently? He thought he was married, so it's the same as if he was. He's an arrogant, slick asshole. He's a type. An archetype. How does his wife being dead get him a pass? He's everything you don't need."

"And you're the expert on what I need? I needed to spend the night with him, and I did." As soon as she said it, she wished she hadn't. "I'm sorry. I say mean things when I'm upset."

"You're upset? How do you think I feel? Did you tell him you spent one helluva night with me in Berlin?" She tried to get out of the car, but he held her back.

"I'm going inside," she said.

He released her. "You aren't sure how you feel. You'll have to sort it out, but here's a fact of military life. I saw his name on the major's list. That means he'll probably get transferred. The Air Force will want him in a job that fits his new rank. If that happens, what will you do?"

She hadn't known about the transfer. "I'll cross that bridge if it happens."

They both got out of the car. "I'd rather you didn't walk me in," she said.

"I'll get you to the elevator. But here's the thing. You're not sure who you want. If he gets orders, he'll be gone." He grinned the cocky grin. "And I'll be right here."

Chapter 17

Dear Brencie,

Thank you for my wonderful time in Weisbaden. The trip home was fine until I got to Houston and they lost my suitcase, but they found it and brought it out, so that's OK.

Wolfgang tries to call every day, but the connections usually are like talking into a paper bag. Speaking of romance, you said Nolan isn't making troubble? I suspect he troubbles you anyway. Don't deny it.

Thanks for the pictures of you and Chase in Paris. He's handsome as can be. Women fall in love with beauty sometimes, you know, like men do all the time.

Love, Bee Bee

When Brencie arrived at work a "flap" had replaced the usual morning calm. The sergeants and officers were clustered in groups held together by muted conversation. Colonel Foss was standing near his desk, speaking to two men in civilian clothes.

"Brencie, these gentlemen are from OSI." Colonel Foss introduced them as Mr. White and Mr. Black, and Brencie struggled not to laugh. If the names were supposed to be a joke, no one else was laughing. Lulu worked at OSI, Office of Special Investigations, and she admitted that people who report directly to the secretary of the Air Force take themselves seriously.

"There's been a security violation, and everyone in the division will be interviewed," Colonel Foss said as he handed her a three-page list. "Could you copy and distribute this, please? Just the first page. That's our people. Make sure everyone knows the times are firm. We're going to General Novak's office. Back in an hour."

The men left, and Brencie scanned the list. Her own name appeared near the bottom of the first page. She didn't know what had happened, but she was responsible for security procedures in the division. When she took the schedule apart to copy the first page, she was shocked to see Wolfgang's name on the third page, on a roster of foreign nationals to be interviewed. It was one thing to interview the Americans, but if the violation involved a local hire, it would be more serious, no matter how long the local employee had worked on the base or how thorough his background check had been.

Brencie copied and distributed the schedule, emphasizing the mandatory nature of the times. When she returned to her office, the telephone was ringing. "Weapons Systems Support Division, Miss Jessup."

"*Guten morgan, Zuckerschnecke.* Here *ist* Wolfgang. *Wie gehts?*"

She didn't know what to say. Since Agnes-Rose went back to Texas, Wolfgang had called Brencie once or twice, but this time he sounded strange. He must have known his name was on the list.

"Brencie? Are you there? Could you meet me for lunch?"

If she was going to talk to him, best to do it in person. "How about one o'clock?"

Colonel Foss's demeanor when he returned increased Brencie's anxiety. He looked worried. Should she tell him Wolfgang had called? She decided against it. He knew about Agnes-Rose and

Wolfgang, and she didn't want to put Foss the Boss in a position to ask her not to meet with Wolfgang.

When it was time she hurried down five flights of stairs, out the door, and into a stinging north wind. In her haste she had forgotten her coat. She arrived at the canteen breathless. There had been crises at NASA, but nothing involving her directly. Her divisional security responsibilities, and maybe her relationship with Wolfgang, made this situation potentially bad. Wolfgang was already there, and as they got sandwiches and found a table, he seemed edgy. "Wolfgang, what happened?"

He looked blank. "What happened about what?"

"The security thing. The OSI guys. You're going to be questioned."

"Oh, that." He took a bite of his sandwich.

He chewed.

She waited.

"The morning read-out went missing. Colonel Foss saw it last and gave it back to Sergeant Anderson. Now that Nolan's in the IG's office, Anderson takes it around, and he on the floor of the men's room dropped it. A *Putzfrau* found it when she went in to mop. She doesn't speak English, but she knew what to do. She hid it in her cleaning cart and went to Captain Crum. It will be sorted out."

"Good grief! How does that involve you?"

"I was supposed to drive the general this morning, and I passed Sergeant Anderson in the hall. They're casting a fat net, so I got caught in it. General Novak canceled, so I'm taking advantage of the consequences, as *Erdbeerchen* would say. I need to talk to you."

"Casting a *wide* net. And you know this before OSI does?" But the local-hire grapevine was legendary. The locals often knew things before the bureaucracy did, classified or not.

He grinned. "Right. I know nothing. I'm making the guess."

"Will Sergeant Anderson get in trouble?"

"*Ach*. You worry too much. Yesterday's report had nothing higher than Confidential. Stuff you can read in *Stars and Stripes*. The report's always handled as Top Secret because sometimes it is, and they don't reclassify it every day. Anderson will be reprimanded, that's all."

"I thought lunch was about the interviews. You seemed nervous."

He laughed. "I'm nervous because I want to propose to Agnes-Rose. I'm here to ask for her hand. If you don't approve, she won't accept me."

Brencie laughed, feeling relieved, happy, excited, and melancholy, all at once.

"So you approve?"

"Of course I do. I want her to be happy. I want you to be happy. I want Jules and Lulu to be happy." She sighed.

"Ah. Everyone's getting happy, and you are not engaged."

"Most of my friends from high school are married. I got a birth announcement yesterday. My best friend had a baby girl. I'll be twenty-three soon. She reminded me the median age for a first marriage is twenty for girls. I'm behind by three years."

By the time lunch was over, Brencie had some idea of her stepmother's future and still no idea about her own. She felt better about the security violation, and when she got back to her office, Colonel Foss's good humor had returned, the air of dread was gone, and the mystery of the missing document had been solved.

"Can you believe it?" Colonel Foss said. "A *Putzfrau* found it in the men's room. That weenie Anderson was carrying a stack of stuff, and he didn't even notice he dropped it."

————))◉((————

Two weeks before Thanksgiving Brencie sat on the floor with Lulu in her apartment, surrounded by cookbooks. "What do you think, Brencie? The cranberry sauce with orange? Or plain?"

"I don't know. I don't like cranberries."

Lulu looked up. "Brencie. You'll have to tell me. Will you and Chase come for Thanksgiving or not? My party will be smaller this year. A lot of people went home this summer. If you and Chase come, it's a buffet again. If you don't, I might manage a sit-down dinner."

"Lulu, do you think I was wrong to forgive Chase?"

"Oh, Brencie, don't ask me. Redemption's a word Jules likes. He believes in it. You forgave Agnes-Rose because you love her and she loves you. Chase lied for months, but you love him, and I think he loves you. Now what about Thanksgiving?"

"I'd love to come, but . . ."

"Yes, Nolan's coming, and he didn't ask about you and Chase. I'm not crazy about the two of them squaring off over the drumsticks, but if Nolan wants to come, he'll come. That's Nolan."

"Oh, God. Will it be the same problem at Christmas?"

"Nope. Jules and I are going to Vienna for the Christmas market. Maybe you and Chase would like to come along. It's a nice train trip."

———◦«◦»◦———

Thanksgiving sorted itself out. Chase's boss invited his team for Thanksgiving dinner, and Chase made it clear accepting was important. His boss lived at the American compound, and although the duplexes were modest, they were well maintained, with freshly shellacked hardwood floors, walls that were painted after each occupant left, and a dining room large enough for a party. The table was set with china, crystal, and silver, and low bouquets of yellow and white chrysanthemums nestled in the center of the table.

Little cards beside each place had tiny rank insignia on them, and the majors were closer to the host. The captains were in the center of the table, and the lieutenants were at the end. Because Chase was on the promotion list, he was at the top of the row of captains, and Brencie was seated beside him.

For all the elegance, something was in the wind. After dinner people stood in groups, heads lowered in quiet conversation, whispers, and sidelong glances that persisted into the evening. It put a damper on the day and reminded Brencie of the security breech that turned out to be nothing. Several people drank too much, including Chase.

When it was time to leave, Chase made no objection when she insisted on driving. They were staying at his place for the long weekend, and when they got there, she asked him about the odd thing in the air, the thing one of the wives called the elephant in the room. "I suspect it's about the war," she said. "Twice I heard something that sounded like Mee Lie, but I'm not sure."

Chase exploded. He swept his arm across his desk, sending a potted poinsettia to the floor, black dirt scattering over the carpet. Brencie had never had occasion to fear male anger, and she was shocked at how threatening it seemed, how visceral the fear felt.

"All right, God damn it, something has happened, but I won't tell you. Maybe you won't ever know. It's on the military grapevine, but for now it's not public, and it doesn't have anything to do with me, not directly. He sat down heavily on the couch, leaning his head back and staring at the ceiling. "In the end it has something to do with all of us. I don't want to talk anymore about it. Is that clear?"

"It isn't clear at all. Did we accidently bomb a hospital or something? A school?"

His laugh sounded bitter. "You think that hasn't happened? You're so stupid. You and your friends. It's a war, not a tea party."

Brencie picked up her coat. "I won't allow you to talk to me like that, even when you're drunk. Call me when you're yourself again."

His expression softened, and he rose from the couch. "No! Don't go!" He reached for her. "I need you. I'm sorry. Please forgive me," he said. "Don't leave. I need you."

She stepped back, still shaken by his anger, and she left over his protests. She was surprised to see taxis at the curb outside. The American facilities—from the Amelia to the Arms, from the golf course in the Taunus Mountains to the community center—all took care to ensure Americans felt at home. Brencie sometimes forgot where she was. Of course there were taxis. Thanksgiving was not a German holiday.

⇒≫«◊»⇐

For days Chase courted Brencie, apologizing, bringing her small gifts, cajoling her into a day trip to Idstein, with its well-preserved half-timbered houses and a palace with a witches' tower.

In the weeks before Christmas, beyond wine at meals, he stopped drinking, and he found new and more tender ways to make love to her. Even so, something had shifted. From *The Book of Agnes-Rose:* "Between a woman and a man, one or the other has the upper hand." Brencie had the upper hand for now, at least, so she decided to bring up the trip to Vienna. They were having dinner at the Officers' Club where once a month, lobsters were flown in from Maine.

Chase pulled a morsel from the fat part of the lobster claw and dipped it into a glass ramekin of drawn butter. "Damn, that's good." He dabbed his chin with a white linen napkin.

"Does the butter get in your dimples?" she teased.

He smiled. "It *is* a problem."

"Lulu invited us to come with her and Jules to the Christmas market in Vienna. We could do all our shopping. I might buy you a pair of lederhosen. You have better legs than I do."

"Thanks, but I'll say no to lederhosen."

"And yes to the Christmas Market?"

He looked away. "You know how I feel. Fraternizing restrictions are not as strict as they used to be, but the trip will include officers and enlisted people, and we would be expected to spend time with the officers. Jules wouldn't give a rat's ass, but it could hurt Lulu's feelings."

The idea of hurting Lulu stung. "You didn't mind going out with Dierdre, Margo, and Jürgen when Lulu and Jules were in Munich." As the waitress removed their plates and poured the last of the wine, Brencie figured it out. "I see. Jürgen von Beckling. Of the officer class."

"What if that's true? But it's more a matter of Jürgen being a civilian. He's neither/nor."

"And Dierdre and Margo? And me? What *class* are we?"

"For a girl, that's determined by her man."

"What about officers like Leah Crum? Is the rank of her man determined by her?"

"That won't happen often enough to worry about. Look, there's a thing on the base next Wednesday, the annual presentation of medals and awards. Flags, a band. Military pomp. I'd like you to come."

⸺•⸻《◎》⸻•⸺

Brencie and Lulu entered an aircraft hangar that was like a cathedral—cavernous, high-ceilinged, full of echoes, and cold.

"Shit," said Lulu. "I can see my stinkin' breath."

Twenty rows of folding chairs had been set up, with an aisle down the center, and down front, below a shiny silver jet, was a wooden podium with a lectern in the center flanked by three American flags. Under the wings of the aircraft were rows of flags, half a dozen American flags down each side, two German flags, and others Brencie didn't recognize.

As they sat down, Lulu tugged at her short plaid skirt, adjusting it before crossing her perfect legs. "I don't come every year," she said. "It's always in December, and cold as hell. Some people from my outfit are receiving awards."

Eight musicians in dress blues silenced the crowd with a brief fanfare, and a master sergeant introduced the base commander.

"Thank you, Sergeant, and welcome, everyone, to the USAFE annual awards ceremony. As you know, most of the honors and medals follow our members from their last post, and their unit commander hands them out as they're received. However, we like to have a formal event once a year. We have a lot to get through, so it's necessary to recognize certain awards by group and then a few special awards individually. We'll start with the meritorious service medals. Sergeant Ark, will you do the honor of calling out the names?"

"What's Chase receiving?" Lulu whispered. "He's sitting down front."

"I don't know. He just said I might enjoy the ceremony. Colonel Foss encouraged me to come. He gave me a ride out. Three guys from our division are getting something too."

Names were read, and people stepped forward in groups. The ceremony was long, but finally the base commander said, "Let's have a round of applause for our outstanding officers, non-coms, and civilians." When the applause ended, he said, "The last honor warrants particular attention. May I ask Major-elect William Chase Dellasera to step forward?"

Chase walked to the podium and stood at attention.

"It's my honor and privilege to award Captain Dellasera the Bronze Star with the V for valor," said the commander. He read the citation, but Brencie could only look at Chase and catch a few words. Acts of heroism. Direct combat. Exposure to enemy hostilities. Grave personal risk. The word *valor* was repeated three times, and Brencie was astonished at the number of combat missions he had flown.

"Figures," Lulu whispered. "In addition to everything, he's a hero. You didn't know about this?"

"I saw the V on a ribbon ages ago, and I asked if it stood for Vietnam. He said he earned it in Vietnam. He didn't say anything about *valor*. He doesn't play up his role in the war."

"Doesn't he? He invited you to the ceremony."

After a round of applause, Chase returned to his seat, and when the proceedings were over, the commander invited everyone to the officers' club for refreshments. Lulu left for the club, and Brencie waited for Chase, who led her forward until they were standing under the planes down front. "Do you remember the first time I brought you out here?" he asked.

"To your sexy jet garage? Sure. You seduced me in the cockpit of an F-4, before we even went to Garmisch. I didn't quite get that at the time, but I'm a lot older now."

"You are. In a good way. This time I'm hoping to persuade you to accept this." He pulled a black velvet box out of his pocket and opened it. "I wanted to wait until Valentine's Day, but the way things are going, I can't be sure I'll be here."

It took her by surprise, but the elation she would have predicted didn't come. Perhaps the cold was making her numb. Looking at the impressive diamond, she almost missed the remark. "What? Do you expect to be transferred?"

"It's a possibility." He put the ring on her finger. "There. Perfect fit, just like you're going to be. The right wife's a huge asset in the military."

She flexed her fingers, and the ring caught the light. It was dazzling, just like Chase Dellasera, and she was to be his asset. Her future would be like the ring, big and shiny. And hard.

He folded her hand into a fist and put both his hands around hers. "I've lined up some friends at the club to celebrate my derring-do in combat and my exceptional courage in popping the question. Let's go celebrate."

As they walked toward the club, she understood. Chase never considered she might say no, and certainly her silence conveyed consent. People were waiting. People expected certain things. Did Lulu know? Brencie doubted it. They entered the club to a round of applause, and Chase's boss raised his glass. "Here's to the future Mrs. Major William Chase Dellasera." No mention of *Brencie*.

As congratulations echoed around the room, Brencie looked at Lulu, who wasn't smiling.

Chapter 18

Dear Brencie,

Boy. A lots happened. Wolf has come to visit and gone. We're officially engaged. He said he asked you for my hand, but he got the rest of me too!

Did you know he's a mechanical genuis? He talked to the VW–BMW place. They want to hire him if he lives here.

Speaking of engagements, congratulations, but I'm worried about you. My instincts are asking questions. Well. Nothing's perfect. Except Wolfgang.

Happy Fasching. I even know what that is, ha ha.

Love, Bee Bee

Agnes-Rose was right. Nothing was perfect, and even the United States of America wasn't ending a troubled year any better than it began. An ex-general advocated the use of nuclear weapons, and the article in *Stars and Stripes* seemed thrilled about it. Jackie Kennedy married a rich Greek toad, as Jules called him.

"When Jules heard about your engagement," Lulu had said, "he made a few negative remarks."

"Should I ask?" Brencie had said.

"I shouldn't tell you, but he said wait till that guy gets a ring on her finger. She'll be done for."

"I don't know what that means. He said it because he's Nolan's friend. What did he say?"

"Nolan?" Lulu said. "Nolan didn't say anything. When Jules told him, he walked away."

Brencie was in Chase's apartment at the moment, where she was spending more time, because he wanted it that way. At least at the American Arms she didn't have to see Nolan run by. She had chosen Chase, an imperfect choice, but how far down an imperfect road should a person go? Compromise? Or selling out? as the hippies said. Chase came back from the Oak Leaf Restaurant with coffee and donuts. "Is that a letter from my girl Agnes-Rose?"

"Yup. With happy Fasching wishes."

"Everybody's happy at Fasching. Did you go to the parade last year?" They planned to walk downtown for the extravagant annual parade.

"No, but everyone's going. Lulu and them. They'll be near the Ringstrasse." She didn't suggest they join her friends. He always had an excuse to avoid it. "We won't see them."

He got his coat and handed Brencie hers. "It's not too cold, but it's a twenty-minute walk."

It had warmed up to fifty-one degrees, unusual for February, and the sun was out. In a few blocks they were in the Kurpark, swept clean of leaves, and comely in its bare bones, the skeletons of the deciduous trees, the brown patches of grass. As they neared the Wilhelmstrasse, the number of passersby increased, many in costume. Chase wore regular clothes, and Brencie wore the dirndl she had purchased from one of the bizarre bazaars at the Amelia, though not much of the outfit showed under her coat.

Chase took her hand as they made their way to Rhein Main-Hallen on the west side of the Wilhelmstrasse, a two-story building, post-war, modern compared to its neighbors. A low wall provided an excellent spot to watch the parade and the passers-by. This year the two most popular costumes were astronaut and Barbarella. *Barbarella*, the movie, hadn't made it to the American theaters in Wiesbaden, but the photo of Jane Fonda in the ridiculous garb was in all the magazines.

The astronaut outfits renewed Brencie's sense of national pride. Astronauts were at public balls and private parties, some surprisingly like the real thing, others concocted from imagination and aluminum foil. Even though the *Apollo* flight in late January had been unmanned, the excitement ramped up with each launch. Could they do it? Could the Americans land a man on the moon?

As a devil strolled by with a pregnant angel, Chase opened his backpack and pulled out a flask. "Wish I'd brought coffee," he said. "It's brandy, but it will warm you." He handed her the flask, and she took a swig. For a while Chase's drinking had dwindled, but in a place with so much partying and cheap booze? As Lulu had said, it's a wonder everyone's not an alcoholic.

Last year everything had been new to Brencie, and so different from home. No flat plains or roaring sunsets. Just hills and muted colors. Military ritual, new jargon—BX, billet, NORS rates, *guten* howdy *wieter* bye-bye parties, retreat, reveille. Now she sorted things into categories. This was good. That was bad. Drinking too much was common, and it was bad.

Every third or fourth float featured live music, and the *Mainzer Narhalla-Marsch* echoed from an approaching float. The parade slowed and stopped, and the band switched from the march to a polka. The crowd began dancing in the street and along the sidewalks, and they didn't stop until the band moved on, making room for the next float. Many floats were suggestive, but one passed that Brencie found offensive.

Like an ugly version of a ship figurehead, a crude caricature of an old man adorned the prow. Probably made of papier mâché, he had enlarged ears, an immense nose, and drool dripping from his mouth. His gnarly hands clutched the front of his pants, so his privates weren't exposed, but the pants were dropped in back to reveal his plump, hairy butt. He was squatting, and gold coins the size of dinner plates issued from his anus. Crouched behind him was a brunette in a bouffant hairdo and a pill box hat, eagerly collecting the filthy coins.

"That's Onassis! And Jackie Kennedy! I've never seen anything so vulgar," Brencie said.

"The Germans are fond of scatological humor," Chase said.

"Is that about bathroom stuff?"

"Right, and you still can't say shit."

"I could. I don't want to." The offensive float passed out of sight. "You would never see that in Friendswood or anywhere in the States." She whispered, unsure if those around her spoke English. When the brandy was gone, Chase suggested they adjourn to Café Europa a few blocks away, where they could get something to eat.

They were heading in that direction when a group of six approached, laughing, dancing, clearly a bit drunk. Brencie recognized Lulu, dressed as a tube of toothpaste. Two long white sheets were suspended from a yoke on her shoulders, and "Colder-gate" was painted on the front. A red pillbox hat, meant to be the toothpaste cap, reminded Brencie of the Ari and Jackie float that she was trying to forget.

Jules had rented the same Pagliacci outfit as he wore the previous year, while Margo and Dierdre had shunned the purple dress-for-two. They were dressed as sexy nurses, in uniforms a size too small, white spike heels, and huge nurses' caps fashioned from white cardboard.

Brencie laughed at the sight of them. "Nurses dressed as nurses. Did you steal those caps from the flying nun? I didn't know fishnet stocking came in white."

Jürgen, in lederhosen, walked behind pulling a wagon. The warming effect of alcohol and hijinks had caused everyone to shed their coats, which were piled on the wagon. "Jürgen," said Chase. "*Wie gehts?* What's with the wagon?"

"I no idea have," Jürgen said. "A little *Mädchen* left it behind. Something wrong with the wheels, but it's good for the coats."

The standout in the group was Father Time, the New Year's Eve image, in a long black robe, a banner proclaiming 1969, and a flimsy cardboard scythe. His face was covered by an old-man mask, but Brencie knew him at once, by his size and posture. Nolan. What a difference a year made. On her first date with Nolan, they ran into Chase. Now she was with Chase, and here was Nolan.

Her friends were delighted to see Brencie, but in their inebriated condition, they were no doubt delighted to see anyone.

Chase was unpredictable when he drank, though it often amplified his mood. If he was feeling down, he became morose. If he was happy, he became delirious. He was in a mellow mood today, so the brandy made him accommodating. When Nolan removed his mask, Chase nodded and said, "Hanik."

"Good afternoon, Captain." Nolan emphasized *captain*, and a pocket of silence descended as the group watched their favorite love triangle.

Chase smiled. "I owe you one, Sergeant. Thanks to you, an unhappy situation regarding my marital status was revealed and resolved."

"We're both happy then," Nolan offered, "about the revelation. As for the resolution, someone said it ain't over till the fat lady sings."

A float with a mockup of the Matterhorn stopped, and a three-piece band dressed as mountain goats struck up a waltz. Dancers took to the streets again, and Nolan held out his hand to Brencie. "I told you I can waltz. Remember?"

"Don't you think you should ask me first?" Chase said.

Nolan smiled, so quick, so effective. "I'd love to dance with you, sir, but it could get ugly. We both like to lead."

The group laughed, even Chase, though it seemed forced. Brencie dropped her coat on Jürgen's wagon, and Nolan said, "The dirndl suits your figure." He embraced her and skillfully maneuvered her away, deeper into the crowd.

"You shouldn't have said that," Brencie mumbled.

"Probably not."

Nolan led her in elegant circles, perfectly timed to the music, and she tried not to think of Berlin. "You're right about one thing," she said. "You do know how to waltz."

"The secret to being a good dancer is to lead with your chest." He held her tighter. "You're thinking about Berlin, aren't you?"

"If I am, it's involuntary."

"Even better. I'm under your skin."

Just like Agnes-Rose, Nolan had the annoying habit of being right. She changed the subject. "Have you heard about law school?"

"I got accepted to Northwestern. I still can't believe it."

"I'm impressed. They say it's hard to pass the bar exam, which makes me think it would be fun to try."

"You could be a lawyer any day of the week. Or an artist. Or a singer. You're smarter and more talented than me." When the music ended, he pulled her closer and kissed her, a lingering kiss.

She finally broke the embrace and said, "What if he saw that? I'm surprised at you."

"I don't care what he saw, and I'm surprised at you. He lied to you for months, and you agreed to marry him, for hell's sake."

She bolted, leaving Nolan behind. The others had moved on, except for Chase. He was waiting, and he wasn't happy. "Is something going on with him? A blind man could see the attraction, and I don't like it."

You know all there is to know about Nolan and me. That's what she wanted to say, but she held back that staggering lie. Better to keep it simple. "No." That was lie enough.

⸺ ((◦)) ⸺

On Monday Nolan called her at work. "Can I take you to lunch?"

"Leave me alone," Brencie said.

"Before you call the Texas Rangers, will you let me explain? I'm not asking you to meet me at midnight by the Rhine. Just a sandwich in the canteen. I want to apologize. Aren't we friends enough for that?"

Brencie sighed. "Yes, of course we are. The canteen at thirteen thirty."

When she arrived Nolan was there, and he had ordered hamburgers. She sat down and waited for him to defend himself.

"Look," he said. "Maybe I shouldn't have done what I did. I was drinking enough to loosen my inhibitions, and I had a fantasy."

"Walt Disney or sexual?"

He laughed. "Fantasy isn't the right word, really. More like I saw a chance to prove something to myself, if not to you. The kiss was deliberate, and I learned what I wanted to know. Brencie, you didn't pull away. You wanted me to kiss you."

"Is there anything else?" She gathered her things.

"Yes. The sight of him didn't make me angry, and that's good. Angry me has become wiser me. When he put you in the hospital, I felt the kind of anger that causes me to make bad choices. I went looking for him, to beat the shit out of him."

"Oh, my god!"

"You said you would listen. Do you remember why I left school?"

"A little girl with a fork in her eye isn't something you forget."

"Exactly. By the time I drove to the American Arms, I had time to think, and I realized it wouldn't do any good to hurt him. It wouldn't change your feelings, and why would I want a girl who doesn't want me? I went back to the barracks." He grinned. "Besides, he's a big, strong guy. Pilots stay fit, or they don't fly. He might have beaten the shit out of me."

Brencie couldn't help it. She laughed. "I don't know what to make of you sometimes, Nolan, but you're interesting."

"I make you laugh and I'm interesting. Not bad." He looked at his watch. "I've got to get back. Thanks for meeting me."

The canteen was almost deserted, so without the usual banging of trays and conversation, she heard him sing an old tune under his breath. "Time, time, time . . . is on my side. Yes, it is." Nolan turned around. "You might come to your senses yet."

"With the help of The Rolling Stones?" she said.

"Maybe. *Tempus fugit*, Brencie. Time flies and things change."

Chapter 19

Leah Crum dropped by to see Colonel Foss, and Brencie invited her to sit down to wait. "He'll be back in about ten minutes. Hey, they got some new tennis rackets in at the BX," Brencie said. "I'm in the market. Any suggestions?"

Leah looked up from the folder she was clutching. "What? Oh, tennis clothes?"

"Rackets. What's up, Leah? You aren't yourself. The IG inspection went wrong, but that wasn't your fault. Colonel Foss said the debrief this morning went well."

"Oh, it's not that. Being the only female officer gets me down sometimes. There's a second lieutenant coming next month, fresh out of training. She'll be on the third floor working with Captain Blair. It will be good to have another 'skirt,' as they call us. If I make major, field grade and all, it might help. It might not."

"Did something happen today?"

"Nothing new. I have responsibilities appropriate to my rank. I supervise two secretaries and three sergeants, but every time I'm in a meeting that requires a notetaker, they ask me to do it. I'm not the lowest ranking person in the room. I'm just the only woman in the room."

Colonel Foss arrived, and Captain Crum went to his desk, leaving Brencie to think about the note-taking business. It didn't seem right, but Brencie had an idea. Leah left, and Brencie called her later to arrange a coffee break.

The canteen was almost empty, so they got coffee and had their choice of tables. "Leah, maybe this is dumb, but I was wondering, when you're asked to take notes, could you suggest they get one of the secretaries to do it?"

"Oh, sure." Leah rolled her eyes. "I thought of that. Then the secretaries would resent me for thinking I'm better than they are."

"It's not a matter of better. We have different jobs, that's all. Listen. Next time you're asked to take notes, why don't you say you're afraid you don't get everything down correctly because you don't take shorthand. Even better, wait until Colonel Foss is leading the meeting. I'll make sure I'm available, and I'll tell Colonel Foss ahead of time. Some of the officers are like him, more oblivious than sexist. They need a little . . . whatchamacallit?"

"*Consciousness raising?*" said Leah.

One week later, Leah called. "It's Colonel Foss's turn to chair the readiness evaluation at fifteen hundred hours. I'm going to take your suggestion. It could be a mistake, but nothing ventured, nothing gained," she said.

Brencie was asked to take the meeting notes, and afterwards, Leah called to say thanks. "The hardest part was getting up the guts to ask. I got a few looks, but no one objected. Colonel Foss seemed to think it was a good idea. You gave him a heads up, I'll bet."

"I did, and he did think it was a good idea."

Brencie left work in an exhilarated mood, like she and Leah had accomplished something. Leah said small changes added up, maybe made a difference.

The guards on duty at the front gate waved cheerfully as she passed by. Chase was back from his latest deployment, and she looked forward to seeing him. She stopped in the flower shop and breathed in the green smell, buckets of tulips and lilacs, daisies and roses, baby's breath and fiddle ferns. She selected a bouquet of white tulips, their heads still tightly closed, and tucked them under her arm, blooms backward in the European style, feeling pleasantly at home in her world. She had adapted, as Jules would say, and even dipped her toe into feminist politics.

Chase was waiting when she entered the Amelia. He was supposed to come over around seven o'clock, so she was surprised to see him. Excitement animated his face and made him look more handsome than ever. "Bren. Something's happened. I can't wait to tell you."

"Yes, it's wonderful," she teased. "Israel has its first female Prime Minister. Golda Meir. And wait till you hear what happened with Leah Crum at work."

He looked confused. "Oh. Right. Well. My news is better. Let's have a drink to celebrate." They found a table, and Brencie was eager to tell him about her day. "I mentioned Captain Crum and the notetaking business. Do you remember?"

"Sure, sort of. But take a look at this." He put a piece of paper on the table. Brencie had seen the like many times, for the officers and men in her unit. It was a PCS notification. Permanent Change of Station. She scanned it, knowing the important information was buried in lines of bureau-speak. When and where? That's what mattered. Who, of course, would be Chase, just as Nolan had predicted.

She read the orders and then looked up at him. "But this is for next month. You weren't supposed to leave until fall. You won't pin on your major's leaves till then." Although the promotion list came out in a certain cycle, it was sometimes many months between the list and the actual promotion.

"It's complicated," he said. "The Air Force doesn't practice frocking, or rarely, anyway, but when a job comes open at the higher rank and you're suited for it, they can send you there, depending on the timing of a lot of things, such as when the incumbent leaves. That's what's happened. That's why I got orders."

Brencie understood most of the terms by then, but *frocking* was a new one. He explained it meant the practice of wearing the insignia of the higher grade before the official date of the promotion or pay increase.

"You get the job but not the pay?"

"It would take hours to explain, but the number of officers of any given rank at any particular time is limited by Congress. The system can't wait around to line up the moon and all the stars. A good job comes open, a guy with the right rank, official or on the list, close to his rotation date, gets the job. We'll be going home next month. We can get married in Texas if you like. I'll be at the War College in D.C. for a few weeks, and then on to Duluth."

How easily he folded her into *we*. Brencie didn't understand her own reaction, a combination of surprise, confusion, and something else, but it wasn't happiness. "The War College? What's that? And Duluth, Minnesota? What's in Duluth? It's way up north, right?"

"The War College got its name a long time ago, but it's an education and training facility. Duluth's on the shore of Lake Superior. I'll be with the 23rd Air Division." He over-looked her lack of enthusiasm, instead talking about travel timing, housing, and possibilities for her to find a job in Duluth. He handed her a folder with some standard literature about the base and the surrounding area and waited for her to open it.

When she didn't, he said, "What is it, Bren? Aren't you excited? I'm sorry. I got carried away. Did you want to tell me something about Leah Crum? Did something bad happen?"

"Not bad. It's just that she's always asked to take notes, because she's the only woman. We arranged for her to ask me to do it, and it worked. We felt pretty good about it. Maybe they got the message."

"Well, you're a woman too."

"I'm a stenographer, not a captain in the United States Air Force. It's the job they hired me for."

"How does it hurt Leah to take notes?"

His lack of interest stung, but she had to concede, his reassignment was bigger news. "Look that information over," he suggested. "It's cold up there, but it will only be for a few years." They ate hamburgers in the bar, and then went to her apartment. It was still early, so they opened a bottle of wine and watched the news on Brencie's tiny TV. *Apollo 9* was midway through its planned ten-day mission.

"Did you ever meet any of those guys?" Chase asked.

"I met a couple astronauts, yes. We had post-mission ceremonies, and I was part of the production staff." She hoped they wouldn't have any further discussions about his orders until she had time to absorb what it meant to her.

But he brought it up again. "We'll have to get going on getting you home," he said. "The Air Force will take over for me, but I'm not sure what will happen about you. It may take a couple extra weeks. Once we get to station, you can get a job on the base, if you'd like, but you'll want to stay home when we start having kids."

"I can't do that." She didn't realize she was actually going to say it.

"Can't do what?"

"Turn my back on the life I've made here. Break my contract. If I go home now, I'll have to reimburse the government for everything, transportation to Wiesbaden, all expenses, plus I'll have to pay my way back to the States. That's in my contract. All expenses paid if I stay three years. If I stay eighteen months, the halfway mark, I won't have to pay anything back, but I'll have to pay my way home."

He patted her hand. "Don't worry, I'll cover any expenses. We could get married here, but there's not time to arrange it. Too bad. Then you'd be my dependent, on my orders. Your expenses would be covered."

When he proposed he had said she would be an *asset* as a wife. Now she would be his *dependent,* just as she felt she had earned her *independence.* "The midpoint is only a few months away," she said.

Her resistance took him by surprise. "But I want you with me. I need you. You know money isn't an issue. I told you. I have an annuity from my grandfather."

"It isn't about the money. It's about a contract. Leaving halfway through goes against my principles. I got here on my own, by making an arrangement with the United States Air Force. I signed a contract. I'm proud of that. Can you understand?"

"No. I can't."

The discussion became an argument, but they finally agreed. She would follow as soon as she reached the eighteen-month point on her contract. "Then we won't have to be apart for so long." They left it that way, but it was a reluctant compromise for him, and it left her exhausted, feeling she had won and lost at the same time.

"I need you so much, Bren." He took her in his arms, and her response, once so natural, was forced. They had sex, but her heart wasn't in it. When it was over, they lay silent and close on the narrow sofa bed, but it didn't feel like afterglow. It felt like ashes.

———⋙⟨◉⟩⋘———

Three weeks after he got his orders, Chase was gone.

———⋙⟨◉⟩⋘———

Ring, ring. Pause. *Ring, ring.*

The annoying sound woke Brencie from a deep sleep. She looked at the clock. Oh eight hundred on Saturday. No one ever called before 9:00 a.m., only when the call had been for Chase, the calls that took him away with little or no explanation. She lunged for the phone. "Yes?"

"This is Lieutenant Overton calling from Base Operations. Is this Brencie Jessup? I have a message from Captain Dellasera."

Brencie sat up, fully awake. "From Chase?"

"He's coming through for a refueling stop, ETA twenty-one hundred hours. He would like you to meet him."

"Meet him? Meet him where?"

"At Base Ops. Here on the base."

"How long will he be here?"

"I'm sorry, ma'am. That's all the information I have." The call ended.

She sat on the edge of the bed, listening to the birds singing in the treetops. She slept with the windows open. The air was warmer now. She counted on her fingers. Chase had been gone for eleven weeks. She went to the lobby for a copy of *Stars and Stripes,* to search for a reason Chase might have been deployed. Vietnam, Vietnam, Vietnam. Martial law on the campus at Berkley. President Eisenhower's funeral. A U.S. plane shot down over the Sea of Japan. Nothing relevant, as far as she could tell. She waited another hour and then called Lulu.

"Lulu. I can't go shopping. Chase is going to be here tonight. Refueling at the base. He got a message to someone who called me. I don't know how long he'll stay."

"That's exciting, but refueling stops are unpredictable. It could be an hour; it could be overnight."

"I wish I knew. Military uncertainty isn't my cup of tea. The ladies know nothing, and I think the men like it that way. Shit!"

Lulu laughed. "Brencie. You said shit! Excellent. You can tell him how the plans are coming."

"What plans?"

"Uh-huh. That's my point. The plans for your wedding, Brencie. Most girls would be knee deep in it. You've done nothing. Don't you wonder what that means?"

⸺⸺⸺◉⸺⸺⸺

The Base Ops waiting area was small, with dingy overhead lighting and the strong smell of burned coffee. She hadn't been in a waiting area since right after Joe O'Barry was killed, and Nolan was waiting for her in Berlin. She didn't want to think about Nolan, but it was only natural to have the current surroundings trigger the memory. Determined to push Nolan out of her head, she picked up a magazine. Every waiting room she had ever been in was soaked in wasted time, like the Salvador Dali print in Margo's apartment, dead clocks and winding roads, roads you can never walk on.

Nothing to do but pretend to read *Aviation Weekly*. She decided to chat up the desk sergeant. Although flight schedules were confidential, they weren't secret. She showed her ID card and smiled, and one or the other worked. The sergeant looked at a list and told her which of the incoming flights was Captain Dellasera's. He was still an hour out.

When the hour passed, she left the building and stood by the high chain link fence along the flight line. Ground lights illuminated the runway, and amber lights near the fence multiplied her shadow into a population of phantoms. The acrid smell of jet fuel. A C-130, props invisible until they stopped turning. Tires skidding and screeching. Mechanical night noises, like beasts in a concrete forest, and then the next aircraft was his.

The F-4 wore camouflage, not the shiny paint of the one she stood under when Chase proposed. The aircraft appeared and disappeared as it passed in and out of low-level ground lights, and then the jet touched down, smooth and elegant, nose wheel suspended for a moment and then lightly kissing the runway, like something organic, a bird not made by man.

The post-landing operation was precise. The ground crew, the refueling apparatus—all danced together around the jet, all knowing their function, all well-trained and sure. When the canopy popped up and two men climbed down, her heart started to pound. In flight suits and helmets, they could have been anyone, but she knew which was Chase by his grace.

He waved when he saw her and removed his helmet. She was mesmerized, as impressed as the first time she saw him. He moved toward her, helmet tucked under his arm, easy gait. She wondered, *What am I seeing? Is it Chase or the idea of Chase?*

She closed her fingers around a link in the fence, and when he reached her, he put his fingers over hers. "I wasn't sure you'd get the message. Back-channel communications are unreliable." They walked along the fence, he on one side, she on the other. There was no gate, no way to get closer, and she remembered Berlin, the family standing on the platform waving across the gap.

Chase entered from the rear of the building as Brencie came in the front door. They met and embraced discreetly, but when he led her back outside, he kissed her, a real kiss, reminding her of what they were to each other. Or what they had been.

"How long can you stay?" she asked.

"Only a couple of hours, and I can't leave the area. I had to call in a few favors to stop here instead of Torrejon. Let's go to the club. We have time for a drink. More if they have to do anything to the plane."

Only a couple of hours, so they couldn't spend the night

together. Sex and love were symbiotic with Chase from the first time in Garmisch. That part of their relationship had captivated her, changed her. Her limited experience magnified his skill, though she had been too besotted to understand. *Until I slept with Nolan.* She shooed that thought away.

They settled at the most private table they could find, but it was Saturday night, and the dining room and the bar were crowded, not ideal for intimate conversation. Brencie wished they could sit side by side, touching, nothing in between them. At the tiny round table against the wall, they sat facing each other.

He ordered wine for her, club soda for himself, and the silence went on until they both spoke at once.

"I think—"

"I wonder—"

"No, you go ahead," she said.

"There's no time for small talk, Bren. When are you coming home? We agreed you would, and the halfway mark on your contract's coming up. Have you started the process?"

She sipped her wine for something to do and then said, "I wish . . ."

She couldn't finish the sentence. He waited, and the space between them seemed to open up, wider and wider, until the table itself became an abyss.

"You aren't coming, are you?" He wasn't looking at her now.

"I'm not coming yet, but—"

"Come home. I need you. I miss you. I'm lonely. If you love me . . ."

As much as she enjoyed working for the U.S. Air Force, and respected it, Brencie didn't want to join it, and that's what marrying Chase would mean. She didn't want to leave her life in Wiesbaden, and maybe she didn't want to get married. To anyone.

"Come home as soon as you can arrange it. I'll pay the cost of quitting your contract. Do you know what you want? Or do you like being just out of reach? I thought that would change if I put a ring on your finger."

"I want to stay who I am. I want to be Brencie. I know that much."

"Look, is this about him?"

"It's about me, Chase." But she didn't pretend not to know who he meant. "I haven't been seeing him, if that's what you're asking. I want my last year here. I've turned into a different person, and I've had the time of my life, a lot of it with you. I want to honor the contract I signed, and I want a clear picture of what's next."

"I'm what's next. Us, I mean. Are you looking for a way out? Is that it?" There was no kindness in his voice. "Or an excuse to be with him? If you haven't been already?"

At the worst moment, the waitress called Chase to the phone, and he left the table.

Us? Brencie thought. To Chase, *us* seemed to mean *him*, what he wanted, what he needed.

When he came back, he didn't sit down. "Bird's good to go."

They walked back, and when they were standing outside Base Ops, he said, "Let's say goodbye here." He kissed her one more time, pressing against her, reminding her. He didn't say he loved her. "Just walk away, Bren."

She didn't want him to see her cry, so she did as he asked, and she didn't turn to look at him when he spoke to her again.

"*Auf Wiedersehen*, Brencie," he said.

She still didn't turn around. "*Auf Wiedersehen*, Chase."

Not on seeing *you* again. Just *On seeing or looking again.*

The shuttle to town ran until the early morning hours, and it wasn't crowded, so she took a seat by herself and leaned against the window. The route ran by the flight line, and a silver F-4 took off. It couldn't be Chase, but she felt an overwhelming sense of loss.

Was it so hard for everyone, to sort out how they felt? It looked as though when it came to love, she could assess real from unreal only when it was finished. What she felt for Chase had been as real as the bus she sat on, not ephemeral like the midnight moon outside, full today, a sliver of itself another night. Love for him was solid. It was meant to last. What happened? And why was the loss tinged with relief?

She thought about the high school boyfriend who once said he couldn't imagine loving anyone but her, and then he had added, "I probably will, though." He had a practical streak. She was certain she had loved him, and a small part of her always would. Then there was Richard Paul Smith, the fiancé who turned out to be a scoundrel, just like her father. Now she was sure she had never loved Rick.

Chase was the prince girls dream about without considering what living in his kingdom might mean. She brushed back a tear, and the engagement ring scratched her cheek. She drew it across her cheek again, hoping to leave a mark, maybe to bleed. She should have given the ring back, but in that last bitter moment, neither of them acknowledged the truth.

Chapter 20

The sound of water murmured at the edge of Brencie's dream:

She floats on an inflatable raft off the beach in Galveston. In one direction the Gulf of Mexico meets the blue sky with nothing to stop it. In the other direction, people walk along the shore as the waves splash over their feet. There's an unpredictable undertow, and in the mystery of time and space, Chase stands over her, as he had on the ski slope at Garmisch, his body blocking the sun. He steps to one side, and there stands Nolan.

"Wake up, Brencie." It was Lulu blocking the sun. "I can't sit down until you take the tray." Brencie sat up on her beach towel.

Lulu handed her the tray and said, "What a view, huh?"

They were on the Neroberg, highest of the Taunus Mountains. The grassy slope was part of the Opelbad complex, and fifty yards away the swimming pool cut an aquamarine oblong in the green hillside. The vineyard on the slope below the pool showed new growth, but no grapes were visible yet. Lulu opened two bottles of Orangina. "Were you dreaming? I looked through your sketches while you were dozing. They're getting better all the time."

"I started sketching to see things better. Maybe it's helping. I was dreaming about Chase. He's been gone three months. He expected to be in Duluth by now, but he's still in D.C. The boss at his new assignment wanted him to extend his training."

"What was your dream about?"

"I was at the beach and skiing with Chase. Nolan showed up. Not too hard to interpret. Should we go swimming?"

"Not me. Too crowded and too cold."

"I'm going," said Brencie. She found a reasonably open area in the pool, plunged in, and lasted a full five minutes. Shivering, she wrapped herself in a towel and sat back down by Lulu. "It was like crushed ice."

"I told you. You have to try everything, don't you?"

"I guess so. Yes, I do." She looked across the town and the valley. "It's odd to see the Amelia from here. I'm used to seeing *here* from the Amelia."

Lulu took a draft of her Orangina and burped. "I shouldn't say anything, but that never stops me. How long are you and Chase going to keep up the fantasy?"

"I miss him, Lulu. It's hard to let go, but at least I'm spending more time with you and our friends. He preferred just the two of us, and we hardly talked about what I wanted. Only about what he wanted. Now I'm the girl he left behind."

"Because you wouldn't go." Lulu pulled the straps of her classic black bathing suit off her shoulders. "What do you think? Is this suit too small?"

"It's fine. Small enough to be sexy, but not small enough to be trashy."

"I've got to cut out the massive shopping trips. I'm spending way too much money," Lulu said. "I'm returning that see-through top, the one we both bought. Wait until Nolan sees you in that."

"I'll wear a camisole, but Nolan isn't going to see me in anything."

"Yet he's already seen you in nothing." Lulu grinned.

"Lulu, I love Nolan. Agnes-Rose thinks it's possible to love two men at once. She thinks I also love Nolan."

Lulu stared. "Did you hear what you said? You said 'I love Nolan' twice. I think you meant to say you love Chase, at least once."

Brencie felt her face get hot. "Well, if I said it wrong, it was a slip of the tongue."

"Has Nolan called? He knows Chase is gone."

"He hasn't, and I'm officially still engaged," Brencie replied.

"I predict that charade won't last much longer," Lulu said. "We saw Nolan last weekend, and he asked when you're leaving. I told him you have no plans yet. He grinned that grin."

"He thinks time is on his side." Brencie stared across the valley. The Amelia Earhart was far in the distance, distinct, though, because it was the tallest structure on the horizon.

"Time is on his side," Lulu said, following Brencie's gaze. "But I'm not so sure it's on yours. At some point he'll walk away. I'm starving. The restaurant here's too expensive. Let's get a hamburger at the Amelia."

All the way back across town in the taxi, Brencie pondered what Lulu said. *He'll walk away.*

⸻ ⦿ ⸻

They changed clothes and met back at the Café Amelia, where the head waiter arrived, pencil and pad in hand. "Yes?" It was Mario, with his Italian good looks and continental arrogance.

Brencie stared at him. "Could we have menus, if it's not too much trouble?"

He looked bored. "Yes, of course, but you know what we have." He came back with menus and left again with no change in surliness.

"Why don't they fire him?" Brencie said.

Lulu shrugged. "He's right. We do know what they have."

On the way in they had stopped for their mail, and Lulu had

a fat manila envelope. "Do you mind if I open this? It's something I sent away for." She drew out pamphlets and thumbed through a magazine with color plates on every page. Her face became animated. "My secret ambition. It's from the Fashion Institute of Technology in New York."

"Really? Let me see." Brencie skimmed the booklet that outlined programs at FIT, as it was called. "Lulu, it's perfect. You're thinking of when you go home with Jules. You've got panache in your bones. You could teach them about style."

"It's just an idea. Jules will go back to City College, but someone has to work. Probably both of us. He has the GI bill, but every cent I made went on my back. I could draw out my retirement fund, but I'm not sure I should."

Brencie held up one of the brochures. "Lulu. This is *you*. Draw out the fund. There are ways to work it out."

"That's what Jules says." They finished eating and rode up in the elevator. As Brencie got off on her floor, Lulu said, "Thank you, Brencie."

"You're welcome. What for?"

"For encouraging me. If you and Jules think FIT can be managed, maybe it can." Lulu smiled as the elevator doors closed.

Brencie entered her apartment and went out on the balcony. She brushed a bit of debris off a chair and sat down. The Neroberg was back where it belonged, as was she.

———— ⬩⟨⬩⟩⬩ ————

Brencie held her racket at an angle and let Leah's hard return bounce off, back to the far corner of Leah's court. She lunged, but it was impossible.

"Ha ha! That's it. My set," Brencie declared. She and Leah had been playing twice a week, and Leah won consistently, but not this time.

"You're getting better," Leah said, "but it will be a long time, like *never*, before you win regularly." She smiled. "See you Wednesday?"

Lulu was on the flagstone terrace that opened from the Amelia and overlooked the broad backyard and the tennis courts. She sipped something tall and cold. Brencie walked over. "Phew! I'm sweaty. Did you see? I beat Leah." She put her racket down and took three balls from the side pocket. She tossed the balls in the air. "Pretty cool, huh?" she said.

"You can juggle. I'm dazed and amazed," said Lulu. "It reminds me of your love life." The tennis balls rebelled in all directions, one rolling out of sight under a low hedge. Brencie retrieved the other two. "Do you have any more hidden talents?" Lulu asked.

"I play the guitar."

"Do you really?"

"No, but maybe I'll learn someday. When you take up tennis."

"I get tired just watching. Cute little skirt, though. I was hoping to catch you. I'm organizing a trip to Rudesheim, and you're invited." It was still cool at night, but the city was blooming in gardens, parks, and window boxes.

"Sounds like fun. Who' coming?" Brencie asked.

"Nolan's coming. I won't tell him you are, in case you change your mind. We'll have to take the train. Jules invited two buddies, so no room in Nolan's VW. We can take the train, or we might take a taxi, if Dierdre and Margo come. The fare split by four would be do-able. Jürgen won't come. Says it's too touristy for his royal self."

Brencie agreed to the outing, and on an unseasonably warm evening, she and Lulu, Diedre and Margo, squeezed into a Mercedes taxi. After Lulu cajoled the driver and convinced him he could catch another fare back, he agreed to drive them down the Rhine road to Rudesheim. Jules and Nolan and two others were waiting at the rendezvous point, and Nolan's look of surprise confirmed he hadn't known she was coming.

Jules introduced the girls to Bob-from-Baltimore and Gary-from-Denver, and they all made their way to the *Drosselgasse*, a narrow ally of outdoor cafes and small shops. It was early in the season, so it was festive, but not as jammed as it would be later in the summer. Loosely hung swags of pale-yellow lights illuminated the way, and many establishments featured live bands on plank dance floors. The group settled at its first stop, and Nolan took a seat directly in front of Brencie.

"Lulu was true to her word," Brencie said. "She didn't tell you I was coming."

"She has a kind heart. She would rather see me surprised than disappointed." Nolan pointedly looked at the ring on her hand, but he said nothing.

A pop band wearing American jeans opened with several rock numbers and then favored the older crowd with a polka. Dierdre and Margo chatted up the newcomers, and Jules and Lulu, Nolan, and Brencie took to the floor. Brencie felt alive in his arms, and when the polka was followed by a waltz, he drew her close. His hand was slightly below her waist, and she thought of Berlin. Her body warmed as his erection pressed into her.

He leaned away, and his smile banished a serious look. "Sorry. What did you call it? Involuntary?"

"You're not sorry," she said.

"And neither are you."

"I'm still engaged."

"In self-delusion."

The band switched to a slightly unusual version of "Angel of the Morning," but with the same longing sounds on the chorus. Brencie sighed, put both arms around his neck, and leaned even closer, conscious of his thighs and his chest.

"Brencie, stop flirting with me with that ring on your finger. It seems to mean more to me than it does to you." He led her back to the table.

By the time the group drank and danced their way along the *Drosselgasse* and back to where they started, it was late. Everyone was drunk or drunk-ish, making the evening hilarious, and the happy crowds around them exhibited the same state of hilarity. Margo and Dierdre were dancing together, and no one cared, except maybe Bob, who looked glassy-eyed and confused. "Time to call it a night," Jules said.

"Can you drive us to a taxi stand or the train station?" Lulu asked.

"Nobody's going home tonight," Nolan said. "I won't risk an accident. I'm going to that hotel on the corner and get some rooms."

"On the first warm Friday night in June? Not a chance, my friend," Jules said. When Nolan came back with a key, Jules rolled his eyes. "Holy shit! How do you get to be a don?"

"Besides joining the mafia?" said Nolan. "You carry a stash of dollars for pirate tribute and hotel bribes. Only one room, though. Two beds. Girls get the beds; boys get the floor."

The crowd had dribbled away, and the band announced the closing number, a favorite of the summer. "Those Were the Days." On the chorus, the lead singer gestured for the remaining revelers to join in. "Yes, those were the days," the crowd sang in delirious agreement.

Lulu, of the beautiful voice and champagne courage, stepped unbidden onto the band platform. She took the mike, and her fine mezzo-soprano silenced all other singers. She delivered the last verse, poised and lovely, in the twinkling lights. She sang of happy and changing times, and the song brought Brencie to tears. She wasn't going back to the States, not yet, and she would never marry Chase.

A week later Brencie stopped at the desk after work, and although she was happy to see a letter from Agnes-Rose and one from her friend Bea in Florida, there was nothing from Chase. The desk clerks, always aware of who, what, when, and where, looked at her with sympathy or satisfaction. It was hard to tell. The decline Lulu predicted had come true. *The men come, they go, they forget. And so do we.*

The bus from the base discharged its passengers, and Lulu appeared at the desk. "Hi. No letter?"

"You aren't surprised," said Brencie. "No letter in weeks." The afternoon happy hour crowd was gathering in the bar to the sound of slot machines and the jukebox, the smell of people and alcohol. The strains of "Red Rubber Ball" bounced into the lobby.

"I love that song, and Chase isn't 'the only starfish in the sea.' Come with me. I'm meeting Jules." They marched into the bar to the beat of that old favorite.

Jules and Nolan sat outside on the flagstone terrace, engaged in an arm-wrestling contest. Nolan saw Brencie and slammed Jules's arm to the table."

Jules looked indignant. "Not fair! I let you win."

"You knew Nolan would be here, didn't you?" Brencie whispered to Lulu. Both courts in the backyard were occupied, and the thud of the balls seemed timed to the song on the jukebox. Brencie was happy to see Nolan, and he was cordial; however, he finished his beer, settled his tab, and left. "Gotta go. I'm charge-of-quarters tonight."

Brencie was disappointed, and she wondered if COQ was a polite excuse.

———●《◉》●———

In the morning the birds were singing so loudly Brencie thought a robin had come into her apartment. She got dressed for work and put on the ring. She looked at the fire in the thing, bright and cold. Finally, she slipped it off and placed it on the coffee table, but thought better of it. The maids weren't known for stealing, but the ring was valuable. Best to put it away.

She took a storage container from a closet and lifted the lid to see the diamond watch Chase had given her, which she had stopped wearing. Beside the watch was the five-year diary Nolan gave her for Christmas, only weeks before she broke it off with him. She opened the diary to the first page. January 1, 1968. *Happy New Year*, she had written. *Had a fight with Nolan. Sent him away.*

She thumbed through the first few pages, most with single-sentence entries, until Valentine's Day, which was blank. There was nothing after that. It had felt unseemly to continue keeping the diary after they broke up. She put the engagement ring into the box and put it away, but she kept the diary out. On an impulse, she found the current date and made an entry: *Chase is gone.*

Time to acknowledge it was finished. She would write to him tonight.

Still, she put it off. Another week passed, and a letter finally came from Chase.

Dear Brencie,

We both know it's over. It has been for a while, if we're honest. The fault is mine, for the lies I told you and the trust we never regained. I've been seeing a girl I knew at Incirlik. She's in D. C. now. Maybe I'll do better this time. She's a little like you, but no one will ever really be like you.

Should I say I'm sorry? As I write this and remember you, I am sorry.

Chase

Brencie called Lulu. "Hi. Can I come up?"

When she arrived, she handed the letter to her friend, who read it and brought out a bottle of vodka. She took two thumb-sized glasses from the kitchen cabinet and filled them to the brim. "Champagne for celebrations," she said. "Vodka for breakups. Here's to love, the good, the bad, and the ugly." They drank. "I'm sorry, Brencie. The fat lady finally sang."

Brencie took a deep breath and asked the question. "He spent so much time at Incirlik. Was he seeing her? Did he play around on his deployments?"

"It's probably a long story. But short version? Wondering is different from knowing. Let it go. It doesn't matter now."

A tear ran down Brencie's face. "Only one tear. Shouldn't I be sobbing? Did I take the easy way out, by just not going with him?"

"The easy way is under-rated. The easy way means no messy scene full of male anger and female tears. Besides, there's infatuation and there's love. If it's the real thing, the insanity changes into something like I have with Jules."

Brencie sighed. "I came here wanting nothing to do with romance, and in the first week I met Chase and Nolan. Now I don't have a boyfriend for the first time since I was thirteen. The Texas boyfriend roundup starts at puberty, and if you don't have one, you're a reject. Now I don't have one, and I feel good about it. I think I'll keep it that way."

"That should be easy enough. Chase's gone, and Nolan doesn't want you if you don't want him. Jules says he's exceptionally mature."

"Does Jules stay up nights summing people up?"

"He does. It's his hobby. When you arrived, you were the unattainable dream girl. Quiet and aloof. You're not the same now, and Nolan wants you more than ever. Chase wouldn't like the new Brencie. Now, what about the ring? You know what Zsa Zsa Gabor said. 'Darlink, return da ring, but keep da stone.' You could buy a new car with that ring."

"I'll send it back. I don't want anything from him."

"Oh, Jesus Christ! I've heard women say that, and that's what they get. The man gets the elevator and the girl gets the shaft. Chase tied you up emotionally for a year. He came between you and Nolan. Wait till Nolan hears about this."

"Lulu, not a word. Promise?"

"Sure, but it will be all over the *Rheingau* by this afternoon. It's a very tiny big community."

Chapter 21

Dear Brencie,

Your letters sound like a travel show. Switzerland next! I'm sorry about Chase. Things change. You did the right thing. You're thriving. Stay there.

Wolfie has come again and gone. The domino affect of that awful thing (you know what) sent you to Germany and then me to Germany, then Wolfgang to me. And one more thing. Stay home Thursday night. I'll call, even if it takes hours to get through.

Lulu's right. Keep the ring.

Love, Bee Bee

Brencie wrote to Chase about the ring and received a letter from his law firm with a receipt enclosed. She couldn't believe how much the ring was worth, or rather, what it had cost. The letter said Major Dellasera wanted her to keep it or return it to the place of purchase. It was a gift, and any further attempts to return it would result in embarrassment to all parties.

Embarrassment to all parties. The coldness persuaded her to view the ring as property, until she remembered. Chase's wife left her ring behind. Maybe he didn't want to see another ring, given in good faith, returned as goodbye. The ring came from the BX, which carried only certified high-quality stones, return guaranteed. Now the ring was a white elephant, and the only one preparing for a wedding was Lulu.

For Brencie, Lulu had chosen a sleeveless sheath of pale yellow dotted swiss, with a scalloped hem. After trying on at least twenty outfits, for herself Lulu chose a light blue silk shantung minidress with piping around the waist, neckline, and cuffs. It came with a fringed scarf that suggested a veil. In the dressing room at Hertie's, Lulu had said, "Very Audrey Hepburn *Two for the Road*, don't you think?"

Brencie had replied, "It's Lucille Greenholt. No one else."

Jules had initiated the paperwork and the date was set, the magistrate in Basel had been notified. Taking his best man duties to heart, Nolan had arranged four first-class train tickets. Brencie and Nolan would stand up with Lulu and Jules. Except for briefly in the Amelia bar, when Nolan made an excuse to leave, Brencie hadn't seen him since the trip to Rudesheim.

After minor alterations the wedding clothes had been delivered to Brencie, and she finished pressing them. It was time for Agnes-Rose's call, and Brencie was pleased when the phone rang only an hour late. After the small talk, Agnes-Rose handed Brencie some news that ranked in the top five surprises of her life.

━━━━━●《◉》●━━━━━

Jules, Lulu, Brencie, and Nolan boarded the train to Basel, Nolan looking trim and fit, and Jules looking like a nervous groom. "If it wasn't for Nolan," he said, "I'd think the arrangements were bound to go to hell. I can't blame him for our wedding getting upstaged by the moon landing."

"You can if you want to," said Nolan, "but blame Brencie. She used to work for NASA."

"And I don't see how they will manage to land on the moon without my superior typing skills," said Brencie.

"Well, it's one way to remember my wedding anniversary," said Jules. "Just days before the glorious United States of America put the first man on the moon. Take that, Commies!"

"Don't worry," said Lulu. "I'll remind you of our anniversary ahead of time. I'll even tell you what I want."

"Thank God," muttered Jules.

The train lurched out of the station heading north. The wedding would be on Friday morning, and on Friday afternoon Jules and Lulu would take the train to Florence. Brencie and Nolan would return to Wiesbaden.

Jules and Nolan went to the club car, and Lulu chattered about their new living arrangements. "We got the apartment on the Ringstrasse. I wanted to stay on at the Amelia to save money, but Jules wants the experience of living in town. Oh, Brencie. Don't look like that. It's walking distance, and we'll still be together all the time."

Brencie stared out the window, watching the scene pass more quickly as the train gathered speed. "It won't be the same."

Lulu shrugged. "Nothing ever is."

————))((————

Nolan had booked two rooms in Basel, and the arrangements were less complicated because Lulu didn't want to spend the night with Jules. She wanted one last night as a single girl, to prepare and uphold the tradition of not seeing the groom before the wedding. Between the two rooms there were four beds, so everyone slept alone.

In the morning Brencie and Lulu took their time. Lulu tucked one of Angelika's handkerchiefs in her pocket for something borrowed, the dress was blue and new, and something old was a bracelet that once belonged to Lulu's grandmother. A touch of pink lipstick, and then Lulu sat before the mirror as Brencie brushed her hair.

Lulu looked at the small book on the dressing table. "Oh my god. Is that the diary Nolan gave you?"

"I came across it. I'm going to write in it tomorrow. *Lulu's wedding day*. And soon after that, *America Lands on the Moon*."

"And after that? Brencie, figure it out. That diary is about Nolan. The electricity between you two is still like sheet lightning. I don't know why you're holding back. Do you?"

"Yes, I do. I think I'm in love with him, but I want to be sure. I want to make decisions, not just let things happen. I can extend my job in Wiesbaden for two years. That's an option in my contract. Or I could go home next year and begin a new phase of my life. Maybe college."

"When we first met, you were wearing that blue-checked *ensemble*, and I thought you were all fluff and flirt. Now I think you can do anything you want, if you ever figure out what that is."

"And so can you."

"No, I can't. I need the right niche. I can be a fashion guru. I could never be a doctor or an accountant. Or an artist or a stinkin' tennis coach. After all, you took off for a job in Europe not knowing anyone. How many people do that?"

"I don't know. How many people catch their stepmother with their fiancé?"

"That's best never mentioned, you know." Lulu turned away from the mirror. "You could have just moved across town to get away from your stepmother, for hell's sake. But back to Nolan. He's nuts about you, but you'll have to go to him."

There was a knock, and a delivery boy handed Lulu a bouquet of white roses and baby's breath, tied with long blue ribbons. The card from Jules said, "For my love on our wedding day."

———◦(◦)◦———

Nolan and Jules taxied to the magistrate's office, so Lulu and Brencie could arrive after them and make an entrance, but two new arrivals almost stole the show. Dierdre and Margo were in the rotunda of city hall, tastefully dressed in Chanel knock-off suits. "Surprise!" they cried in unison.

After embraces all around, Lulu said, "How did you know where and when?"

"We called Nolan a few days ago," said Dierdre.

"We're taking the train back this afternoon . . ."

"But we wouldn't have missed this wedding for the world."

Their group peeked into the wedding chamber. Jules and Nolan were there, and other couples and family members filled the room with corsages, black suits, wedding gowns, and pastel summer dresses, all adding up to a congregation, a real wedding. White lilies and roses in silver urns stood beneath the windows, their scent decorating the air. On the wall behind the judge hung a large tapestry featuring a bride and groom on a winding path, suggesting the journey they were about to undertake.

Brencie, Dierdre, and Margo went into the room, but Lulu insisted on staying in the antechamber. Couples were called one by one, and an elegant white-haired judge spoke the traditional words in perfect English, German, or French, as requested by the bride. When the judge called for Greenholt and Pasternak, Jules and Nolan stepped up, handsome in dark suits with white rose boutonnieres, and Dierdre and Margo stood behind them like two volunteer bridesmaids. Brencie summoned Lulu. As Lulu had coached her,

Brencie then walked slowly to the front, and Lulu paused, framed in the doorway, light falling on her face, then came slowly toward the judge.

When the ceremony was over Lulu untied the fringed scarf, shook out her lovely hair, and received a kiss from her husband. Brencie feared the ceremony might be sterile, but it had been charming.

Lulu and Jules signed a record-keeping ledger, and Brencie and Nolan signed as witnesses. Whatever happened, the names of Lulu Greenholt, Jules Pasternak, Brencie Jessup, and Nolan Hanik would be side by side, tucked away in a wedding book in Basel, forever.

Nolan had arranged lunch at an enchanting restaurant by the river, and after everyone was served champagne, Jules stood and tapped his spoon against a glass. "Ladies and gentlemen, I'd like to offer a toast to this beautiful young lady who became my wife today." There was a polite round of applause in the small restaurant, as the other patrons enjoyed the romantic interruption.

"When I proposed, right after she said *yes*, Lulu asked me a question. 'Will you get tired of me? I'm not smart like you. So why me?' I knew why in my heart, and I know you won't believe I was ever speechless, but I couldn't come up with the words. I've had time to find something that expresses how I feel. As Lulu would say, it's a long story, but I'll stick to the short version."

He opened a piece of paper. "I'd like to reference something by the great Russian poet, Yevgeny Yevtushenko, a poem called *Colours*. My grandfather used to read it to me in Russian, and then translate it in his own way. The poem is about a lover's face casting a glow on seas and rivers, and showing the beloved a truer way of looking at the world. With her style, her warmth, her compassion, and her love, that's what Lulu brings to me. So. Here's to Lucille Marie Greenholt Pasternak, my bride."

Jules raised his glass, and everyone in the room did the same. As the other patrons went back to their meals, Jules sat down. "Now, one more thing," he said. "Here's a wedding gift from our friends, collected by Brencie, who made me swear not to open it until later, but she didn't define *later*. She also said she hoped we won't be disappointed because it isn't another fondue pot."

Everyone chuckled as he handed Lulu an envelope. "Mrs. Pasternak—Lulu—would you do the honors?"

Lulu removed a check from the envelop, with a note attached. She read the note aloud. "In lieu of bath towels and bed sheets, crystal vases, and carving knives, here's something to add to your tuition fund for the Fashion Institute in New York." Lulu looked at the check and couldn't speak.

Jules took the check. "Holy shit!" He looked around the room. "You must have hit up Howard Hughes. Where the hell did this much money come from?"

Nolan stood up and shook Jules's hand. "Say thank you and shut up, my friend, or we'll forget you're a trained fighting man."

Brencie admired the grace with which Nolan had arranged everything, and how deftly he lightened the emotional moment. Lulu would figure out where the money came from, but for now, it was good to change the subject.

Lulu disengaged from Jules and invited Brencie to the ladies' room, the kind of female flocking Lulu usually hated. "Just come on," she said. They stopped before they went into the WC. "Brencie, you didn't collect anything. The money came from the ring. You returned it and gave the money to me. I don't know what to say, except I'll never forget this."

"I'm embarrassed. Jules wasn't supposed to open that until much later, like when you got back to the States. I didn't want to give you the chance to refuse."

"Well, he thought later was up to him, and I'm not going to refuse. I am going to thank you."

"Just become the American Mary Quant. You're already a better fashion designer than she is. That's all I ask, and you can do it." They hugged, cried, composed themselves, and returned to the table.

Lulu sat down, but Brencie remained standing. "Everyone, there's one more thing I've been saving." She paused to determine all were listening. "This is Jules and Lulu's day, so I debated whether to tell you or wait. After much inner debate and deliberation, soul searching and head scratching . . ." She looked at the wedding party, one by one. "I decided it would add to the celebration, not take away from it."

"All right already," said Jules. "Our breath is bated."

"Well . . . OK. Agnes-Rose called me last week to tell me she's the happiest women in the world. I'm going to be a big sister. She's pregnant, and that rascal Wolfgang Ritter is the proud papa."

<hr />

Dierdre and Margo left after lunch, and when it was time to put the bride and groom on the train to Italy, Nolan and Brencie stood side by side on the platform and waved them goodbye. "And so," said Brencie.

"And so." Nolan looked at the clock overhead. "We have a few hours to kill before our train goes. Should we get something to eat?"

The Bahnhof café had a television in one corner, broadcasting news of the upcoming mission to the moon, photographs from Cape Kennedy, pictures of the astronauts, and stock photos of the mission control center in Houston.

"Were you ever inside mission control?" Nolan asked.

"Once, during my orientation the first week. They walked a group of new employees through it. A guy in a space suit sneaked up behind us and scared the crap out of everyone. If things had been different, I would probably still be at NASA."

"If you were there, you wouldn't be here, and you wouldn't have been at Lulu's wedding. You wouldn't even know Lulu."

"Or you," Brencie said.

He looked away from the TV to stare at Brencie's face. "Or me. Is that important?"

"Nolan, I don't want to go back tonight. I want to stay in Basel. With you."

"I'll be right back."

He was gone long enough for her doubts to kick in. Maybe she had miscalculated. Maybe he was done with her. When he came back, she said, "Was it a mistake? Have your feelings changed?"

He laughed out loud. "There's not a single reason you should doubt how I feel about you. If you can't see it, I'm a damn good actor. I had to change our train tickets and telephone the hotel. After I threatened to burn it down, they found a double bed with a room."

When Brencie laughed, he said, "Oh, crap. I hope I didn't really say that."

<hr />

Brencie woke up wondering why she ever stopped being with Nolan. As the sun filtered through the shuttered windows, throwing bars of sunlight along the faded carpet, he made a sound somewhere between a deep breath and a soft snore.

She dressed quietly, took her bag, and left the hotel, walking toward the river, breathing in the fresh smell of dawn and the stillness of a world still asleep.

In Basel the Rhine changed its westerly direction, turning north to flow through the *Rheingau* and on to the North Sea. She took her sketch pad from her bag and drew two parallel lines representing the river, then rubbed the charcoal with her knuckle, producing watery shapes between the lines. Watching the river wind away, she knew. She loved Nolan, and maybe she had all along.

She began to sketch the bridge and the shops across the river when Nolan materialized beside her. "People who grow up on the coast always head to the water," he said, handing her a cup. "Coffee. I had to move the world to get the kitchen to give me these. Why didn't you wake me?"

"You were sleeping so soundly. I didn't want to disturb you."

"Brencie, disturbing me is what you do." He looked at her sketch. "That's good. What do they sell in those shops? Let me buy you something, a keepsake from this trip."

"I won't need a keepsake to remember."

He looked serious. "Some things are hard to forget. Brencie, why did you take him back? He lied about the most important thing he could lie about. I'm not sure what happens next with us, but I have to ask. Are you really done with him?"

"It's complicated, but here's the short answer as Lulu would say. You met Agnes-Rose. She's generous and kind. She's wise. She loved me, no matter what. She did something bad. Maybe someday I'll tell you what, but the thing is, I didn't forgive her. I didn't even give her a chance. Then she accidently shot herself. She could have died, but even before that, I was ashamed of not forgiving her. I just didn't know how to fix it until I went home."

He finished his coffee and turned toward the river, watching its steady flow. "So it was about forgiveness?"

"Forgiveness. Second chances. Whatever you want to call it, it led to the right outcome. Because I took him back, I'll never wonder if he was the love of my life, and I didn't give him another chance. It's not over because he left, or because you're here and he isn't. It's over because I took him back, and whatever we had, it played itself out. It's over because it's over."

Still facing the river, Nolan leaned his elbows on the guard rail and turned his face up toward Brencie. "I didn't think if you tried for a hundred years, you could make me understand. But you have."

She smiled. "Do you remember a conversation we had the day we met? You asked if they would put a man on the moon by 1970. I said yes. You didn't think there was any way that could happen, either."

"That conversation seems like a long time ago," he said.

"Yes, it does. I'm a different person than I was then. Everyone has dreams, but now mine seem more like chances I could take. Opportunities."

"Vietnam changed me like that. When I got there, I was just head down, 'get 'er done.' By the time I left I owed something to my future, just because I had one."

"And in a few days, if nothing goes wrong, a man will walk on the moon," she said. "Will that take the romance out of moonlight?"

"I read some quotes in *Stars and Stripes* about NASA and the space program. One person said, 'America! What a country!' All that's happened this year, riots, assassinations, all of it, but still. 'America! What a country!' Maybe that kind of achievement makes things even more romantic. And anyway, Jules and Lulu are still on their *honeymoon*."

"Once in a blue moon. Mooning over you," said Brencie. "Moonbeams. Moon pies."

"Moon pies? Is that edible?"

She laughed. "There's some debate about that, even in Texas."

Nolan grew serious. "Moonstruck. You hung the moon."

She saw the tenderness in his eyes. "Do you remember what you said at the end of our very first date? About the future? Five years from now, I think you said."

"About becoming a lawyer? I remember. I was trying to impress you."

"You also said we would be married."

"Still trying to impress you. Now I think we have a chance for something. When we know each other better. When we know ourselves better. When we go back to the States, where everything isn't . . ."

"Where everything isn't like this?" She looked at the slow-moving boat traffic on the river and the gentle contours of the beautiful town. "Where it isn't so easy to imagine you're in love?"

"Yes. Exactly," he said. "This place will just be a foreign country where we used to live. Life will get serious, harder, full of problems and responsibilities."

Brencie looked away from the river and into Nolan's eyes. "I love you, Nolan. We'll both be here another year at least. Like you said, time is on our side. Time to figure out what we want."

"I know what I want," he said, "but you can't always get what you want."

"*Rolling Stones* philosophy? 'Sometimes you get what you need?'"

"Sure. Why not? Take good advice where you find it, from Agnes-Rose to the Stones. From Lulu-no-doubt to Jules the Genius.

Brencie looked up at the moon, still a sliver in the morning sky. "But what do you think?"

"About the moon landing?" Nolan asked. "Or about us?"

Brencie smiled. "Yes."

The End

CPSIA information can be obtained
at www.ICGtesting.com
Printed in the USA
BVHW040911110921
616115BV00015B/309